these

numbered

days

Anna E. Collins

These Numbered Days
Red Adept Publishing, LLC
104 Bugenfield Court
Garner, NC 27529
https://RedAdeptPublishing.com/

For my children, who will always have my heart.

CHAPTER 1

Today was day 2,902. I wrote it down, and the screech of the marker against the wall calendar made the skin on my neck prickle. I'd been counting the days since the Tuesday morning I'd said goodbye to my kids. Walked away for their sake.

It was an awful number—too high by any mother's standards, of course, but also disconcerting from an aesthetic point of view. The double twos offered a fleeting illusion of balance that was quickly butchered by the nine. I itched to scribble over it but instead, I mustered the strength to cap my marker. Facing my choices head-on, as Dr. Samson would say.

I should have never let it get this far. It had never been the plan.

Blinds drawn to the impending New Mexico daylight, I made my coffee in the semidarkness as usual. Each clang of the spoon against the ceramic mug marked time ticking further and further away from my past. Or maybe closer toward it depending on what happened next. There was change in the air.

I squeezed my eyes shut and counted backward from twenty. A deep breath in, a deep breath out. *Steady now.*

The cell phone on the table chimed, startling me enough to send my coffee splattering across the laminate countertop. Only two people knew where to find me, and it was early for either of them to call. 8:08 a.m. The numerical symmetry gave me the boost I needed to pick up.

"Hello?"

"It's true. They're looking into adopting them." Kara, my childhood friend and the only remaining connection to my past, didn't waste any time. "My sister saw Brandy at Safeway yesterday, and she told her. They've contacted an attorney."

I clutched the phone to my ear and forced a breath. "Oh."

She was quiet for a beat. "What are you going to do?"

Something close to a giggle, or perhaps it was a sob, clambered its way up my throat. Eight years I'd been away. Eight years of waiting for the inevitable end I'd been so sure would come—of antidepressants, therapy, and periods of impenetrable darkness. A half-life I'd not thought I would survive. *Had* barely survived.

When I'd had my children, they'd taken over my heart. They'd pulled it out for me to carry in the open, pulsating and vulnerable, because they were *it*—a piece of me roaming free. I'd left Grace and Connor to protect them. Abandoned my heart because I thought they would be safer without me and my treacherous brain. Safer with just Joel. And now everything had changed.

"Annie?" Kara's voice came from somewhere far away.

I bit down hard on my lip. "I don't know."

She sighed. "You know I love you, and I think I've been very understanding over the years, but this? Annie, they're your kids. They've lost their dad. You're the only parent they have left."

I resisted the urge to shatter my coffee mug against the wall. I already *knew* that. But I'd only barely regained my footing after finding out he'd died. Yes, I wanted to go to them—had wanted to for a while even through the haze of the last six months of recovery. I just couldn't see what good I would be to them at this point.

"It's not that simple," I finally said. "They don't know me anymore."

"That can change."

"*I* don't know *them*."

"Again—"

"And you said they seem okay with Brandy and Shane."

Kara raised her voice. "That's not the point."

She was right of course. I paced between the threadbare recliner that came with the sublet and the kitchen, waiting for her to continue. What I really wanted was to put on my headphones and escape into the cymbals, horns, and massive choirs of Orff, Wagner, Mahler, and Dvorak. When the outside world tried to impose, only music could temporarily drown out reality.

Kara continued, more gently now, "Sure, they're with family, but an aunt and uncle are not the same as a mom. In spite of everything, you should know that. This might be your last chance."

There was a voice in the background on the other end, and Kara gave a muffled response before she got back on the phone. "Shit. Listen, I've got to help Logan get ready for school. T-shirt crisis. I'll have to call you back later. Please, think about it."

"It" being me somehow leaving Albuquerque to go back home to Snohomish, Washington.

I told her I would, and we hung up. It wasn't a lie. I'd thought of little else since the rumor had reached me that Brandy and Shane were considering adopting the kids. Leaving them with Joel had been one thing. *But this?* Adoption would be a final surrender.

With a shaky hand, I reached for one of the two glasses taking up space in my nearly empty cabinets. They shared the shelf with three mismatched plates and a dulled cheese grater left by a previous tenant. I filled the glass from the tap, ignoring its chlorine tang as I drank. A cheeky ray of sunlight had broken through the seam where the two curtain panels met. It danced across the floor, illuminating the specks of dust suspended in midair as I shook out my daily doses of Wellbutrin and Lexapro from their amber bottles. After years of experimenting with medications and dosages, I'd finally found a combination that worked well enough.

My first three years away, almost every waking thought revolved around how I would leave this world. I'd overdosed but not enough. I'd swerved into the wrong lane but lost my nerve at the last minute when my headlights lit up the fear in the other driver's face. General recklessness hadn't worked either. Walking the streets of downtown Albuquerque alone at night turned out to be much safer than rumors had it. Three suicide attempts my first four years away and only one in the last four spoke volumes. And I'd regretted the last overdose right away. Ended up in the ER. After that, I'd had no choice but to find a therapist.

I briefly considered adding a Xanax to the cocktail in my hand. I was only supposed to take it on really bad days, but if this one didn't qualify, I didn't know what did. In the end, I decided against it, and I swallowed the two pills in one gulp. Then I leaned across the table and opened the drapes with a decisive pull. The morning sun shocked my pupils into tiny pinheads, but I didn't shy away. The outside wanted in. The question was if I would let it.

Kara's words echoed in my mind. *What* am *I going to do?*

I turned, rubbing at the crease between my brows while the sun warmed my back. Before me lay the paltry pieces of my life. I named each item as if they were part of a childhood rhyme—bed, closet, coat hook; stove, bookcase, reading nook. *No Mother Goose idyll, that's for sure.*

My gaze caught on my laptop, askew on the crate that served as a coffee table. The education platform I used as a virtual classroom for my online students sat open, displaying the draft of today's introduction, which I'd started typing last night. *Guten Tag. Heute ist Dienstag, der 6 September.* After sitting down, I minimized it then glanced at the time. 8:40 a.m. The evenly divisible digits stirred something inside me again. The concord was unusual. First 8:08 then this. I took it as a good omen and clicked open the article I'd found last week.

Joel McLaren Remembered: School Names Baseball Field after Late Coach

I squinted at the flickering text. Yes, it still said his name. It was still true. My throat went as tight as it had back in February when Kara had called me with the news.

"You were supposed to always be there for them," I whispered. Then, louder, "Do you hear me?" The words only resounded for a split second before being absorbed into the carpeting.

Maybe I needed to be there for them like Kara said. Or maybe the kids would do great with Shane and Brandy, who knew them better than me. There was no way for me to be sure. All I knew was, if I let the adoption happen—let someone other than Joel take over permanently—and it turned out poorly, I would never be able to forgive myself. At the very least, I owed it to them to check in. I wouldn't have to meddle—maybe not even tell them I was there—but if I could only see for myself that the kids were all right, I wouldn't have to risk hurting them again.

I closed the laptop with a snap and reached for my phone. My therapist, Dr. Samson, had given me her cell number a while back, knowing I would only call if I really needed her. She answered on the third ring.

"Annie?"

"Hi."

"What's going on?"

I told her what I'd learned.

She was silent for a moment. "Ah. And how do you feel about that?"

I picked at a thread coming loose on the frayed knee of my jeans. "I shouldn't feel anything. The kids are already living there. It's not like much would change."

"But?"

"I don't know. What if it's a sign?"

"You've talked about returning before."

My cheeks heated as the memory surfaced. About four years into my self-imposed exile, I'd called Joel. The pain of being away was torture. He'd heard me out, or so I'd thought, but when he spoke, I barely recognized him.

"We're doing fine now," he'd said. "Stay the fuck away."

So I had.

"I don't want to mess it up," I told my therapist.

A long silence stretched out on the line. "Where are you at today?"

I'd been seeing Dr. Samson long enough to know she didn't mean physically. We used a scale—zero meant I was in a good place, and ten meant she would drop everything and get me emergency psych care. My last ten happened seven months ago when Joel died. I didn't remember what zero felt like.

"About a four."

"Good."

"You think I should go?"

"That's not for me to say."

I suppressed a groan. "Yeah, yeah. But could I handle it?"

Dr. Samson let out a low chuckle. "I'm all the way across town. You're the only one who can answer that question."

"In your professional opinion. Come on, please."

"Annie." Dr. Samson's voice was almost tender. "You alone can decide what happens." She seemed to hesitate. "But we've done some good work this year. You don't give yourself enough credit."

"So I should go?"

She let out a sharp sigh. "I wouldn't tell you not to. Though that's not to say I'm unaware of the impact your presence there might have on all of them. Tread lightly if you do."

I let her words sink in, and clarity hit me so hard I rose from my seat. I *had* to go. If I didn't, I would always wonder, and Joel wasn't there to tell me not to this time.

"I can still call you?"

"Any time. You know it."

The flutter of a thousand butterfly wings jostled my insides. I was really going back.

CHAPTER 2

The Snohomish Valley hadn't changed much, but the colors surprised me. Eight years near the desert will do that. I'd forgotten green could be so green. As I closed in on the town, I slowed to take in the fields, the sky, and the glittering river. My chest tightened. Familiarity wasn't always a good thing.

I made my way through downtown on autopilot while my panic rose like bubbling yellow acid in a test tube. Maple Avenue to Pine. A right on 16th Street. Our old house came into view before I was ready for it, shocking despite its unassuming gray hue. Once, I had come and gone as I'd pleased there. Not anymore.

A For Sale sign with a diagonal stripe across announcing Sold sat near the mailbox, but there was no sign of life. I didn't know what I'd expected. The kids didn't live there anymore, and even if they did, they would be in school right now. Connor would be a sophomore in high school and Grace in her last year of middle school. *Would I even recognize them if I saw them?* Shame made my skin tingle, and I swallowed hard against the lump that was forming in my throat.

"You're not their mother anymore," I whispered. "You had your chance."

No, I needed to make every effort not to see them—unless I could make sure they wouldn't catch me looking. *Or they give me a reason to think they want to see me.*

"Stop it." I slammed my palm onto the steering wheel and grasped it tightly. My foot came down hard on the gas pedal, the sudden influx of fuel whipping the car away from the curb. In this town of burnt bridges, there was only one person I could be reasonably sure wouldn't kick me out on sight, and that was Kara.

AS I DROVE THROUGH the streets where I'd grown up, passing old hangouts and new stores, the sense of déjà vu was overwhelming. It had now been 2,904 days since I'd left, but something about the light and the neighborhoods resonated deep within my bones. I almost missed it more seeing it again than I had while away trying to forget it.

I parked in a side alley off the main shopping street then joined the throngs of shoppers moving from store to store with the hesitation of a captive animal finally set free in the wild. The undulation of the crowd made the world pitch slightly. The sensory overload—a blaring car horn, exhaust fumes, a crying baby in a sling, old lady perfume, two young girls laughing, freshly brewed coffee, and even the murmured backdrop of voices—was too much. I hurried back to my car, gasping for breath. After digging out a Xanax from my purse, I swallowed it with a gulp of day-old coffee. *A few more minutes. No rush.* I rested my head against the seatback and willed my heartbeat to slow.

An hour later, I pushed open the door to The Fudge Factory, the candy shop Kara had opened together with her sister after college. The brass bell jingled, announcing my entry, but the counters were crowded. No one paid me any attention. Traces of burnt sugar and popcorn wafted over me, rewinding years too swiftly gone by. I was twenty again, playfully arguing with Joel about the merits of milk chocolate versus dark chocolate. He'd liked the bitter stuff. I did not.

From behind the relative safety of my sunglasses, I scanned the space on the other side of the counter. Three girls were helping customers, and a guy was washing measuring cups in the industrial sink. Kara was nowhere to be seen. She was probably downstairs, then.

Before anyone could intercept me, I retreated past two strollers and headed to the cordoned-off staircase in the middle of the store. The old wood creaked under my feet as I hurried down the steps.

It was murky in the lower hallway, but bright light shone through a partially opened door to my right, a familiar voice talking animatedly in the room beyond.

"I don't really care what your excuse is. You're supposed to pick him up today, not me. I'm working."

Through the crack, I could make out Kara hunched over the phone on her desk.

"Well," she went on, "you should have thought of that earlier."

Feeling bad about eavesdropping, I knocked on the door, pushing it open farther.

Kara held up a finger in my direction with a glance toward me before she returned to her phone. When her head jerked more fully my way, it was clear she'd expected someone else to be interrupting her call, and for a moment she just stared.

"Holy shit!" Her face paled. "No, not you," she said into the receiver. "I'm going to have to call you back." She hung up and spun her chair toward me, eyes huge. "You're here already?"

I nodded, afraid my voice wouldn't carry. I'd texted her my decision before I'd left Albuquerque, but since I'd had no idea either how long the drive would take or how many stops I'd have to make, I'd been vague about my arrival time.

She pushed out of her chair and crossed the room. "It's really you."

I nodded again. Smiled. "I'm sorry, I—"

She cut me off with a hug.

"It's good to see you, Kara." My voice was muffled against her shoulder, and my arms hung limply at my sides. I knew I was supposed to do something with them, but her proximity caught me off guard. *How long has it been since I hugged another person? Since another person hugged me?*

She held me at arm's length and shook her head. "When did you—I mean, how...?" She pulled me to the decrepit love seat in the corner. "Sorry. I'm babbling. Sit. Coffee?"

"Sure."

Kara grabbed two mugs from a shelf above the desk and filled them before she sat.

"Tell me everything. I was expecting you next week maybe. I would have picked you up from the airport."

"I drove."

She choked on her coffee. "You drove?"

"Seemed faster. Plus, do you know how much they charge for last-minute flights?"

"Point taken. Gosh, I can't believe you're here." She cradled her mug between both hands. "Did you see the kids already?"

"I just got in. Came straight here."

"But you are going to talk to them?"

Normally, I appreciated Kara's no-bullshit manners, but being so far out of my comfort zone, they took me aback. "Like I said before, I'm going to find a way to make sure they're okay. That doesn't mean they need to know I'm here."

Kara studied me. "Brandy and Shane, then?"

Up until that moment, I'd told myself I might be able to sneak a peek at my children's lives from afar. Get in, get out. No one would be the wiser. Now, I realized just how unrealistic that was. Snohomish was a small town, and most people there probably assumed I was long dead. The jungle drums would start beating as soon as I ran into someone I knew. "I suppose I should."

I sipped my coffee, watching Kara over the brim. For the first time, I noticed the subtle changes in her face—the thinner jawline and the faint crow's feet around her eyes. Kara and I had been inseparable in high school, our friendship peaking in an epic summer of ice cream, bonfires, and suntans before junior year. So much time had passed.

"Here." Kara reached for a pad on her desk and scribbled something before tearing off the paper and handing it to me.

I read the note. Shepherd's Christian, it said, with rough directions scribbled underneath. "What's this?"

"The school where Brandy works. In case you want to get it over with."

My eyes widened. "She's a teacher?" Brandy, the sorority girl with the lofty event planner dreams. That couldn't be right. "Wasn't she in marketing?"

Kara smirked. "You'll find she's had quite the change of heart."

Something in her voice implied I had a surprise in store. As if she could sense how disquieting that was to me, Kara took my hand and squeezed it. The feeling was so foreign I had to force myself to hold still.

"Don't worry. We're all older now. A lot can happen in eight years. If I were you, I'd just rip off the Band-Aid."

"Today?"

"No time like the present. If you're going to talk to her, do it before someone else tells her you're in town."

She had a point. I sighed. "But what should I say?"

"Well, what do you want to know? If the kids are doing well in school? If they're coping with Joel's death? If they have friends? If they're happy?"

"You're right. Just ask." I tried straightening in my seat as if that act would enforce the notion that I actually had a spine. It kind of worked. *I can do this.*

"By the way, you're staying with me, right?" Kara asked.

"I was going to check at the River Motel. I don't want to put you guys out."

"You really did leave in a hurry, didn't you?" She smiled. "The motel burnt down two years ago. Come on. It'll give us more time to catch up. And it's walking distance from here, so nowhere near Brandy's."

I squirmed in my seat. "But your family. Won't they mind?"

She wrinkled her nose, and for a split second, she looked sixteen again. "Mike and I are kind of separated right now. It's just me and Logan."

"Oh. Sorry. I didn't know." She'd never said a word about it. Not that we spoke often or even regularly. *Crap.* That was why. That was the kind of friend I was. Irregular.

"I haven't told many people. It's pretty recent." She shrugged. "So, what do you say? My couch is very comfortable."

With some reluctance, I accepted her offer. She wished me luck for my meeting with Brandy, and for that I was grateful. I suspected I would need it, considering my whole mission there depended on it.

CHAPTER 3

From the shade beneath a giant cedar, I watched as parents picked up their kids from within Shepherd's Christian. As the crowd thinned, two straggling moms emerged engulfed in deep conversation with a third woman who appeared to be the teacher. But surely more than one teacher worked there. Surely, the woman in slacks and a Peter Pan-collared blouse wasn't Joel's little sister. The severe blond bob looked too adult.

"Bye, Mrs. Hemingway," one of the little boys called as the grouping dispersed.

I stood corrected.

A soon as Brandy went back inside, I freed myself from the trunk of the tree and approached the building. It was attached to a Catholic church and shared an entrance with the administrative office, which meant that, once in the foyer, I was faced with a gated glass door and a buzzer. Before I could press it, a white-haired lady with cat-eye glasses across the hall smiled and waved me in. The vague smell of full vacuum bags and Clorox wipes made my nostrils twitch.

"Um, hi. I'm here to see Brandy Hemingway."

"And do you have an appointment with Mrs. Hemingway?" the lady asked. The nametag on her desk said *Sec. Maura Kilkenny*. "Parents must have appointments or the teachers would get nothing done. Nothing at all." Maura tilted her head coquettishly.

Perhaps I should smile. I forced the corners of my mouth up, the muscles twitching at the unfamiliar motion. "Oh, I'm not a parent. I just need to see her."

She scrunched up her face. "Oh, dear. Well, let's have a look-see at her schedule for the rest of the week, then."

One of the benefits of not interacting with people daily was that I didn't have to deal much with red tape. Maura was my rude awakening, and now, I had to make a snap decision whether or not I'd let her get in my way. I planted both hands on the counter. "I'm sorry, but I really need to see her now."

Maura kept flipping through pages. "Need or want?"

The temperature of my blood rising, I contemplated making a run for it. If not for the door down the hall, which was likely also locked, I would have. "Mrs. Kilkenny—Maura—you don't understand—"

"Patience is a virtue, dear." Maura leveled a pointed stare at me over the brim of her glasses. "I can't let just anyone in. That simply wouldn't do, as I'm sure you agree. And *Mrs. Kilkenny* will do just fine." She closed the ledger and put it aside.

Something fierce and decidedly alive stirred within my core. If a simple plea wasn't enough, I had no choice. "Please, Mrs. Kilkenny. She'll want to see me. It's about her brother." My voice quivered as the white lie slipped out.

Finally, she looked up. "Mr. McLaren? That poor man."

"What's going on here?" a voice behind me said. I'd been so focused on the argument at hand I hadn't noticed we had company.

"Ah, Mrs. Hemingway. You have a visitor." Maura smiled sweetly at the person behind me as if she hadn't just refused my very presence in the building.

"How can I help?" Brandy's voice was even and polite, a far cry from the lazy inflection she'd perfected when last I knew her.

I turned slowly, forcing my shoulders to relax. "Hi."

She gasped and took a half step back. Then she crossed herself.

Brandy "Bee" Hemingway. Crossed. Herself.

This was not the twentysomething woman I'd known. Up close, she was even more put together than she had looked out in the schoolyard. Diamond studs in her ears, a discreet crucifix on a silver chain around her neck, and barely any makeup.

"Annie?" she whispered.

"Sorry. I didn't mean to shock you."

"Everything okay, Mrs. Hemingway?" Mrs. Kilkenny asked behind me. "You look like you've seen a ghost."

"Um." Brandy kept staring at me. "Um, yes. I'm all right." Her gaze flicked to the secretary. "Thank you."

I needed to act fast before I was thrown out or Brandy fainted. I took a step toward my sister-in-law. "Can we talk? In private?"

Brandy sucked in a breath and, with visible effort, raised her chin. "Of course. Come with me." She took off down the hallway, her Mary Janes moving silently across the carpet. I followed as fast as I could into unchartered waters.

Brandy's office was no bigger than a glorified closet with books and binders stacked everywhere.

"I can't believe you're here." She cleared a chair for me before sitting down at her desk. "All this time..." She fiddled with the religious charm resting at the base of her throat. "We thought you were dead."

Clearly, Joel had kept my call to himself. "No, still here. A bit of a surprise to me too," I mumbled then tried for a conciliatory smile. I wasn't sure what kind of ground I was on with her. "Look, I'm really sorry to be showing up like this out of the blue. I would have called, but I don't have your number."

"Uh-huh." She was still staring at me as if she thought I might vanish into thin air any second. It was starting to worry me.

"Can I get you some water or something?" I gestured to the dispenser by the door.

"Sure."

I filled a paper cup and set it down in front of her. She drained it right away. Perhaps some small talk would snap her out of her stupor. "So, you're a teacher now. What grade?"

"It's a second and third split." She closed her eyes and pressed her fingers to her eyelids, shaking her head. "What are you doing here, Annie?" She met my gaze with renewed intensity. "Where have you been? What the fu—" She bit off the word before it could pass her lips. "Why are you here?"

So little Bee wasn't entirely gone.

"I heard about Joel. I'm so sorry." A shadow crossed her face upon hearing his name, but I continued, "And I also heard that Grace and Connor are living with you."

Brandy's face reddened. "If you think for a minute I'll let you anywhere near those poor kids, you are sorely mistaken. Haven't you put them through enough?"

A chill ran down my sides. I needed to make her understand. All she saw in me was a bad mom. A horrible person. But maybe she was right.

"That's not—" My voice caught. I got up and helped myself to some water too. After a few sips, I was reasonably sure I could speak again. "It's very kind of you and Shane to take them in."

Her lips pursed. "It's the Christian thing to do."

"Hm." I twirled the cup between my fingers. "I heard, uh, you're considering making it permanent?"

"Who told you that?"

"Does it matter?"

"So I suppose you're here to interfere, then? I should have known."

"No." I set my cup down. "No. That's not it at all."

She frowned, her hands linking in her lap. "Oh?"

"I know what you must be thinking of me. And that's fine. I left them. I left Joel to care for them—counted on it, even—and now he's gone." Brandy's lips quivered, but I pushed on. "You might not believe me, but I didn't leave for my sake. I had good reasons. But there hasn't been a day I haven't thought of them. And I am still their mother—"

"Debatable," she muttered.

"By blood." I forced myself to hold her gaze until she looked away. "All I want is to make sure they're okay. Not that I doubt you and Shane," I hurried to add. "For peace of mind."

"But to come here and disturb everything? Don't you care about how they'll react?"

I raised my hands in defense. "They don't need to know. That's why I came to you."

That left her speechless for a moment. "You won't seek them out?"

"I promise."

She exhaled. "Oh." Blinked. "Okay."

There. A fragile truce but a truce all the same. Perhaps that meant I could finally ask the dreaded question that had brought me there. "Please. Will you tell me about them? How are they?" I steeled myself for her response, her accusations perhaps, and her judgment. I deserved all that. Leaving had been the right thing to do, but I wasn't so naive that I didn't recognize it might have caused some damage. I would happily own up to that any day because I knew that leaving them had been the lesser of two evils.

Brandy's brow smoothed out. "They're good." She offered a half smile. "Really good. Finally. Losing Joel was incredibly hard, of course, and the past seven months have been a roller coaster, but with school starting, they seem to have settled into a routine again. Connor is in soccer. Grace in choir. They have friends."

Without noticing, I'd brought my hand to my chest at the mention of my kids' names. As if that made them real again. For so long, I'd thought of them only as memories—it was odd to have someone else speak of them as actual living, breathing people.

"Here." Brandy handed me a tissue from the box, gesturing to my face. Once I'd cleaned myself up, she spoke again. "I'm glad you understand you can't see them. Not now when they are finally getting back to normal."

I nodded.

She leaned forward, resting her arms on the desk. "Where have you been, Annie?" Her eyes burned into me. "How could you leave them?"

"I'm sorry." My voice was barely more than a whisper. "I—"

"Knock knock." Mrs. Kilkenny pushed the door open and stuck her head in. "Mr. Wolston, Darren's father, is here," she announced, ignoring me. "I thought you should know."

Brandy checked her watch. "He's ten minutes early."

"So I should tell him to wait?"

"That would be great."

The secretary glanced at me. Hesitated. "He does seem in a hurry—"

Brandy's chin jerked up, and she spoke in sharp consonants. "Mrs. Kilkenny, I'm in the middle of something, and I'll be with him shortly. Thank you."

"Oh. W-Well," Mrs. Kilkenny sputtered. I only just caught a glimpse of her crimson face before the door closed.

Brandy sighed. "Sorry about that. She's a *competent* administrator. Where were we?"

How could I leave them?

"No, you're busy. I should go." I stood and threw my cup away. I did owe her answers, though, and I hoped she had more for me. "We could meet tomorrow?"

She considered that. "Sure. Where are you staying?"

I told her about Kara's offer of a couch, and that seemed to satisfy her.

"But let's not meet here. People talk."

I didn't question her. Small town and all that. "You can come to Kara's. She won't mind."

"I'm off work at noon tomorrow. I'll be there as soon as I can."

"Okay."

As I moved toward the door, she put her hand on my arm to stop me. "But after that, you have to leave. Promise me."

I told her "yes." And in that moment, I meant it.

CHAPTER 4

I spent the following morning responding to questions from my online students to keep the nerves about seeing Brandy again at bay. I'd taught various virtual classes through the years—mainly German and SAT prep but also some ESL. It didn't make me rich but checked all the boxes as far as allowing me to do my work alone and from home. Incidentally, it was also how Kara had tracked me down a few years back.

I was deeply engrossed in a chat with two students about the German gender rules when the doorbell rang at noon. I hurried to log off before running my fingers through my hair and taking a calming breath. *You don't need her to like you*, I reminded myself. As long as she told me about the kids, she could cuss me out to her heart's content.

I braced myself and opened the door, but my pasted-on smile vanished upon seeing she wasn't alone. She'd brought Shane.

My brother-in-law squinted at me, but there was no trace of hostility on his features. "Hi, Annie." He stuck out his hand.

Not sure how to react, I took it. The formality of the handshake made me sweat. "Come on in." I opened the door wider.

Shane placed his palm at the base of Brandy's back and steered her inside. I couldn't tell if he did it out of habit or to prevent her from taking off in the other direction.

Shane had aged worse than his wife. He'd been a newly minted accountant when I'd left, and judging by his paunch and pallid complexion, my bet was that his choice of careers hadn't changed. He looked almost a decade older than his thirty-five years.

"I hope you don't mind that I brought him," Brandy said as we sat down. Today, she wore a different pair of slacks and a short-sleeved blue turtleneck. The silver crucifix was still around her neck. "I figured two people would be better than one at answering your questions, and the sooner you're satisfied the sooner—" She cut herself off and cleared her throat.

"So, Annie. You look good," Shane said. "Life treating you well?"

An odd question considering they'd thought I was dead for eight years. I didn't know how to respond. Then again, he'd always been an even-keeled, don't-rock-the-boat kind of guy.

"Can we just get to the point?" Brandy opened her purse and took out a stack of photos.

Something inside me jolted. *Are those...?*

"These are from this summer. You can keep them or give them back. It's up to you. Whatever's easier." She held them out for me.

With trembling fingers, I took the stack from her and set it in my lap. Part of me ached to tear through them that very instant but another sensed a need to wait, to prepare myself first. The edges of the photos cut into my palms.

"Honey, why don't you tell Annie what we talked about last night?" Brandy looked at Shane before scooting back on the couch.

"Right." Shane clasped his hands. "Right." He pressed his lips together and inflated his cheeks before letting the air out with a pop. "So, Annie. Obviously, we understand your urge to come back in the wake of Joel's, um, demise."

I wished I'd remembered to offer them a beverage. The severity of the three of us facing one another across the small coffee table with no distractions made my scalp itch.

Shane turned to Brandy, who nodded encouragingly at him. He continued, "Even though he was no longer your husband,

I—we—can sympathize with a certain sense of grief perhaps, and a need for, uh, closure. For asking forgiveness."

I looked from one to the other, not entirely sure where the conversation was going.

"Now, the Lord tells us to forgive, to welcome the prodigal son upon his return. And in time, I'm certain *we* will get there. The children, however—" He shook his head, morosely. "We simply cannot have their lives upended again." When finished speaking, he nodded once, leaned back in his seat, and placed his hands on his belly. Brandy reached for his shoulder, and they exchanged a contented glance.

"Okay." I braced my elbows on my knees and scrubbed my hands across my face. I had forgotten how complicated conversations could be when the person speaking said one thing but meant another. "Thank you for that, I guess. And for everything you've done. But like I told Brandy yesterday, I have no intention of disturbing the peace." I turned to face Brandy. "I told you, I just want to know they have what they need."

"Oh." Shane frowned. "Bee made it seem like—"

"Better safe than sorry." Brandy pursed her lips.

"Well, now." Shane chuckled. "Let's not turn to argument."

Brandy gave him a glower that I thought best to nip in the bud.

"I really appreciate you both taking the time to see me," I said, turning to face Brandy. "You asked me yesterday where I've been and how I could leave. The short answer to the former is, I've been in New Mexico. As for the second question..." I sighed. A fly buzzed behind the curtain to my right. "I'm sure you already know of my mental health struggles, and I don't really want to get into that right now, but I was *able* to leave because of Joel. In my mind, he was always going to be there for them. The best dad. The best parent. I didn't add anything to the equation. That might have been wrong. It might have been right." I shrugged. "If they're happy, that would suggest the lat-ter. That I solved the problem all those years ago."

Brandy started to say something, but Shane put a hand on her arm to stop her.

I gave him a thankful smile. "So, me coming here now is more of a... a lingering instinct, perhaps. You know, to protect them."

I searched Brandy's face for understanding but found none. It struck me then to wonder whether they had kids of their own.

"Protect them from *what*?" Brandy spat. "What do you think of us?"

I raised my palms, taken aback by her sudden hostility. "I meant no disrespect."

Shane cleared his throat. "Now, now. Annie, what I hear you say-ing is that you want reassurance."

I nodded, grateful to have him translate.

He looked me square in the eyes. "I do think Joel's accident stirred up some old hurts for the kids. They were really young when you left but old enough to remember. They saw a grief specialist through the summer, but now that school has started, we've given them the option to only go as needed. They talk to us—as much as can be expected of teenagers—and they have good friends and teach-ers who look out for them."

I let out a shaky breath, allowing myself the most cursory of glances at the top photo in the stack in my lap. Two happy faces greeted me, and I would have known those smiles anywhere. The years hadn't mattered. I knew them in my soul. Against the backdrop of a snow-clad mountain—Rainier perhaps—Grace wore her still-blond hair piled on top of her head in a messy bun, fingers forming a peace sign in front of her chin. Connor, a spitting image of his dad, grinned self-consciously at the camera from behind knockoff Ray-Bans. *My children.*

No. They weren't *mine* anymore.

I let the tips of my fingers caress the picture. It wasn't the same as seeing them in real life, of course, but it would have to do. The closest I would let myself get.

Shane briefly rested his hand on Brandy's knee, ending with a pat. "At our house, they have their own rooms, chores, allowances, and family time. We take them to church every Sunday—"

I looked up.

"We realize that wasn't yours or Joel's thing," Brandy interjected. "But since they're in our home, that's something we expect."

I nodded even as I wondered when religion had become a fixture for them. It didn't fit with how I remembered things.

"I guess what I'm trying to say, what I'm trying to *assure* you of"—Shane leaned forward —"is that they are indeed happy and cared for. There's no need to worry. No need to..." He strummed his fingers together as if searching for the right word.

"Linger," I said. "Gotcha."

Brandy straightened. "You said you'd leave once you knew."

I nodded. "I meant it. I'll leave tomorrow."

She seemed to relax at that, but Shane's eyebrows went up. "You don't have any other questions?"

"Better not." I gave him a tight smile. The photos burned in my hand. I knew I would look at them, knew I would plunge right back into that initial despair I'd suffered after leaving them in the first place, but when I did, I intended to be far away from there. Far away where I couldn't hurt them. I didn't need to add details of their real-ness to those images.

"Well, then." Brandy stood, hoisting her purse onto her shoulder. "I wish you the best, Annie. God bless."

I walked them to the door and saw them out, willing Brandy to hear my unspoken wishes. *Be good to them. Take care of them. Be there for them.* Then I waved and closed the door, tears blurring my vision.

My job there was done, but in my heart, it felt anything but.

CHAPTER 5

After a night of much talking and little sleep, Kara saw me to my car late the following morning.

"Are you sure you don't want to stay over the weekend at least?" She handed me a bottle of water for the road, her eyes following my every movement. "You drove all the way here." She didn't say what I knew was on the tip of her tongue—that she was worried about me—but it was in her voice.

"I'll take my time heading back. Might as well start today." I set my backpack on the passenger seat and closed the door before facing her. The weight of leaving Snohomish once again rested heavily on my shoulders, and my head was pounding. I asked if Kara had some painkillers to spare before I hit the road.

"Yeah. Be right back." She disappeared into the house.

I waited, leaning against the side of my car, sucking in deep breaths of the earthy air. It felt so different going down my lungs than the dry New Mexican equivalent. More alive. I'd missed it.

"You're in luck!" Kara came down the steps with a small canister in her hand. "I had three left."

I was about to respond when she froze midstride. "Oh, shit."

"What?"

"Annie." She moved slowly toward me, her eyes darting between me and the street at my back. "Annie, maybe—"

"What's going on?" Her odd behavior was putting me on edge. Her voice sounded more like she was warning of an imminent bear attack than handing over painkillers.

She took my hand, a concerned crease marring her brow as she glanced behind me again.

I turned, and my whole world tilted on end.

"Mom?" Connor had stopped his bike on the other side of my car, face in shadow beneath the brim of his Seahawks cap.

Kara's grip tightened around my fingers as if sensing I needed physical support to remain upright, but I still reached for the roof of the car to suppress the illogical instinct to crouch down and hide. My heart pounded a rhythm of *flee, stay, flee, stay* against my ribs. Not that I could have run if I tried. My son's sudden appearance was either my wish come true or the worst thing that could have happened.

"It *is* you," he said. "It's me, Connor." He took his cap off, large gray eyes searching my face.

"Connor." His name came out whispered, and one of my hands flew to my mouth to stifle a sob. My son, right there in front of me. When I'd last seen him, he'd barely reached my elbow. Eight years later, he towered a whole head above me—tall like his dad. He wore his light-brown hair in a trendy quiff, so sleek compared to the messy second-grader I'd known.

Connor pushed his bike up onto the curb and parked it.

"Um, I should probably—" Kara pointed her thumb toward the house and started backing away from us despite my pleading look. I wasn't ready for this. This was not supposed to happen. She had to know I could break. Or worse, break him.

"You remember me, right?" Connor asked, stepping closer.

A nervous sound rippled up my throat. "Every day." I shook my head slowly, my brain grasping for something predictable to steady me. All I could think of were prime numbers. *Two, three, five, seven, eleven, thirteen... easy, Annie.* "You look so much like your dad."

As soon as I spoke, a shadow crossed his face.

Damn. I skimmed my sides for pockets in which to hide my shaking hands but came up short because of the useless sweatpants I was wearing. "I'm sorry. I shouldn't have—"

"It's okay." Connor's lips curved upward, that wide Cupid's bow that had always puckered in his sleep as a baby now stretching into a reassuring smile. "I heard Aunt Brandy on the phone last night. I don't think she knew I was still up. I had to come see."

"But aren't you supposed to be in school?" I blurted.

He shrugged and glanced at my car. "School's not going anywhere."

Right. I was supposed to be hitting the road.

As if he could sense where my thoughts were headed, he said, "Can we talk?"

Can we?

"Sure." I motioned for him to join me on the front step. I might have imagined it, but I thought I saw Kara moving by the curtain.

"So," Connor said after we sat down. He even sounded like Joel.

"So."

"Were you really not going to come say hi?"

I swallowed. "We thought it best. Considering."

"Because you're leaving again."

His words cut deep, even though there was no anger in them.

"Well, yes." I took a deep breath. "Because you're settled now, and it wouldn't be right to interfere."

"Huh." He gazed off down the street. "Says who?"

I studied his profile—the sharpening jawline, the curve of his ear, the cowlick at his temple that used to drive the hairdresser nuts. I had no idea where he got his hair cut nowadays, whether he'd had braces, or who his friends were. That realization stung.

Before I could stop myself, I reached out and let my fingers skim the side of his head. He flinched at my touch but didn't move away.

It was still enough for me to apologize and tuck my hands into my armpits.

"Grace doesn't know you're here," he said after a moment.

"Good."

"I wanted to make sure first. But if you can wait until tonight, I can bring her by. Brandy has book club."

Yes, yes, yes, my insides screamed. I bit down on my cheek. I'd promised. "I have a long drive. It's probably best not to."

For the first time since he'd shown up, Connor's expression darkened. "You still don't want us, then. I should have figured." He got up from the steps. Paced a few feet before turning to me. "When I was in fifth grade, we had to do our family tree for school. We never talked about you—Dad didn't want to—but for that project, I needed birth dates and stuff. So, I asked him for yours, and then I—" His voice cracked. "Then I asked him what date you had died. That was the first time I realized you might still be alive. Somewhere." His eyes had me pinned. "Just not with us."

The yearning to comfort him was no weaker than it had been years ago. I'd been there through nightmares, tears, scrapes, and bruises. For a while. Of course, I was the one causing his distress now. *Can a boogeyman offer solace? Should it try?*

"Connor." I rose to my feet, one hand outstretched, which he ignored. I let it fall back to my side. "It's not that simple."

"Then what?"

"Leaving you and Grace was the hardest thing I ever did, but you have to believe me—I did it for you."

He scoffed and pulled his hat back on. "Because you were depressed or whatever. Yeah, Dad said. But that makes no sense to me. If you're sad, wouldn't being with us, your family, make you feel better?"

"It should. I don't have a great explanation, but I want you to know—"

Connor's phone rang, interrupting me, and he pulled it out of his pocket. "Crap."

"What is it?"

"Brandy. School must have called her. What should I do?"

"You have to answer."

He walked away from me, clutching the phone to his ear. While he was talking to her, Kara stuck her head out the front door. "Everything okay?"

"We're about to find out. Brandy was notified that he ditched school."

Kara scrunched up her nose. "Oh. Oh, that's bad."

Connor returned, his face a deep red. "I have to go."

"What did she say?"

He sighed. "What didn't she say? I'm grounded for two weeks."

"For seeing your mom?" Kara asked. When Connor and I both glared at her, she retreated. "Sorry, I'll be inside." She closed the door again.

"I'm sorry, bud. If there's anything I can do..."

Connor awarded me a wide grin out of nowhere.

"What?"

"You called me 'bud.' I'd forgotten you used to do that."

My mouth tugged up at one corner. "I guess some habits never go away."

After a brief moment of shared mirth, he turned serious again. "Mom, I have so many questions. Do you *have* to leave today? What if you stay for the weekend? I promise I'll try to understand if—I mean when—you leave after that, but—" He took a breath and looked into my eyes. "Please don't go."

He looked so young right then, my son. Still little. Still uncertain and finding his way in the world. Beneath the adolescent surface, he was still the boy I'd known, and I had no doubt in my mind that had he spoken those same words to me eight years ago, I would have never left. They held ancient magic, the power of blood bonds, and my blessed curse was no different than that of any other mother—I had to heed it.

I stared at him for a long while. "Okay. But only for the weekend. And only if Shane and Brandy agree."

Hope lit his pale eyes. "They will. I'll make sure of it." He moved toward his bike. "And you promise you won't leave without letting me know, right?"

I followed. "I promise."

He released the kickstand but then paused and put it down again. After a brief hesitation, he hurried to me and wrapped his arms around my shoulders. It took me completely by surprise and was over before I could reciprocate, but his embrace imprinted deep within me. He didn't hate me like I'd hated myself. *Why?*

"See ya!" he called over his shoulder pedaling away.

"See ya," I whispered back.

ONCE INSIDE, I SAGGED to the floor, in need of air but getting none. I rested my palms on the hard tile, willing my lungs to cooperate. Cool tendrils of fear scurried up my neck at dizzying speed, then hands were on my shoulders.

"Annie? What's wrong? Do you need some water?" Kara made a move to pull away, but I managed to get hold of her wrist.

"Stay," I managed between gasps. "Panic." As if that alone could explain how my inner defenses were crumbling. "Will pass."

She sat down next to me and took my hand in hers. My fingers had gone numb, but when I focused my gaze on the outline of her thumb across the back of my hand, I could will myself to feel it there. Minutes passed—I could tell, since her wristwatch was in my direct line of sight. 11:23 a.m. Not helpful. I closed my eyes and focused instead on calming my runaway heart by conjuring Ravel's "Bolero" inside my head. Its slow crescendo had returned me from the brink more than once.

After going through each movement of the music, I cleared my throat. Still, my voice came out thick and hoarse. "I'll take a drink of water now."

Kara sprang into action as if she'd been waiting for my request the whole time.

"Thanks." I chugged the whole glass when she handed it to me. "I'm so sorry."

She took the glass back and set it on a side table. "Don't worry about it. What happened?"

"I had a panic attack. Connor—it was too much." Slowly, I flexed my fingers, relieved to find they did what I asked.

"I believe it. Are you okay now?"

I took stock. Breathing worked, my pulse had settled, and the cold sweat was subsiding. "I'll be fine."

Kara let out a sigh. "Gosh, you scared me. Does it happen a lot?"

"It depends. I wasn't prepared. Seeing him—" My voice cracked, and I blew out a shaky breath.

"Yeah, I get it. Lots of memories."

Memories? No, that was barely the half of it. Meeting Connor again was the closest I'd ever come to having my whole life flash before me—every high and low wrapped into a handful of minutes. No wonder it had sent me spiraling.

And yet, I couldn't wait to see him again.

CHAPTER 6

I spent my afternoon in quiet trepidation over the possible consequences of Connor's visit and my subsequent promise to stay for a few days. I wondered if that meant I would get to see Grace too.

I called Dr. Samson in emergency mode, but as she always did, she managed to settle me somewhat.

"Let your children set the pace. Accept what they offer, but don't ask for more. Answer their questions as best as you can. Be honest. And call me whenever."

I could do that. At least, I thought I could.

Shane called that evening, and after a courteous greeting, he got straight to the point. "This is less than ideal."

Harsh whispers from his end of the line told me Brandy disapproved of his choice of words.

"*Really* not ideal," he emphasized. "Yet, here we are."

I waited for him to continue, but when he didn't, I said the only words I could say—words I was quickly getting used to. "I'm sorry. I had every intention of leaving earlier today. I didn't know Connor would show up." I wanted to add that if they had been so worried about the kids finding out I was in town, they should have taken greater precautions not to mention my name in the house. As it was, I held my tongue.

"So he says." I could make out sounds of footsteps and a door closing on Shane's end. "Ah, well. What's done is done. I take it his little visit must have been a bit of a shock to you, too, perhaps?"

I relaxed. "You can say that again."

"He wants to see you. Bee is not keen, especially since he's supposed to be grounded, but in light of the circumstances, I think an exception can be made."

"I'd appreciate it."

"On our terms, of course."

"Terms?" My eyebrows furrowed.

"We'd like to invite you over for brunch tomorrow morning. Eleven. We'll speak to Grace tonight and let her know what's going on."

"Oh." Well, that was a better offer than I'd expected. More terrifying too. The mere thought of entering into their domain a visitor made my stomach clench.

"That way, we can all sit down together. Have a chat."

I was pretty sure that was code for "Don't try anything. We'll be watching."

"Brunch sounds great." I forced lightness into my voice. "Thank you so much for doing this. It means a lot."

"Don't mention it. 'Do not withhold good from those to whom it is due, when it is in your power to act.' Proverbs 3:27." Shane cleared his throat.

It seemed I'd become a religious charity now. Well, I wasn't about to knock it, considering.

MY PULSE WAS A FLIGHTY pitter-patter by the time I made my way to the other side of town the next morning. "She's your daughter," I said into the empty air. "It'll be fine."

It was raining hard, and by the looks of the graphite sky on the horizon, hail might be imminent. I should have brought a warmer sweater if the goosebumps on my arms were anything to go by. As my car approached one of the elementary schools, I reached to turn up the heat, briefly taking my eyes off the road. A stop sign appeared out of nowhere, but by some miracle, I was able to slam on the brakes at the very last moment. A split second later, I was shoved forward to the accompaniment of a grinding crunch and a honk.

"What the fuck?" I heard through the pelting rain. In my side mirror, I saw a figure in sweats surveying the damage where our cars had kissed. I took a deep breath and opened the door.

"How bad is it?"

"I don't have time for this shit," the guy muttered, ignoring my question. I could barely see his face beneath the hood of his soft-shell jacket. "The stop sign too hard for you to see?"

My brow furrowed. "You do realize *you* hit *me*, right?"

"Because you slammed on the brakes. It's not like I had anywhere else to go. If you had paid attention, it would have never happened." He caressed his dented hood. "I'm going to need to take this in."

Is this guy for real?

I leaned past him to examine my car and noted with some satisfaction that the extent of damage on my end was a deformed license plate. No biggie. I turned to face the guy. "Totally avoidable if you had kept a greater distance, in my opinion." I held his gaze, ready to defend myself further.

He was about to rebut but instead clamped his jaw shut. "Hold on." He pushed his hood back and squinted at me through the downpour. "Annie?"

The anger gave way to suspicion. I wasn't accustomed to random people knowing my name.

"Yeah?"

"Annie Wolff? From Centennial Middle School?"

The rain was starting to seep through my jacket, but I didn't move. I'd hoped for a longer respite before someone recognized me, but now word would get out, and people would start talking. I was about to deny it, but before I could respond, his previously glowering features broke into a wide grin. "It *is* you." He pointed at himself. "Wic Dubray. We had math and PE together."

Wic Dubray. The name rang a faint bell, but I still couldn't place him. "I'm sorry," I said, shaking my head.

"Aw, that's all right. I have a thing about faces, but I know not everyone does, and it has been a while. If it helps, I was the kid who nailed that three-pointer the first day, and then Ms. Curraugh called me 'lucky shot' for a month. You gave me a high five actually. Made my day." His teeth flashed white through the wet. He was rather striking despite the currents of water streaming down his dark hair.

The penny dropped. I remembered because that kid had huffed and puffed quite a bit about luck not having anything to do with it. "That was you? But you were—" I stopped. I'd been about to say "tiny."

He chuckled as if he knew then shrugged. "Late bloomer."

"I'll say." Heat washed over me as soon as the words passed my lips. "Um, I'm actually running late."

His expression fell. "Gotcha. Well, nice seeing you." He seemed to remember then where we were. "Or, you know, sorry about the..." He gestured toward the point of impact.

"Right." I hesitated for a split second, but then I got in the car and pulled away. When I checked the mirror, Wic had already disappeared into his car.

SINCE I'D BEEN TOLD Brandy had the food under control, I'd only brought a bouquet of tulips from Safeway. As I walked up to the house, I second-guessed that decision a dozen times. Maybe flowers were too formal. Maybe I should have chosen a box of donuts instead. Before I could come to a conclusion, Connor threw open the door, a toothy grin on his face.

"Hi." His deepening voice was so full of excitement that I couldn't help but smile back. "She's here!" he called into the house. Then he noticed my melted appearance. "What happened to you?"

Brandy came out from the kitchen, an apron tied around her waist over dark blue jeans. She stopped in her tracks when she saw my drenched cat impression.

"It's a long story," I said simply.

"Clearly." She gave me a curt nod and a disapproving glare, but when Connor turned to her, her expression instantly shifted into that of a Hostess with a capital *H*. "Get your sister, please." To me, she said, "The egg casserole has ten more minutes. Why don't you make yourself comfortable in the family room in the meantime, and I'll fetch you a dry sweater?"

I almost expected her to show me where to go as if I hadn't spent countless hours there in the past.

Left to my own devices, I meandered from the foyer through the arched doorway into the heart of the Hemingway home. I was relieved to discover the same mismatched sofa and recliner they'd had back then and too many throw pillows to count. It seemed Brandy's transformation had yet to reach her humble abode. That was if I ignored the oversized wooden cross above the mantel. *Seriously, when did this one-eighty happen?*

"Mom?"

I turned toward Connor's voice, still pondering my sister-in-law's personality swap. I'd taken my mind off the most important part of today, and as punishment, the past once more punched me in the gut.

Connor stood in the doorway, his hands resting on the shoulders of a girl at least a foot and a half shorter than him. Grace. Also, not Grace—at least, not the girl in the photos Brandy had given me. The version of my daughter slouching before me had short, uneven bangs and wore a black vest with the hood up even though it was plenty warm in the house.

I opened my mouth to greet her, but nothing came out.

Her glare reflected all my defects and failures, every squandered minute, and rightly so. If not for Connor's smile, I might have granted her unmistakable wish and left.

"Hello, Grace," I said with as much feigned confidence as I could muster. *You're the adult,* I reminded myself. *Act it.* "It's really good to see you."

She met my gaze, her expression one of defiance. "Hi." Then quietly to Connor, "I was kind of in the middle of something upstairs. I'll be down when the food is ready." She almost collided with Brandy in her hurry to leave.

Brandy handed me a pair of track pants that I suspected were Shane's and a University of Washington sweatshirt. She frowned at the stairs. "What happened?"

"I'm not sure." *Eight years?*

Connor offered an apologetic grimace. "Don't take it personally—she's crabby most of the time nowadays."

So it wasn't just me? I turned to Brandy for an explanation, but she avoided eye contact. I thought she'd told me the kids were doing "really good." If that was the case, she and I must have different definitions of the phrase.

"It's fine," I said. "I don't want to make her talk to me. That was never my intent."

"That may be well and good for you, but in this house, I expect manners. Grace?" Brandy hollered up the stairs. When there was no response, she walked up a few paces. "Grace McLaren, come downstairs, please!"

Connor and I exchanged uneasy glances.

This is my fault. Showing my face after such a long absence was bad for them. *I* was bad for them. Still.

"Do you like waffles?" Connor asked, watching me carefully. "I made the batter from scratch."

Oh, sweet boy. Ever the mediator. I had forgotten about that too. Forcing my misgivings down, I smiled, turning all my focus on him.

"I love waffles. Just let me get changed, and I'll meet you in the kitchen."

FOR A LONG WHILE, THE only sound in the dining room was silverware clanking against china and the occasional hum of approval from Shane when he ingested a particularly tasty morsel. I tried to find a rhythm in it, something countable to hold on to, but failed. Instead, I focused on my food, hyperaware of Grace across from me, pushing a single strawberry around in circles on her plate. The tines of her fork scraped against the enamel.

After Connor helped himself to a second heap of waffles, he looked from me to his sister and put his fork down. "Did you know Grace is a really good singer?"

Grace's shoulders stiffened.

"I heard she was in choir." I glanced at Brandy. "Do you like it, Grace?"

My daughter peered up at me from beneath those uneven bangs. She lanced the strawberry with one final stab. "I guess."

Shane chuckled. "You're too humble, Gracie." He turned to me. "She sings like an angel."

Grace leveled her icy glare on him. "I've asked you before not to call me Gracie. Only Dad did, and you are not my dad."

A pink flush crept across Shane's cheeks at this alleged faux pas, but he didn't respond. Instead, he wiped his mouth once, twice, three times with the cloth napkin he'd spread across his lap.

"Grace," Brandy cautioned, dragging out the vowel.

Grace dropped her fork with a loud rattle. "What?"

"Come on, guys." Connor tried a smile, his gaze flickering between them. "Who wants more food? Should I get the casserole from the kitchen?"

For a moment, it seemed Brandy would take Grace's bait and start something, but then she pressed her lips together. "Sure, Connor. That'd be great."

With some effort, I willed the knot in my chest to ease. "It's delicious," I said, forcing a light tone. "I'd love some more."

Connor disappeared into the kitchen, leaving me to figure out how I could possibly swallow another bite. I'd known coming back was a risk, but I hadn't prepared myself for outright hostility. At least I wasn't the only recipient. Grace distributed her displeasure fairly and evenly around the table. To me, that suggested there was more to her rancor than my presence.

More than once, the thought struck that I could get up and leave, that perhaps this was a mistake. But every time it did, a nagging tugged ever stronger at my insides. I'd come back to assure myself all was well.

With one look at Grace, I'd just confirmed it wasn't.

CHAPTER 7

Connor had a soccer game Sunday afternoon to which I more or less invited myself. He seemed excited I would be there, Brandy less so.

The cold steel and unforgiving edges of the high school bleachers made spectating as uncomfortable as I remembered, but the turnout meant good people watching. Kara had warned me that morning that I would probably see plenty of familiar faces—we were in a small town of less than ten thousand, after all. Consequently, I'd borrowed one of her caps that, together with my sunglasses, covered most of my face. I had no desire whatsoever to be recognized.

"Can I have money for chips?" Grace asked Shane a few minutes before kickoff.

I instinctively reached for my purse and pulled out my wallet. "How much do you need?"

She aimed a silent question toward her uncle, who gave her a nod. "Five dollars?"

I smiled at her and handed her a bill. "Here's ten. In case you see something else you want."

She hesitated then shoved it into the pocket of her black jeans. "Thanks."

"Hurry back!" Brandy called after her.

Grace reached the end of the row, head downturned, feet ambling. I watched uneasily, not only because she'd only spoken a few curt words to me so far. In my gut, I knew something was off. My little Grace had been a social butterfly, always making friends and chatting away. She talked to old ladies at the store, dressed with the sole purpose of "feeling fun," and was always quick to smile. The version in front of me had lost its colors.

I wasn't dumb. Five was different from thirteen. But although Connor clearly had grown up and changed, he was still Connor. Grace felt altogether foreign. Whether it was because of me, Joel's death, or everything put together, I couldn't yet tell.

"How is she doing in school?" I asked Shane after we settled in.

"Great." He waved to someone he knew a few rows down from us. "She would have had straight As last year if not for..." He glanced at his wife before turning to me. "You know."

"Right. Of course."

"Most of her teachers were very understanding through it all. Only one or two insisted the incomplete assignments at the end of the semester meant they couldn't, in good conscience, retain her grade."

"Completely heartless," Brandy muttered next to her husband.

"Well, it was seventh grade. Not really high stakes." Shane shrugged.

"But she likes school?"

"Sure." He nodded. "Except for PE. Says it's a waste of time."

"I tend to agree," Brandy said, "but I don't tell her that."

The game started, and for a while, everyone's focus was on the field where the local team set out to clobber Redmond early on. Connor was fast, dancing around the opposition with the ball. I didn't know much about the sport, but I couldn't keep my eyes off my son.

"He's good, right?" I asked Shane after our team scored its first goal off an assist from Connor.

"Sure is." Shane grinned. "God-given gift."

"Sports take up too much time," Brandy said. "He only has a few more years of high school and should be focusing on his studies. And now with the drama club too—"

Shane put a hand on his wife's arm. "We've talked about this. He needs it."

"He's playing, isn't he? I didn't put my foot down."

I got the feeling Brandy putting her foot down meant the end of most arguments. Seeing Connor on the field made me appreciate even more Shane having his back over the last few months, but that might only last until Brandy had had enough. *And where's she getting all these ideas about schooling versus extracurriculars?* From what Joel had told me, Brandy herself hadn't been a model student way back when.

"Weren't you on the cheer team in high school?" I asked her, pretending not to notice the way her nostrils flared at my question. When Brandy didn't respond, I scanned the entrance of the field where two concession carts were drawing lines of people. "I'm going to go look for Grace. She should have been back by now."

I found my daughter watching the game from the far end of the bleachers, snacks in hand and her phone balancing on her leg. She flinched when I said her name but didn't object when I sat next to her.

"Find anything good?" I asked, pointing at her small bag of Doritos.

She tilted it my way without a word.

"Thanks."

We watched the game together in silence until halftime. The home team was still leading 1-0, and spirits were high.

Grace opened a bottle of cola.

"Do you like soccer?" I asked. "Or do you prefer basketball like your dad?"

She glared at me before turning away. "Don't talk about him."

She was treacherous as a bog—one wrong step, and I'd be gobbled up.

"Okay." I scanned the sidelines for Connor's team. He was talking animatedly with two other players. All three of them laughed. "Maybe I should go back to the others?"

She shrugged. "Up to you."

At least I wasn't banished.

Another girl came up the steps nearby, and instantly, my daughter's demeanor changed.

"Hi, Chrissy." There was something obliging in her voice. Something eager that I didn't recognize.

The girl stopped. "Oh, hey. Have you seen Lucy and them?"

"Um, no. I didn't know you guys were—"

"Never mind, they're probably late again." Chrissy tapped something on her phone and sat down. "Oh, you've got chips?" She reached for Grace's bag, but it was already empty. "Aw, but I'm hungry. Mom wouldn't let me buy anything."

"I got a Twix too." Grace held it out.

Chrissy took it. "Thanks."

"So, what are you—"

"Hold on." Chrissy cut Grace off, typing something on her phone. She stared at it, let out a sharp "Ha!" at the response, then typed again. This went on for several excruciating minutes.

Meanwhile, Grace picked up her phone. She looked at the dark screen, put it down again, glanced at Chrissy, then off into the distance.

Something about Grace's friend rubbed me the wrong way. I leaned forward past my daughter. "Hi, there."

Grace froze as her friend's eyes cut between us.

"Um, hi?" Chrissy finally put her phone down.

Grace glared at me. "This is my... This is Annie," she said, grudgingly. She pointed at the girl. "Chrissy is a friend from school."

"Nice to meet you."

Chrissy blew a bubble with her gum then popped it loudly. The two girls looked at each other and giggled as if I wasn't there. It didn't matter. At least Grace was smiling. I didn't even mind that she'd avoided introducing me as her mom. I hadn't earned that yet.

Yet? I shook my head. There would be no more chances. Tomorrow, I would head back to New Mexico, and life would resume for everyone involved. That was how it was supposed to be.

The game started back up. I watched, unseeing, while the girls whispered and laughed next to me. I pictured saying goodbye to Grace and Connor tonight, getting into my car in the morning, then driving all those long hours back. *But to what?* Nothing was waiting for me in Albuquerque that I couldn't handle with a phone and a computer for a while.

The crowd around me cheered for another goal as I visualized walking into my studio sublet. The faint smell of frying grease that permeated the building hallways and seeped into the apartments. The noiseless sound of empty space after I shut my door behind me.

The image filled me with such dread, I couldn't move.

"Are you okay? You're all white." Grace's voice registered faintly to my right.

What if I stay for a bit? Will that help? I tried out a different scenario in my head—one where I came to Connor's game next weekend, too, maybe took the kids for ice cream after school one day, and got Grace to open up. *Yes, that's better.* I could breathe again.

"I'm fine," I said out loud, surprised my voice carried.

Grace turned back to Chrissy with a shrug.

I asked myself if I was sure. Tested my resolve by picturing the two scenarios again. The stark truth was that, in the end, I couldn't fathom leaving them yet. I wanted more time, and I needed to get to the bottom of what was going on with Grace. It might have been selfish and foolish and futile, but that unexpected warmth infusing my heart whenever I looked upon the two lives I'd once created had me shackled and unwilling to break the bond.

Just then, Connor scored the third and final goal of the game, and the crowd went as wild as the butterflies inside me.

THE BLEACHERS CLEARED before I could move again. Grace had left with her friend, and only the coaches and a few players with their parents remained on the field. I flinched as if waking from a dream, a sudden urgency to find the others propelling me forward.

I caught up to them in the parking lot, where they'd gathered in a small cluster, talking to a tall man in sunglasses. The sunlight glinted off the straight black hair that spilled past his broad shoulders.

Just as I reached them, he said something to Connor and patted him on the back. Connor grinned at him. A compliment about the game, I assumed.

"Oh, there you are." Brandy checked her wristwatch. "We've been waiting. Grace said you were right behind her."

"Annie, this is my cousin. I don't think you've met." Shane gestured to the man.

I squinted up at the stranger, extending my hand.

He enveloped it with warm, tan fingers that made mine disappear. With his other hand, he propped his sunglasses up on his head. "We meet again." He pointed at himself, grinning. "Wic, remember?"

My eyes widened despite the bright light. *No way.* "You're Shane's cousin?"

"You guys know each other?" Connor asked, confusion in his voice.

Wic said "Yes" at the same time I answered "No."

"We don't." I cringed at how harsh that sounded. "I mean, not really." *Ugh, why is this so complicated? Be normal.*

"Annie is actually Bee's sister-in-law, and the kids'... um, mother," Shane said.

I saw the moment of understanding hit—a fleeting hesitation in Wic's smile—but he recovered quickly. "What do you know? Small world. Turns out we had classes together in sixth grade. And then we *ran into* each other again yesterday morning." He winked at me.

The nerve.

"Actually, he ran into me is more accurate." I pulled my hand out of his, surprised I hadn't noticed him holding it this whole time. "He's the guy who hit me at the stop sign."

Connor's eyebrows drew up as he turned to Wic. "That was you?"

"You can't slam the brakes last minute and expect traffic behind to follow without consequence. Back me up here, cuz."

"Okay, well, um..." Shane laughed uncomfortably.

It was impossible to tell if Wic was being serious or messing with me, and I didn't care for walking into traps. I tried to match his expression when I retorted, "The key word being *behind*. You were *behind* me. You're supposed to leave enough space, especially in bad weather."

Our eyes met—whether a challenge or an effort to take measure, I wasn't sure—but the glint in his dark brown ones broke my defenses just a little. Enough to make me forget what I was going to say.

"She's not wrong." Brandy interjected, thereby interrupting whatever connection Wic and I had shared. "If you keep enough distance, you still have time to brake."

I gave her a nod of appreciation, but Wic just laughed. "Okay, okay. For what it's worth, I'm sorry. I'd had a bad day and was in a hurry to get to the pharmacy to fill Mom's prescription, but I should have paid attention. Truce?"

I had a feeling he could have swayed even the coldest heart with those dimples, and now it appeared he'd also had a good reason for being in a hurry. All I could do was nod and let it go.

"Good." He turned back to Shane. "Anyway, the deck."

"Right." Shane shifted where he stood. "The deck."

"I have some time on my hands like I said, so hit me up if you decide to do anything with it." Wic bumped Shane's shoulder with his fist and took a step back. "I should go. Enjoy the rest of your Sunday." He strode away, not even acknowledging me.

Which was fine, of course.

"So, your cousin, huh?" I asked Shane as we made our way to the cars.

My brother-in-law grimaced. "He's a good guy. Going through some stuff with his mom—my aunt—right now."

"Oh." I wanted to ask more questions, but it was none of my business. I wasn't there to socialize with anyone but my children anyway. Couldn't if I tried, really, judging by the underwhelming interaction with Wic that had just taken place.

"Dinner tonight before you head back?" Brandy asked as if she'd read my mind.

A shiver coursed through me. *Head back.* I dreaded what she would say when I told her I would be extending my stay. I hoped she would understand my concerns for Grace but knew I couldn't count on it. To prepare for what was coming, I needed some time to clear my mind and a call to Dr. Samson.

CHAPTER 8

I told them two more weeks, since that was about as long as I could impose on Kara's hospitality, but judging by everyone's reaction, I might as well have said I was staying forever, running for mayor, and starting an underground escort service.

"You promised you'd leave!" Brandy all but yelled over the phone. "I knew we shouldn't have let you in, but Shane, he—" She huffed. "This is not appropriate, Annie. Not appropriate at all."

There was a chance she was right, of course. I *was* messing with the status quo. But Grace was not okay. No matter how I twisted and turned what little I'd seen of her behavior around in my head, I knew I wasn't imagining things.

"What's your main concern?" Dr. Samson asked during a call a few days later. "You know you have my support. I just want you to be very clear on why you can't leave as planned."

I considered this, replaying all that had happened in the days since I'd returned. "I keep coming back to the photo Brandy gave me. The one from the summer. And how much Grace has changed since. I know they see it, too, even though Brandy tried not to let on at first. Connor does for sure. I suppose it could be puberty, or Joel's death, or friend stuff, or even a delayed reaction to me leaving all those years ago, but"—I wrapped my arms tighter around the pillow in my lap—"What I'm really worried about is that she might be like me. And my mother and grandmother." The hair on my neck rose as the words crossed my lips.

Dr. Samson didn't interrupt, so I continued, "What if no one else can see it? What if I'm the only one who can help her? I always thought leaving them meant saving them. That if I wasn't here and they never had to go through what I did—never had to beg me to get off the couch to make them food, remind me to take my pills, wipe my tears, or watch as I—" I shook my head to get rid of the imposing memories. "I thought they'd be better off. But now I don't know."

Dr. Samson was silent for a while. "I understand," she said eventually. "And you're right, of course. It's likely depression runs in your family."

"But what if...?" *I was wrong? Made a mistake? Failed?*

"Yes?"

"What if me being here makes it worse? She's clearly mad at me."

Dr. Samson seemed to consider this. "It's possible her immediate reaction to you coming back and a potential depression could be two separate things. After all, the changes you've told me about—her appearance, her demeanor—that started before your return, no?"

"I guess. Somehow it still feels like my fault, though."

"Annie, it would be no more your fault than the color of her hair, her musical talent, or her opinion on the taste of olives. Like it or not, genes are a lottery." She paused. "It would mean there's double to deal with, however. What if you don't find the answers you're looking for before these two weeks are up?"

I rubbed my forehead. "I know." Brandy had stopped speaking to me after I told her I wasn't leaving as agreed, and with her, Grace. It was unclear how I would ever be able to get close enough to my daughter to find out what was really going on. "All I know is, I can do even less from Albuquerque."

There had to be a way to get Brandy and Shane on my side. They loved the kids—that I didn't doubt. They'd wanted to adopt them for goodness sakes. "If two weeks isn't enough, I'll deal with that later."

IN ALL OF THE TURMOIL, at least one person in my family was happy I was still there, and that was Connor.

In the week after the soccer game, I saw him twice away from the house—once when he came by Kara's and again when we met up for coffee after school. He was quick to smile and eager to talk, but it always felt like we were on borrowed time, sneaking around. From the way he repeatedly checked the time on his phone, I could tell I wasn't alone in that feeling. It wasn't fair to him.

That was why I asked him to bring Shane to our next meeting.

On Saturday morning, my brother-in-law was waiting for me at one of the unassuming brown tables in the corner cafe on 1st Street. The place was about half-full, the sound of voices an even murmur. I scanned the space for Connor but didn't see him.

"He'll be here in a bit. I wanted a word first." Shane gestured to the seat across from him after I got a cup of coffee at the counter. I'd considered the full pastry case as well but decided against anything sugary. My stomach was too tight from nerves to be able to handle it.

I sat, weighing my words. I had no business asking him to take my side over Brandy's, but that was what I needed to do. Only a week remained of the time I'd allowed myself, and I was not a smidge closer to solving the riddle that was Grace. I needed a man on the inside, so to speak.

"I know what you must be thinking. Who am I to meddle in your affairs? The kids were settling in, they have every material comfort anyone could ask, and you and Brandy are already their guardians." I wrapped my fingers around the warm mug.

"Hmm." Shane steepled his hands together on the table.

"I mean, I get that me coming back isn't what you planned for. But I'm worried about Grace. I can't leave until I know what's going on." There, I'd said it. "I realize you might not like that, and I get it, I promise. I'll try not to overstep—I really am grateful to you guys for everything you're doing."

Shane put a hand up to stop me. "Did you know Bee is pregnant?" he asked, his brow furrowing.

My mouth snapped shut. Not what I'd expected.

"We've been trying to start a family for years. Three miscarriages." His lips pursed.

That answered my question of why they didn't have children. "I'm so sorry."

"And you know, I'm convinced God has a plan for us. I can feel it. But it's been real hard on Bee. Real hard." He nodded solemnly, lost in some far-off place. After a long moment, he cocked his head and gave me a faint smile. "You're their mom, Annie. It's not my place to judge or to tell you what to do. Of course, you're not wrong about them settling in and all that. But if you want to stay—if you feel strong enough to stay then, by all means, do. It has certainly brought some joie de vivre back to Connor." He paused to scoot his chair in so another customer could pass behind him. "It used to be all soccer talk, and now it's Mom this and Mom that. Between you and that drama club at school, I'm really seeing some of the old Connor come back."

I smiled. That alone meant my presence wasn't for nothing.

"And don't worry about Grace. She'll come around. She's thirteen."

My smile froze. An age thing, then. I wasn't convinced. "Yeah, maybe. And Brandy? Think she'll come around too?"

"She's just concerned about them. Joel's death was a hard blow for her—she's the only one left in her family now."

Deep inside, I knew he was right. Brandy's aversion to me wasn't really rooted in my person. We had been quite friendly in the early days of my and Joel's relationship. No, it was what I represented—an uncontrollable threat, an unpredictable element in their lives—that bothered her. She had said so herself when we said goodbye one of my first nights back, if in not as many words: "At least tell them before you leave this time." I'd have to work harder to show her I, too, had the kids' best interest at heart. Even if that, in the long run, meant they might stay with her and Shane.

Shane ran a hand over his dark mop of shaggy hair as if attempting to flatten it down. "Here's Connor." He nodded past my shoulder.

I turned to see my son weave between the square tables. "Hey."

"Hi, Mom." He cut a casual figure in a soccer jersey and skinny jeans, but his hair was impeccable as always.

"Want anything?"

He glanced toward the counter. "Maybe."

Shane adjusted the cuffs on his windbreaker. "Lunch is in an hour. You know your aunt doesn't like you eating too close to meals." To me, he said, "It was a bit of an adjustment at first. The regular meals. Vegetables. Joel sure liked his carbs." He chuckled.

In my peripheral, I saw Connor's eyes flash, but he didn't say anything.

"I'm sure a cookie won't make much of a difference." I smiled at my son. "It is Saturday, after all."

Shane's chin bobbed. "I suppose you're right. Just this once." He stood. "Well, I'm off. Mulching duty calls. See you at home, Connor? And why don't you come around for dinner in the next few days, Annie? I'll put something on the grill."

"Are you sure?"

A conspiratorial wink. "I'll talk to Bee. It'll be fine."

How about that? I'd hoped for something small that would reassure Connor he wasn't breaking any rules by seeing me, and now Shane was turning into an unexpected ally to boot.

"Can I have a cinnamon roll instead?" Connor asked when Shane had left. "I'm starving."

I considered what I'd just learned about Brandy's food rules. As much as I didn't want to undermine her, I also failed to see the harm. He was a growing boy. "Sure," I said after a beat.

Connor lit up.

I watched him order at the counter—a young man now but still finding his posture as such. At first glance, he seemed content with his current situation, but something still had me not entirely convinced. As he regaled me with stories from his latest soccer practice, my mind was stuck on that dark glare he'd given Shane a minute ago after the offhanded comment about Joel and on whether or not he liked living with his aunt and uncle. Of course, I couldn't ask. The situation was a balancing act. Keep Connor *or* Brandy happy. Get to know Grace, *or* give her space. The problem was, learning to walk the tightrope took time and patience, neither of which I had.

"We have an away game in Bothell next weekend," Connor said. "Will you come?"

I wanted to say yes, but it wasn't that simple. I hid behind a big gulp of lukewarm coffee and a shrug to avoid answering. I doubted Shane talking to Brandy would make anything better. No, with time running out, this situation required action of a different kind.

Brandy and me, all our cards on the table.

CHAPTER 9

Done hedging, I called Brandy early that week to take the bull by the horns. She answered with a curt "Hello," that made me break out in a sweat before I'd even spoken, but when I asked if we could talk, she reluctantly told me to come over.

"Ground rules need to be established," she said. "Might as well get it over with." It wasn't exactly a peace offering, but I was game. To reach Grace, I would need her on my side.

IT WAS A DIFFERENT Brandy who opened the door when I knocked. Her face was pale and bare, her hair pulled back with a hairband. "Feeling a bit under the weather," she said in response to what must have been my look of concern. "It's nothing."

She let me in and brought me into the kitchen, where freshly made cookies lined the countertop. "PTA bake sale. But you can have one if you'd like." She poured two cups of coffee.

"Thanks." I sat down at the kitchen table. The trees outside the window were turning more and more orange by the day.

She pulled milk out of the fridge and set it down between us before taking a seat herself.

"Sorry you don't feel well," I said. "Let me know if there's something I can do."

She brought the coffee mug to her lips, but after a sniff, she promptly set it down again.

"I'm not actually sick." Her hands went to her temples, rubbing circles. "I'm pregnant."

I stopped chewing one of the delicious cookies and watched her. For a moment, I considered pretending to be surprised but decided against it. "Shane told me. How far along?"

"Eighteen weeks."

Instinctively, my attention was drawn to her midsection. She could have fooled anyone in her sweats, but then again, she'd always been petite. "That's great news. I'm really happy for you."

Her chin trembled as her fingers fluttered to her eyelids and pressed down. A small sob escaped her lips. I sat paralyzed, unsure what to do. Eventually, I reached for the roll of paper towels in the window and handed her a sheet.

She sniffled into it and pulled in a shaky breath. "Sorry, I'm just scared. Did Shane tell you it's the fourth time?" Her face crumpled again.

I leaned over and patted her arm awkwardly. "He did. And I'm really sorry."

Brandy blew her nose again. "The doctor says everything looks good. Heartbeat is strong. My levels are normal."

"Well, that's good."

"There was nothing wrong the other times either. They just didn't want to stay no matter how I prayed."

I frowned. "You know it's not your fault, right? Sometimes it takes a few tries."

She glared at me then, with a hint of a challenge, said, "Not for you and Joel. You barely looked at each other and *bam*. It's not fair when *I* want this so badly."

I finished my cookie, chewing slowly to allow the implication in what she'd said to run off me. It didn't work. "For the record, Connor and Grace were both wanted. In case that's what you meant by fair."

"At the time, perhaps," Brandy said, more to herself than to me. She'd stopped crying.

"Excuse me?"

"Well, you have a strange way of showing it, don't you think? Abandoning them?" Her voice took on an edge. "Do you have any idea what that did to them? What it did to Joel? Of all the selfish, misguided impulses. You're supposed to tough it out. That's what parenting is."

Each one of her words hit home like honing arrows, and the pain made me bristle. "Yeah, you'd know?"

Her suddenly slack expression made me wish I could take it back. *Damn it, Annie.*

"I'm sorry," I said instead. "That was unnecessary."

"Whatever." She pushed her chair back from the table and went to the sink to fill up a glass of water.

I had to fix this. "Bee, you know why I left, right? Joel told you?"

She turned and leaned against the countertop. "Depression, you didn't love him anymore, had to figure out some issues, yada, yada, yada."

I cocked my head. "Have you ever been depressed? And I don't mean sad because the quarterback dumped you for your best friend. Or"—I held up a finger to stop her from interrupting— "even devastated with struggling to conceive. I'm talking the pervasive erosion of your very self. When nothing matters, and you're just trapped inside your head where no one can reach you."

She rolled her eyes. "That's a bit melodramatic, don't you think?"

"I'll take that as a no, then."

"But you had a family." She shook her head. "I'm sorry. I will never understand."

At ten years old, I'd found my mom's dead body in the bathtub. She had been thirteen when her mother had hung herself in the barn. Shortly after Connor's sixth birthday, I stole my mother-in-law's sleeping pills and gorged myself on them while Joel was at work. I stuck my fingers down my throat right away that time, and when Grace woke up from her nap, I was still there. But after that day, I knew I had to do something drastic.

"I was in a dark place," I said. "I thought if I didn't leave, the kids would go through the same trauma I did. I had to stop the cycle somehow."

Brandy stared at me for a long moment. "Joel told me about your mom." She reached for one of the cookies and took a bite before putting it down. "No," she said after a long minute. "As horrible as that must have been, it's still no excuse. When you left, you might as well have been dead."

"You don't think it's better to grow up knowing your mother loved you enough to know when to leave than to watch her die?"

"But you didn't, did you? Die."

I scoffed and stood, preparing to leave. "Not for a lack of trying. What do you want me to say? You want to know what it feels like to have your stomach pumped in the back of an ambulance? You have no idea what it's been like, and I refuse to sit here and take your judgment." There was also the fact that I might have been back for the past four years already if not for Joel. Though I doubted at this point it would matter to her that he'd told me to stay away.

"I would never claim to know what's happened to you to turn you into this"—I waved my hand in her general direction—"version of yourself. I feel for you, and I sincerely hope things work out this time, but don't pretend I'm the root of all that's gone wrong and you haven't also made questionable choices along the way. We're human. All of us. Including me."

I headed for the foyer, but she caught up to me when I reached the door.

"You're going to hurt them again. They've been through so much, and I worry you being here will lead to nothing good."

I spun. "Is that so? Then how come Shane says Connor is finally coming out of his shell again? *He* sought *me* out? And you know something is going on with Grace."

"What are you talking about? Grace is fine."

"I disagree."

"She's a teenager. You don't know her like I do. She was five when you left. As far as she knows, she doesn't have a mother."

I deflated as if she'd punched me. "I take it you see yourself as the stand-in?"

Her lips pursed.

With a resigned sigh, I met Brandy's gaze. "Look, I don't want to fight with you. I know it doesn't seem like it, but I am deeply grateful they have you and Shane. You've picked up the pieces and put them back together. But I'm here now, and I intend to see them—as long as they want me to. Can't you at least try to think of it as a good thing to have one more pair of eyes on them, one more person to help? Especially now that you're pregnant."

After a moment, she nodded. "Pregnant" must have been the magic word. "I suppose so."

"I promise, I'm not here to mess things up. I'm happy to drive to activities if you need to rest, and maybe I can take them for dinner or ice cream every once in a while. Surely you and Shane could use some time together."

Brandy relaxed her stance and let her arms fall to her sides. I took it as a good sign.

"And if the time comes for me to leave, I'll make sure they are prepared and understand why." The hair at the nape of my neck rose at the thought, but I pressed on. "I know you don't like me very much, and that's fine. But do you think we could be a team for now at least? Work together? If Grace is fine, I'll stand corrected, but—"

"No, I agree." A small crease appeared between Brandy's brows. "She's different lately, quieter. Doesn't see friends as often. I've been preoccupied with this pregnancy and school starting and everything. The nausea was horrible—never-ending—but the last few days, it seems to have receded slightly. Though that scares me in a different way."

I nodded. I recognized the ailments and worries all too well.

"I'll see if I can get her to talk," she continued. "But you have to do something in return."

"Anything."

"You need to commit. None of this 'if I decide to leave' crap. If you want to see the kids, get to know them again, you need to show them you mean it."

"But—"

"No. Nonnegotiable. I may not understand what your life has been like, and I don't know that I'll ever forgive you for what you did. My only option, then, is to trust that God has a higher purpose for bringing you back. You're here. So be it. You need to promise to stay."

It was as if she knew Dr. Samson's question had haunted me. *If two weeks weren't enough, what would I do?* Even if I somehow miraculously managed to settle Grace's case in the next seven days, there was still Connor. He and I were already building something that would be very hard to leave behind. The fantasy was already there, of staying and somehow being part of their lives; I'd glimpsed it in brief moments of weakness throughout the past week. And there Brandy was, suggesting it could be made a reality.

My throat tightened. "What if I fail?"

"This time, we know. Ask for help."

I stared at her. It was the most unexpected olive branch.

"If you mean what you say, wouldn't you do absolutely anything to make it work this time?"

I nodded. "I would."

"Good." She crossed her arms. "Then that's my deal. If you stay, you plan on staying for good. Adoption would no longer be necessary, but we are still their guardians. I don't see that changing any time soon, if ever, considering. Show you are willing to try, and in return, I will accept you being part of their lives."

It was more than I'd hoped for. And she was right. There was no need to interfere with current living arrangements. My mom had been thirty-eight when she'd ended it, her mom thirty-seven. I'd turned thirty-six two months ago—I knew I was by no means safe. "And you'll help with Grace? Keep me posted?"

"I will."

Finally, some form of progress.

"She actually has a violin recital next Saturday," Brandy continued. "Maybe you can come?"

"She plays?" So many moments missed.

"Fourth year. She's pretty good."

"And you think she'll be okay with me there?"

She shrugged. "We've got to start somewhere, right?"

CHAPTER 10

"Do you think I'm making the right decision?" I asked Kara the following weekend on what would have been one of my last nights there. The weight of knowing I had to figure out what was going on with Grace as fast as possible rested firmly on my shoulders.

Kara had brought work home with her. She popped a fudge sample in her mouth then handed me the plate with the rest. She sucked on the sweet until it dissolved, like a sommelier identifying notes in a new wine. "Too much brown sugar. Pass me one of the peanut butter ones."

I returned the dish then curled up on the couch, pulling a blanket across my lap. The summer heat had finally given in to the crisp, fragrant air of late September.

She studied me for a long while before speaking. "It's not my place to say. You know I've loved having you here. It's felt like—"

"Like old times." I smiled at her.

"You still haven't talked to Grace?"

I shook my head. "Not yet. Brandy has promised to help."

"What does Connor say?"

I allowed myself a small smile, but it battled with the tightness forming in my chest. "He's excited but keeps asking if I'm sure. Kind of breaks my heart. But I guess that's fair."

"Does he know? About you, I mean—why you left?"

"I think he knows more than I've told him."

Kara squinted at me. She opened her mouth as if to speak but hesitated before the words came out. "I might be overstepping here, but you just don't seem depressed to me. I don't want to downplay anything, and I know you're worried, but maybe you're fine. Maybe things are just different now. Have you thought of that?"

I wrapped a strand of the throw's fringe around my finger and watched as the tip turned blue before releasing the tie. Outside the window, a car drove by too fast. "The medication is doing its job right now. And I've been sleeping better on your couch than I was back home." That had been a surprise. The sleep issues were one symptom of my depression the meds had not been able to fix before. "I'm good right now. But I've been good before, and it never lasts."

"Maybe this time it will."

Oh, how I wanted it to—wanted to be freed of the fogged-glass prison that had been my home for so long. Shatter its limiting walls. Abolish the lurking shadows haunting the other side of the panes, stalking me. Therapy and medications had cleared the glass, poked breathing holes in the ceiling, and let some warmth seep in, but I'd never completely escaped. I could never fully stand up straight and set my sights on the horizon. There was always the question of what if.

"It's not that simple."

"Okay." Kara reached for another piece of fudge, sniffing it before putting it on her tongue. "But you do want to stay?"

"Yes. I need to." I may have abdicated my role as a mother eight years ago, but its essence still ran thick in my blood. "I love them. And now that they're older, they might understand when—*if* I dip again." A heat wave rolled up my torso, and I rubbed my neck absentmindedly. "I'm taking the risk. It's time."

"Wow." Kara beamed at me. "I'm in fucking awe of you right now. Good for you. So, what's next, then? I'm really sorry I have to kick you out soon. You know I don't want to."

"I do."

"Logan needs his normal back, I think. Going back and forth between me and Mike is not ideal."

"You don't have to explain. I get it." While I spoke, her question echoed inside my head. *What is next?* I pressed my fingertips against each thumbpad, both hands moving in synchrony, faster and faster. *How will Grace react? Where will I live? What do I do with my sublet in Albuquerque? Do I have to find a new therapist? When will I crack?*

My field of vision started shrinking at the same time my heart picked up speed. The stampede in my chest made it difficult to catch my breath, but I closed my eyes, willing the panic to retreat. In, out. In, out. *Not now.* I ran through a new sequence, starting with four and adding three. *Seven. Ten. Thirteen. Sixteen. Nineteen...* It didn't help. The pattern was too mindless to offer relief.

"Ah, I can't!" I tossed the blanket aside with numb fingers, cold sweat breaking out on my neck. My hands clutched at the couch.

Kara got up on her knees and leaned over me, but that only made the air denser.

"No, I need to—" I flung myself forward and tucked my head between my knees, focusing on the singular point of contact between my nails and my palm. The pain shone like a red beacon through the haze, something to hold on to while my brain raged.

"I'll be fine," I managed between counts of four. As long as I didn't think at all.

"I'll get some water." I felt the couch shift as Kara got up.

I could hear Dr. Samson's voice in my head. *Breathe, Annie. Just breathe.* I tried to do what she said. Tried so hard.

Time stood still.

When at last the iron fist released me, I rubbed both hands over my face and slumped back on the couch. Kara's face was pale, but she offered a small smile and handed me the glass.

"I'm sorry," she said. "If it was something I—"

"Not your fault," I mumbled between sips. "Sometimes I wake up to it. It's like a cipher with trigger words no one is meant to know ahead of time. When I came back, I wasn't prepared for any of this. It's good but still pretty overwhelming."

She patted my arm. "You know I'm here for you, right? I'm your friend. When things get tricky, you can talk to me."

"I know."

"But I want you to *really* know."

I blinked at the sincerity in her expression, the concern. "Thank you," I said. "For everything. You've always been the best."

"Aw." She pulled me into a hug and, this time, I hugged her back. "My Banannie."

I laughed at the old nickname. "I completely forgot about that, *Karamel*."

She giggled. "Do you remember when we lost the oars and got stuck in the middle of the lake that time, and Josh and Dan and them would only come get us if we agreed to tell Mr. Sellers those were our actual names at roll call."

"Oh my gosh. And then for a solid month, he called himself *Mr. Celery*."

"Yeah, the joke was on them. Silly boys." Kara chuckled. "I liked Mr. Sellers. He was a good guy."

"Only reason I didn't flunk biology."

We fell silent in the midst of reminiscing. I looked around the room at the flowy white curtains, the shag rug, crate table, and the portraits of Logan on the walls. Neat and tidy. Kara's house growing up had been a cluttered mess on account of a grandmother with some hoarding tendencies, so I could see why this minimalist style appealed to her. We all had histories, I supposed.

"I love what you've done with this place," I said. "It's very peace-ful."

"Again, I wish I had more room. I—"

"I'll be fine. You've already done so much." I reached for a left-over piece of fudge and let it melt on my tongue. "I guess I'll have some phone calls to make tomorrow."

CHAPTER 11

The first order of business was finding a place to rent. With few contacts and zero experience in leveraging the ones I had, I set off cold-calling ads in the paper.

Over the next couple of days, I saw five places—four in town and one at a farm just outside of it. Number one reeked so badly of mold, my nose hurt just stepping inside. Number two showed promise until the tenant above turned on the TV and I could hear the dialogue from down below. Number three had a shared bathroom and kitchen—something I wasn't opposed to until the owner explained she was vegan and would not tolerate any carnivorous activities in her home. I politely bowed out of that one too. By the time I got to number four, my expectations were significantly lower, though not so low as to accept a door with no lock and holes in the walls that I suspected the old creep used to spy on his tenants. That left the farm, and while situated picturesquely between two cornfields, it was simply too far away. I was back to square one.

Feeling increasingly more uncomfortable taking advantage of Kara's kindness, I bit the bullet and called Brandy. After all, she had told me to ask for help.

Shane picked up instead, and when it turned out Brandy wasn't home, I relayed my struggle with finding a place.

His voice instantly brightened. "You know who you should call? Wic."

"Why?"

He must have picked up on my skepticism because he cleared his throat then said, "I know, I know. He can be a bit of a tease at times, but he's really a great guy who happens to have a room to rent."

My chin retracted. "He does?"

"Well, technically, it's his mom's house, but still."

I couldn't help but smile at that. "He lives with his mom?"

"He moved back when Mina had a stroke. He takes care of her."

"Oh."

"Anyway. He's fallen on some hard times with work from what I gather. He's had to pick up odd jobs here and there, and he mentioned wanting to rent the room above the garage. He just finished fixing it up. I could put you in touch."

I cringed, imagining how awkward that conversation would be. On the other hand, I didn't exactly have a ton of options. *Renters can't be choosers.* I rested my forehead in my hand. "Okay, thanks."

"Great. I really think it could be a win-win. I know you got off on the wrong foot, but give it a chance, yeah?"

I told him I would, knowing full well the likelihood of me ending up living with Wic and his mom was slim to none. Not in a million years.

I waited a couple of hours to allow Shane to contact Wic first and to prepare mentally, but eventually, I swallowed my pride enough to dial. *Maybe he won't pick up. It's the middle of the day. Surely he has better things to do than—*

"This is Wic."

I squeezed my eyes shut. "Oh, hey. Hi. This is Annie. Shane's sister-in-law. We met at—"

"Annie." He almost sounded happy to hear from me. Like he was smiling. "Hey."

For some reason, I'd expected the inconvenienced, hurried version of him from our first encounter. No matter how much he'd laughed it off at the game or apologized, I still suspected he thought the accident was my fault.

"Calling to lecture me some more about traffic rules?"

There's the jab. But he was definitely smiling. *How odd.* "Ha ha. Very funny."

"No? Then to what do I owe the pleasure?"

As if he didn't know. "I heard you have a room to rent."

"You heard correctly."

"Is it still available?"

"Sure is."

"Does it have critters?" I wasn't sure why the question popped out of my mouth, but I regretted it right away. I needed a place to stay. Offending the landlord was probably not the best approach. "Sorry. I've seen some bad places in the past few days."

"So, it's not a reflection of what you think of me?" He was smiling again.

It was true he had a bit of that grungy look. As the weather got colder, I wouldn't be surprised if he pulled out flannels and beanies. But he hadn't looked unkempt, and he'd smelled nice. Not that I had really noticed. It was just a general observation—he didn't stink.

"That's not what I meant."

"I know. I'm just yanking your chain."

"Oh."

"So you want to see the room?"

I pinched the bridge of my nose. A headache was coming on. "Sure. Yeah. When's a good time?"

"I'm home all day. How about in an hour?"

"Um, I..." Objectively speaking, I supposed he was nice enough, all the teasing aside. But it might be easier to rent from someone who didn't know me at all. *Maybe I should go through the classifieds again for new listings.* On the off chance that I found something, I could bow out of Wic's option before it went any further.

"Hello? You still there?"

I tapped the back of the phone with my fingertips. "Sure," I said finally. "That works."

He gave me the address, and we hung up.

"You don't have to take it," I muttered as I went into the bathroom to clean myself up. "You're just looking. Doing Shane a favor."

One of the lightbulbs above the sink was out, casting my face in asymmetric shadows. I grabbed a hand mirror instead and went to the window to apply my makeup. I needed to moisturize more. In the stark light of day, I could see every fine line forming webs around my eyes. *Four years left until the big four-oh. If I last that long.* My tongue clicked against my palate with the thought. I froze, staring at myself in the mirror. *If* was new. *If* was—dared I think it—a possibility. I could turn forty.

Before that notion could settle within, I shook my head, chasing it off. I sucked in a deep breath and focused instead on the face I was constructing. It had been a long time since I'd had reason to care about my appearance, and though part of me still didn't, a bit of added color helped put me in a more open frame of mind for meeting people. Dr. Samson called it "fake it 'til you make it." Having been isolated for so long, I definitely needed the boost.

The mascara clumps cleaned off, I considered some blush, too, but thought better of it. No need to go overboard. I didn't care what Wic thought of me anyway.

WIC'S HOUSE WAS IN a cul-de-sac, set back a fair distance from the street. The sizeable yard in front sported large cedars and oversized rhododendron bushes, offering privacy from the neighboring properties that were made up by an eclectic collection of ranch homes and split-levels. The next-door neighbor to the left had a motorhome almost the size of the actual home beneath a tarp, and in the yard to the right was a dilapidated playset that clearly had not been used in at least a decade. If the browns, grays, and greens were any indication, the whole area had been conjured by a city planner in the seventies.

I parked behind Wic's car, which, to my guilty satisfaction, still exhibited a convex hood from our first encounter. Kara had helped me hammer out my license plate in her garage over a week ago.

"Admiring your handiwork?" Wic came down the makeshift ramp that covered the front steps, an apple in hand. He wore his hair in a ponytail tied with a leather string today. *What conditioner does he use to get it that shiny?* I could never get my dishwater-blond waves to stop frizzing.

I ignored the implication of his question. "Just surprised you haven't gotten it fixed yet. Makes you come off as not that good a driver."

His eyes widened slightly, making me blush. I hadn't intended for it to sound that harsh. Before I could apologize, a loud guffaw rumbled out of him.

"Damn." He bobbed his head a few times in appreciation. "Good burn."

"I—" *Oh crap.* "I didn't mean..."

He planted himself in front of me and bit into the apple. He ate it like a cartoon character, each bite taking a solid quarter of the fruit. As he chewed, I latched on to the sharp turn of his jaw, its slow, decisive movement followed by the vertical bounce of his Adam's apple as he swallowed.

"Were you going to finish that sentence?"

I blinked. "Huh?"

"You didn't mean...?"

What were we talking about? Right. "The burn. That was unnecessary."

He waved off my half-assed apology and tossed the mangled remains of the apple into the bushes. "No, it's fair. I *was* a bit of a jerk that day. Again, I'm sorry. Shall we?" He extended an arm toward the house and started walking. But instead of leading me to the front door, he headed to the side of the garage.

"It has its own entrance. Dad used it as an office a long time ago for his business."

My own entrance? I liked where this was going. "What did he do?"

"Contractor. He actually built most of this house himself."

"Should I be concerned about DIY wiring or anything like that?"

Wic chuckled. "Are you always this optimistic? You heard me say he was a professional contractor, right?"

"Sorry."

He opened the exterior door, and we stepped into a tiny hallway at the bottom of a staircase. "There are stairs on the other side leading into the house, too, but you can always keep that door locked."

"Okay." I trailed behind him, intently focused on each step. If I looked up, my line of sight would be level with his jean-clad behind.

"Here we are." Wic swung open another door at the top landing, and we entered the room in question.

Judging by the worn treads of the stairs, I expected something equally dated like brown carpet or paneled walls. What greeted me instead was a bright space with a semivaulted ceiling, new laminate flooring, and white walls. It smelled a bit damp, likely from disuse, but that could be remedied with a good airing-out and a scented candle. There was a trundle bed that doubled as a couch, a table with two chairs, a dresser, and a wide modular bookcase that spanned most of one wall. The sunlight slanted in through the two windows that faced the front yard, making the room feel bigger than it was.

"There's a small bathroom over here." Wic opened a door next to where we'd entered. "I'm afraid it hasn't been updated yet, and there's no shower. You'd have to use the one in the main house."

I peered past him into the closet-sized space where a green sink and toilet battled for space.

"Works, though," Wic added. "And I've scrubbed the shit out of it. Pun intended."

A snort escaped my lips. "Sounds lovely."

I couldn't have cared less about the color of the fixtures. The room was perfect, as was the location. I walked back to the windows and looked out. Too bad there was no way I'd be able to afford it.

"So, what do you think? It's not much, but Shane said you were just on the hunt for something temporary."

The last word startled me. *Do they think I won't honor my promise or that I'll soon find something permanent?* The answer would come down to their faith in me.

I forced a smile on my face as I turned to him. "Honestly, I love it. But you could probably find someone tomorrow who'd be able to pay twice what I can. My budget is really tight. The other places I looked at were all in the five-hundred-dollar range."

"Who says I'm asking more?"

I stared at him for a moment. "You should. Five hundred would be stupid for this place."

"Ah, now I'm stupid too?" He smirked and crossed his arms over his wide chest. "Annie. The room is five hundred a month. Do you want it?"

And that was that. I picked up some towels, sheets, and a microwave at the local mart then moved in the next day.

CHAPTER 12

That first week of actually living in Snohomish again was surreal. Each day, I woke up momentarily disoriented, the same hollow indifference I'd made my companion during my years away lingering on the sidelines.

Can I come in? it asked. *Should I?*

And each time, I opened my eyes to the photo of my kids and replied, *No*.

In that room above Wic's garage, there was no need for numbness or distraction. No "Carmina Burana" or "Requiem." I allowed myself to be present, and it felt good. Liberating.

I kept up with my online work—emails, grading, the biweekly live chat, the recordings—but outside of that, my days were completely different. I went for walks through my old neighborhoods, did lunch with Kara, went to Connor's practice, and tried to think of ways to reach out to Grace.

I didn't see Wic much. He came and went, picking up jobs where he could, I assumed. Connor told me he did custodial work at the school from time to time, and I knew, from Shane, that he helped with some construction projects. I wondered if that was what he'd gone to school for but hadn't had a chance to ask.

"SO, WHAT'S IT LIKE living with Wic the Dick?" Kara asked when I joined her for lunch in the back room of her shop one day. The smell of cocoa powder was so thick it was almost palpable. A new batch of truffles had just been poured, and my mouth was watering.

"I haven't seen him much, actually. The car's been gone a lot, and when he is home, he's mostly inside. I assume because of his mom." I had yet to meet Mina, and I had a hard time picturing Wic as a caretaker, so I was curious to see them together. But it wasn't my place to impose. "Anyway, no need for derogatory nicknames. He's been nice enough."

Kara looked up from her yogurt and cocked an eyebrow. "Oh, it wasn't meant as an insult. You do know that's what he's known as, right?"

"An asshole?"

"No, 'Wic the Dick.' Oh my God. How do you not know this?" She pushed the rest of her lunch aside and leaned forward, eyes sparkling. "Not that kind of dick—*that* kind of dick." She made a circling motion over her crotch area. "He used to be a catalog model. Someone found out after he moved back."

"No way."

"Here, look." She popped a grape in her mouth and opened her laptop. "Wic Du-bray," she mumbled as she typed. A few clicks later, she turned the monitor toward me with a salacious grin. "He earned that nickname, baby."

Wic must have been fifteen years younger in the photo, face baby smooth, his straight dark hair even longer than it was now. But what stood out the most was what the impossibly chiseled expanse of his tan chest led down to. "Oh my."

"Mm-hmm." Kara smirked at me. "Guy knows how to fill out a pair of boxer briefs."

I pushed the laptop away from me, cheeks heating. "It doesn't feel right to be, I don't know, digging up old stuff like that."

Kara leaned closer to the screen. "What are you talking about? A fine male in his prime. Feels right to me."

I attempted to push the lid closed but failed. "Come on. Let's not."

"But—"

"No. It's weird. I have to go home and know about... that." I wrinkled my nose. "Do you think they used padding?"

Kara laughed. "I sure hope not." She leaned back in her chair. "You know, you can always find out. You're single. He's single. Plus, you're already living together."

"Definitely not. And we don't live together."

"You shower in his house."

"That's not the point." Without thinking about it, I'd raised my voice, and it surprised us both.

Kara held her palms up to me. "Calm down. I'm joking."

"I don't even like him."

"Correction, you don't know him enough to know if you like him. Which can be rectified."

"Not why I'm here. And can you put that picture away?" Objectively speaking, Wic was not bad looking. And he *had* offered me the room, even though he could have easily found someone to pay more. Shane seemed to have been telling the truth—Wic was a good guy. That said, I was certainly not trying to find someone in that respect and didn't care one bit for Kara's insinuation.

She wiggled her eyebrows playfully, but all that did was make me vow to keep my distance. No one was getting to know anyone any better if I had something to say about it. I had my kids to focus on.

"Oh, relax, you prude." Kara tossed a candy wrapper at me. She did, however, finally close the laptop and put it away.

"Thank you. And I'm not a prude."

For a few minutes, we ate in silence, Kara with an introspective smile on her face that I chose to ignore. I was very much aware that as soon as she opened her computer again, that image would still be there. It made my jaw clench.

"Let me ask you something." She threw the empty yogurt container in the trash. "You've come back. You plan to stay. It's reasonable to think someone might ask you out eventually —is it always going to be no?" Her face grew somber. "Are you still thinking of Joel?"

A piece of bread lodged itself in my throat, and it took some effort to cough it into the right pipe. "No," I croaked between swigs of water.

"No, what?" She studied me.

"I put him out of my mind a long time ago. I had to. But I don't want to talk about that right now." *Or ever.* We'd married young, loved fast, and drifted faster. Mainly because of me. I'd never forget those last bitter words of his on the phone.

At least Kara had the decency to look remorseful at that. "Okay, fine. I get it. Just one more thing, and then I'll shut up."

Perhaps sensing I felt crowded, she swiveled her chair away from me and reached for a pile of documents on her desk. "It's okay to live a little." The *O* in *okay* was elongated as if she were talking to a child. She glanced at me before returning her attention to the paperwork. "You don't need anyone's permission to do normal things. I think maybe you need to hear that."

"No, I know that."

"Do you really?"

I frowned, but before I could respond, she chuckled and held up an order form. "Thirty Jack Skellington cake pops for a classroom Halloween party. I swear, it gets more outrageous every year."

The moment had passed. "Um, right. Good for business, though."

"You can say that again."

We chatted for a while longer until she needed to return to the store, and before I left, I told her about Grace's recital coming up and how much I hoped that would be the icebreaker I needed. At Brandy's urging, I hadn't pushed anything with my daughter since deciding to stay. "Let her get used to the thought," she'd said, and it wasn't like I'd had a choice but to comply.

"You'll be fine." Kara offered a reassuring smile. "Teenage girls are wily creatures. We should know, right?"

That was exactly the problem—I did know. And Grace being like me was my worst nightmare.

CHAPTER 13

I was more nervous than I thought I would be, getting ready Saturday afternoon to go to the church where the recital was being held. Brandy had told me to meet them there, since Grace's call time was forty minutes before the start, and I was running late. I had purchased a few outfits just for the sake of having a change of clothes, since all my stuff was still in Albuquerque, but they were all much too casual for a concert. I debated whether or not I had time to stop to pick something else up, but then it was half past one, and I had to go.

In all black except for a multicolored scarf, I entered the church five minutes ahead of the performance start time. A few stragglers were still mingling in the lobby, but everyone else was already seated. I pushed through the double doors to the nave and scanned the crowd for my family. *My family.* There was a brief clenching in my stomach at that, an adrenaline spike. Joy and trepidation muddled together, but I pushed both emotions down. This was not a time for self-analysis. I needed to find them.

The musicians were in the front row, and I could see the back of Grace's head but none of the others. Finally, I spotted Connor's arm waving in the fourth row and made my way there.

After taking a seat next to Brandy, I said, "Quite a turnout. How are you doing?"

"You're late."

"It hasn't started yet."

"We said one forty-five. I was starting to think you wouldn't show."

I tucked my purse between my feet. "I'm here now. Is there a program?"

"Here, you can have mine. I'll share with Shane." She handed me a slip of paper.

"Thanks."

"Shh."

"Thanks," I repeated in a whisper. "And I'm sorry I didn't get here sooner."

She waved me off, and I took her dismissal as a cue to stop talking altogether. I browsed the program for Grace's name. She was listed fourth and would be playing Huber's "Student Concertino," a piece I'd never heard of.

The teacher took the stage, and the crowd settled.

The first student was the youngest one—a boy of six who had only been playing for a few months. Needless to say, it wasn't all that enjoyable to the ears, but the crowd still applauded him with vigor.

When it was Grace's turn, she got up and walked to the stage with poise, nodding to her teacher, who was at the piano. She was so pretty in a black-and-white recital dress and a matching black hairband, and for a split second, I saw my five-year-old again. Then the piano started, and Grace put her violin up. She scanned the audience while waiting for her cue and smiled at someone she knew, but when her eyes slid across me, she did a double take. Instantly, she froze, the bow perched on the strings. Her face paled. The piano stopped.

She'd missed her start.

"Oh crap." I scooted down, the whispered words reaching no one but myself and Brandy.

"What?"

"Did you not tell her I was coming?"

Brandy looked from me to Grace, who was saying something to the teacher. "I didn't want to risk her throwing a fit."

Great. I kept my eyes down as the piano started up again, not daring to look Grace's way. I had ruined her moment by merely being present. Not a good start.

The second time, the violin did join in with the piano. I snuck a glance every once in a while, and when Grace was no longer paying attention to her surroundings, I allowed myself to really admire her again.

My daughter was a beautiful musician, swaying slightly with the rise and fall of the music while her bow arm gracefully coaxed notes from the strings, making not a single error. When the final tone rang out, I realized I was holding my breath. It escaped me in a rush as the applause rose. There were more skilled players, of course, but to me, she was it. She'd played from within, and that was what made a great musician.

When she joined us afterward in the lobby, I told her as much.

"I messed up the double-stops, though."

Brandy put her arm around Grace's shoulders. "Practice makes perfect. You're on the right track."

In response, Grace shrugged off her arm with a glare.

"So. Ice cream at Sal's Sundaes?" Shane asked, holding the front door open. The sun was trying to break through after a few morning showers, and it bathed the parking lot in a hazy-gray light.

"Is *she* coming?" Grace nodded my way.

Brandy frowned. "Grace!"

My steps faltered. Perhaps I'd already done enough damage for today. "Um, maybe I'd better..." I hoisted my thumb toward my car.

"Everyone is going." The tone of Shane's voice didn't invite argument, and when Connor hooked his arm through mine with a "Yeah, Mom, you have to come," I reluctantly agreed.

To my relief, Grace didn't object further.

"I'll take my car." I hoped the offer might help to give her a bit of space to calm down. "I'll meet you there."

"Can I ride with you?" Connor asked.

I aimed a silent question at Brandy, who nodded, then the two of us veered off toward my car.

"You'll have to tell me where it is." I turned the key in the ignition after Connor climbed into the passenger seat.

"It's on Cedar just past Pearl."

"Where the barber used to be?"

"Next door."

I made a right out of the parking lot, and we drove in silence for a few minutes before I cleared my throat and glanced at Connor. "Does Grace talk to you at all?"

"Not really. I mean, yeah, about school stuff maybe—when she's frustrated with a teacher or has a lot of homework."

"Is she frustrated a lot?"

"I don't know. I don't think so."

"But you said before she's been a bit crabby lately?"

Connor thought about it. "I don't know. She used to be happier before Dad... you know."

"I guess that's normal."

"She used to be fun, but now she'll bite your head off if you look at her the wrong way." He turned to me. "Did you know she cut her own bangs? Brandy freaked out."

"Has she said anything about me?"

He hesitated.

"If you don't want to tell, that's okay. I understand."

"Yeah, I don't think I should. She'd kill me in my sleep."

I leaned forward to peer through the windshield. "Is this it?"

"Yup. Parking's in the back."

Once I found a spot and turned off the engine, I turned to Connor as he unbuckled. "Can I ask you something?"

"Sure."

"Why aren't *you* mad at me?"

"Oh." He blew out a sharp breath. "I was. Sometimes. But Dad told me not to be."

My eyebrows went up. "That's all it took? Joel told you to shake it off, and you did? Wow, you are something else." I resisted the urge to ruffle his hair.

Connor studied the hands in his lap while he spoke again. "He always told me you loved us very much, and if you could have stayed, you would have."

So he refrained from badmouthing me to the kids despite how he felt. To protect their memory of me? I swallowed with some effort. "He was right."

"I know." He paused, glanced up at me, then looked back at his hands. "Mom, are you sure you'll stay this time?"

The caution in his voice cut straight through me, draining me of every word I knew I should tell him. The safest thing to do would be to avoid absolutes, to make sure he didn't get his hopes up in case the situation proved to be an indulgence on my part and I failed. Only, each day that went by forced upon me a new conviction that I could never go back.

"I..." I started, struggling to string the syllables together. "I plan to." It was the best I could do right then and there, and I hoped it would be enough. I tilted my head forward, searching for his eyes. When they made contact, I smiled. "Now how about some ice cream?"

His smile was slow to bloom, but eventually, his features relaxed, and we went to join the others.

"What's your favorite flavor?" I asked Grace while scanning the offerings. There were at least thirty tubs of ice cream in the windowed freezers lining the wall, and they all looked delicious.

"Why?"

"Just curious."

I could almost feel an eye roll emanating from her.

"Are you more of a fruity-flavor kind of person or the chocolaty kind?"

No response.

"My favorite is the strawberry-cheesecake one. Anything with strawberry really."

Her head flinched in my direction, but she caught herself. "I *hate* strawberry."

Connor snorted on the other side of her. "No, you don't. You always get strawberry."

She punched him in the arm. "Nuh-uh. Not anymore."

Shane called out from the register, "Connor, Grace—know what you want?"

"Oh, it's my treat."

"Wouldn't hear of it." Shane winked at me. "Pick your poison, everyone."

We ate at two small tables, in silent reverie of the cold treat. Connor had a cone with two scoops of chocolate and Moose Tracks leaning precariously to the side, Shane had a cup of Coffee Toffee, Brandy nibbled on a cookie from the counter, and Grace stirred her cup of plain vanilla as if she was infusing it with every curse she could come up with. The strawberry cheesecake was delicious.

"Ugh," I said after finishing half. "I'm so full. Anyone want the rest of this? Connor?"

He bit off a large part of the cone and gave me a garbled "I'm good."

"No?" I rubbed my belly. "Shame to throw it out. Maybe this is better than the strawberry flavors you've had lately, Grace. Want to try it?"

She stabbed her ice cream a few times for good measure and peered up at me from beneath dark lashes. "Maybe."

"Well, I'm not going to eat it. Kind of a waste." I pushed my cup toward her.

"I guess." She glanced at Brandy to see if she was paying attention, but she and Shane were talking about something to do with the house and were in their own world. "Okay."

I turned back to Connor to ask about his upcoming game, but out of the corner of my eye, I saw Grace take a heaping spoonful of my ice cream then another.

"Thanks," she said into the cup.

It wasn't much, but it was more than nothing. A whisper of a promise.

CHAPTER 14

I stepped out of the shower the following morning with a newly minted confidence that Grace would come around despite Brandy not quite keeping her word of helping to bridge the gap. I had considered calling her out on the whole concert fiasco but decided against it. I was in her debt and not really in a place to make demands. Plus, she had the pregnancy to deal with. I was heading over there for dinner later anyway, an opportunity to turn a new page, but first, I had someone I needed to talk to. I still had to visit Joel's grave.

Opening the bathroom door in the downstairs hallway, I almost ran into Wic, who was carrying two large garbage bags outside. I jumped back, apologizing.

"No worries!" he hollered, pushing through the front door. "You're up early today."

Eight in the morning on a Sunday—I supposed that could count as early.

I was halfway up the stairs to my room when he came back inside and called for me.

"Since you're up, you want breakfast? I just made a fresh pot of coffee for Mom and me."

I paused midstep, the thought of a real breakfast making my mouth water. I had a mini fridge in my room and enough milk and cereal to last a few weeks, but that seemed paltry by comparison. *Is that bacon I smell?* There was also the lure of finally meeting Mina. This would be as good a time as any.

I turned to face him. "Sure, that would be great. Just let me get ready, and I'll be right there."

"Cool."

I took the last few steps two at a time, pulled a brush through my hair, then gave it little more than a once-over with the hairdryer. Rushing back and forth between my dresser and the vanity, I suddenly stopped, scowling at myself. *What am I doing?* For some reason, I had just tried on and discarded two perfectly good shirts. I was holding my toothbrush in one hand and mascara in the other, an urgency filling me I hadn't experienced in a long time.

I tossed the mascara on the bed and finished getting ready. *Damn that Kara for planting ideas in my subconscious.*

The kitchen was small but functional, with a square table that was pushed toward the front-facing window and a woven rug covering linoleum flooring. A faint smell of sautéed onions lingered in the walls but not so strongly as to make it unpleasant. It was a lived-in space, and after so many years in a builder's-grade apartment, I could appreciate that.

Wic made formal introductions. "Annie, this is my mom, Mina Dubray. Mom, this is Annie Wolff." He waved the spatula he was holding between us. "Or do you go by McLaren?"

"It's Wolff. I took back my maiden name."

"Cool. Coffee is on the table. Milk and sugar?"

"Both, thanks."

The fan above the stove wheezed and sputtered as Wic returned to the cooking. I sat down across from Mina, who was in a wheelchair by the window, an orange tabby cat purring contentedly on top of the quilt covering her lap. Mina's left arm was in a brace on the armrest, and the left side of her face drooped slightly, which was made more obvious by the smile that pulled the right side up. Her round face was framed by long, dark hair streaked with silver.

"It's good to finally meet you." Her voice was surprisingly strong if a tad slow.

"You as well."

"I'd get up, but Biscuit here is sleeping." Her eyes twinkled.

I stared at her, puzzled.

Wic put a plate of still sizzling bacon on the table and patted his mom's shoulder. "A regular jokester, you." He chuckled. To me he said, "Dad used to be the funny one. Mom was the disciplinarian."

"Lord knows you needed it."

"Then she had the stroke, and now it's one quip after the other. Go figure."

"Glad I amuse you. Now where's my coffee?"

"Just a sec, Mom." Wic grabbed a pan filled with scrambled eggs then set it down in the middle of the table. "There. Here's a plate. Help yourself, Annie." He tucked a napkin under his mom's chin and lifted her coffee mug to her lips.

"Mm, that hits the spot," she said. "I'll have some eggs too. Did you remember the chives?"

"Of course." He loaded up a forkful and brought it to her mouth. "Mom is the best cook. When I was little, she could turn three ingredients into a gourmet meal. I didn't know how good I had it until I went off to college and had to subsist on ramen."

"I bet."

Mina lifted her right hand and swatted at her son's shoulder. Noticing my gaze trailing her movement, she said, "Yes, I can move. But I spoon-fed him once upon a time, so I think it's only fair he does the same for me."

"Mom." Wic scolded her with a crooked smile then turned to me. "The paralysis is partial and on the left side. She has no real use of the leg, the arm twitches constantly, and there's some weakness in the face. It's less messy if I handle the utensils."

"I see."

I sipped my coffee and nibbled a piece of bacon while watching the two of them interact. Mina had the same prominent cheekbones and kindly eyes as Wic, but she was tiny, five feet at most. Next to her, he looked like a giant, his hand as big as her whole face.

A flash of the picture Kara had shown me popped into my head unbidden, and I had to turn away to hide the color in my cheeks. *What does he do to stay in shape?* There was no way that body had come courtesy only of random construction jobs.

"Wic tells me you're Shane's sister-in-law who disappeared," Mina said, interrupting my thoughts.

Wic let out a sputtering sound, choking on the mouthful of coffee he'd just taken. "Mom!"

She turned her head toward him with a jerky movement. "What? We're all adults here. We can handle the truth."

With lips pursed in a terse smile, he leaned closer to her. "But you just met her, and she might not want to talk about it."

"No, it's okay," I said.

"See?" Mina raised her chin.

After a moment's hesitation, Wic stuffed a whole strip of bacon into his mouth. He looked from his mom to me as if giving us the go-ahead but making it very clear he was washing his hands of the whole thing.

"Why did you do it?" Mina asked, her intelligent gaze fixed on me.

Wic let his chin fall to his chest in defeat, muttering something under his breath.

I took another sip of coffee to stall. The only people I'd ever talked to about this in detail before were my therapists and Kara, and I had no idea why I'd just agreed to widen that circle. Perhaps it was something about Mina. Her lack of a filter was refreshing after having people tiptoe around me for a long time.

"Why did I leave my family?"

"Yes, that. Assuming there are no murders you also want to admit to—the question could go either way."

Wic pushed his chair back with a loud grating sound. "It's too early for this. I need more coffee. Anyone?"

I handed him my mug in response then ran my hands across the smooth wood of the tabletop before me. "Because I loved them," I said eventually. "Staying would have hurt them more. Or I thought so back then anyway."

Mina's lips parted as if she was about to say something else, but she stopped herself. Wic brought my refill, and I took my time adding milk and sugar before I continued. "Depression runs in my family. I've never been able to picture myself growing old because none of the women in my family do."

Wic leaned forward, his elbows on the table. "What? Do you guys get sick, or what do you mean?"

"She means they off themselves." Mina's voice held more compassion than her words suggested, but I still startled as she said it.

Wic's gaze flew to mine. "Oh."

"Shane's never told you?"

"Nah, we're not that close. Yeah, he's my cousin, but I moved away from here when I was twelve and didn't come back until a few years ago. I thought maybe Joel was... not that good a guy."

"Oh, no. He was. It was me. Turns out, it's very difficult to love someone when you don't love yourself. He deserved better."

Wic's brow furrowed. "But you're good now, right?"

"I have ups and downs." *Probably always will.*

"I see." His eyes held mine a little longer as if he had more he wanted to say, but when Mina spoke again, he returned his attention to the coffee.

"And now you're back."

"Yeah." I stirred my coffee, watching the deep brown turn mocha. Somehow, a month had gone by since my return. I vacillated between feeling like it should have been longer and marveling over the accomplishment of having made it a *whole* month. "It was an impulse. The rest just sort of happened."

"Huh." She mulled that over for a bit. "And are you still planning on killing yourself?"

"Oh, come on!" Wic groaned. "That is *not* an appropriate question. *At* all. Can we please change the subject now?"

"Men. Always so sensitive about the emotional stuff." Mina shook her head and smacked her lips together. "Fine. I withdraw the question. But let me just say one more thing."

Wic asked, "Do you have to?" at the same time I said, "Sure."

"The other women in your family—you are not them. You know that, right?"

"I'm like them."

She squinted and tilted her head slightly. "I think not." Then she pursed her lips and gave a final nod to mark the end of the discussion.

"Are we done?" Wic glared at his mom, though an indulgent trace of a smile was playing in the corners of his full lips.

"Yes. May I have some more eggs, please?" Her good hand went to Biscuit's shiny fur, making his purring rev.

I hid a smile of my own behind the rim of my mug. I liked Mina. A lot. Enough to allow for the possibility that she might be right. I'd felt relatively well before but always with a sort of jellied core, wobbly and insubstantial, easy to compromise with changing conditions. Something in me had solidified when I'd come back, because of the children, perhaps, and human interaction. More and more, the evidence pointed to my leaving eight years ago as having been a huge mistake. For everyone involved.

I RAN INTO WIC IN THE driveway a little later as I was leaving, and he immediately apologized for his mom's questions.

"I had no idea she was going to go there. It's the stroke—ever since it happened, she says whatever comes to mind."

I assured him there was no lasting damage and that I'd really enjoyed meeting her. "I think it's really admirable, you moving back here to take care of her. Not all sons would do something like that."

He shifted his stance. "Well, in all honesty, it wasn't a completely unselfish move, but more on that another time." He gave me a blinding grin that once again brought to mind the old model picture. It was a very nice smile.

"I'll hold you to that." I got in my car and set my purse on the floor.

"Actually..." He rubbed at the back of his neck and looked away. "I was thinking of grilling some burgers later if you'd like to join us. It's such a nice day." His gaze flicked to me then off toward the street.

"Um, thanks." My mind worked furiously to orient myself in the week. *What are my plans?* "Actually, I'm having dinner at Brandy's."

"Ah, family dinner." He did a two-handed, all-finger snap and backed away a few steps. "Another time?"

"Definitely."

"Well, good. Then I will just—" He pointed in the direction of the house. "See ya."

I frowned, watching him head back inside. *What was that about?*

I started the car and put it in reverse. For a moment, I thought I saw Mina in the window, but at a second glance, she wasn't there. *What an interesting woman.* As I drove off, I couldn't help but look forward to talking with her some more. I was curious if she would be as straightforward in answering questions as she was asking them. If she wanted to spill some dirt on Wic, I'd be more than game. It would be worth it just to see the alarm on his face. I smiled to myself.

But that was for another day. My immediate destination was the cemetery. I had some overdue explaining to do to my late ex-husband.

CHAPTER 15

Joel's headstone was plain granite with black lettering in a sea of similar markers. He never liked flowers, so I hadn't brought any, but faced with colorful bouquets left and right, I wished I'd at least brought a pine wreath. I didn't think he'd have objected to that.

I read the sparse inscription over and over until the letters jumbled. A plump, lazy fly buzzed by, shimmering in the sun, but it did nothing to interrupt the breathless stillness of the place. It was all wrong. I'd never thought he would be the one of us to die young.

I sat down, hoping the conversation might flow better that way. It didn't. I'd pictured explaining everything—my flight, my years away, my reaction to his death, and what was going on now—but faced with the silent stone, my mind went blank. Aside from a whispered apology, words didn't seem worthwhile. Instead, I closed my eyes and pictured us the way we'd once been. It felt like a more appropriate tribute.

I wasn't sure how much time had passed when a voice pulled me out of my reverie.

"Mom?"

I turned, blinking against the light. Connor was approaching between the graves, his cap in one hand, a water bottle in the other.

"Hey."

"What are you doing here?" He sat down next to me and crossed his legs.

I checked the time—11:30 a.m. "I could ask you the same. Aren't you supposed to be in church?"

He shrugged and leaned forward to pull out a wily tuft of grass right next to the headstone.

"What's that supposed to mean?"

"Means I'm not in church."

I took in his profile, the thick eyebrows, the birthmark in front of his ear, how the set of his jaw gave away that he was not indifferent to my scrutiny. He didn't want to talk about it—that much was clear.

I turned back to the headstone. "Do you come here a lot?"

"Once or twice a week."

"It's my first time."

Finally, he looked at me.

"It's complicated," I responded to his silent question.

"Thirsty?" he asked, holding out his bottle.

"No, I'm good."

We sat side by side by Joel's grave, letting the fall sun warm our heads as the minutes ticked on. Ours was a comfortable silence, not one that needed to be filled with words. My legs eventually fell asleep, so I lay down in the grass, hands behind my head. The earthy scents of decaying leaves and chlorophyll enveloped me. Not a cloud in the sky.

"Did you love each other?" Connor asked when I'd been lost in my thoughts long enough to have nearly forgotten he was there.

I pushed myself up on my elbows. "We did. For a while at least."

"But not when you left?"

I splayed my fingers in the grass, pulled up a few blades, then let them drift back down one by one. "I honestly don't know. We'd stopped talking. I was terrible company. I still cared for him, but—" I pressed my lips together.

"But not enough?"

I sat up fully. "Maybe."

He nodded.

My turn to ask now. "Did he ever, you know, date anyone? After I left?"

"If he did, I didn't know about it."

I hoped he was wrong. I would hate it if I was the last Joel knew of companionship. I'd failed him as a wife, and I'd told him as much in my parting letter. I'd encouraged him to move on, both for his own sake and for the kids. "I'll have some of that water now if you don't mind." I reached for the bottle. When I'd finished drinking, I asked, "Were you close?"

Connor shrugged again. "The baseball stuff took up a lot of his time. He was excited when I got into soccer, though."

"Yeah?"

"Mm-hmm."

"Well, you're really good. Anyone can see that." I bumped my shoulder to his.

He smiled slightly, but the expression disappeared almost instantly, replaced by the same wrinkling of the brow I recognized from my reflection. "Mom, I think there's something you should probably know. Shane and Brandy don't want me to tell you, but—" He glanced my way and adjusted his legs under him. "I heard Brandy tell you about Dad's accident—the black ice, how he hit a tree."

"Yeah?"

Conflict warred in his eyes. He closed them briefly and cleared his throat. "What she didn't tell you was that he was drunk when it happened."

"Drunk?"

He nodded.

"But it was a Wednesday. He barely even drank on the weekends."

Connor looked down at his hands. "Dad actually drank kind of a lot. More the last couple years."

I took in the words on the headstone again, my thoughts spinning. *This is Joel we're talking about, right?* I reached for Connor's arm. "What are you trying to say, bud? That he was an alcoholic?"

He must have heard the alarm in my voice because he placed a hand on top of mine. "Don't worry, he wasn't mean or anything. And please don't tell them I told you. But yeah."

All the blood drained from my face. Joel driving drunk in the middle of the week. With the kids at home. Nothing made sense anymore. "Holy shit!" The words were out of my mouth before I could stop them. I pushed off the ground and started pacing. "But—"

"Mom." Connor rose too.

"How could...?"

"Mom."

I stopped. "You don't understand. I called him. He was—he said—oh my God."

I'd trusted him when he'd told me they were fine. Instead of insisting on a change, I'd slunk away, tail between my legs, after one phone call. All it took was him telling me to "stay the fuck away." Never mind that those harsh words had been out of character for him. I'd been so stupid. Or perhaps willfully ignorant because I'd needed them to be fine. In my mind, he was the one to see to that. He was *the* parent. Not me.

Connor stared at me. "It wasn't that bad," he tried. "He didn't drink every day. At least, I don't think so."

I crouched down in front of the headstone and covered my mouth with my hands.

Joel Robert McLaren
Beloved father and brother

Not a *beloved husband*, I noted. Because I'd left.

By leaving, I'd placed an added burden on him. I'd known that but had never questioned him being up for the challenge. I'd only known that I wasn't. In my mind, he was already parenting on his own long before I left. And he loved being a dad. He'd wanted kids since he was little more than a child himself. That was why I'd believed him when he said I was no longer needed. A mistake, as it turned out. My fault.

Sweat beaded at my neck. "I've got to go."

"No, you—"

"I'm sorry. I'm not mad at you. I just have to." I started walking away, my legs moving of their own accord. I was past physical feeling. *Away, away.* I needed silence to sort out the fractured thoughts in my head.

"Where?" Connor trailed me as I hurried toward the parking lot where the blissful solace of my car awaited. "Mom, you're coming back, right?" he called out, voice breaking.

I spun at his question, a snare tightening around my throat. With the last ounce of self-control I could muster, I gave him a tight "Of course I am," hoping that was enough. I hated that I was scaring him and that I couldn't stay to settle him, but the illusion of righteousness I'd built up around me was cracking. I couldn't let him see me when that happened.

If I'd ever before questioned my decision to leave them, there was the answer. All the people judging me were right—in this story, I was the villain.

I DROVE AROUND FOR an hour, the jarring sound of a conscience in turmoil pressing at my temple. I wasn't paying attention when I turned into Wic's driveway, and neither, it appeared, was he as his car zoomed toward mine in reverse. Once again, we met with an unfortunate bang. Unlike last time, it was my front to his rear, and even I had to admit it was mainly my fault. Not that I was in any mood for owing up to that out loud.

Wic was faster than me, making it to the point of impact before I could do more than open my door. "We have to stop meeting this way. I haven't had time to fix the hood yet."

I gritted my teeth as I climbed out of my car. "You're supposed to be paying attention when you're backing out."

"But not when you're driving forward?" Wic raised an eyebrow. The calm he exhibited was an impressive contrast to our first meeting.

"Not according to you if I remember correctly," I said under my breath.

A clever grin spread on his face. "So since I was the one driving forward the first time, I was not to blame? Do I understand you correctly?"

I straightened with my hands to my sides. "No, that's not..." My voice trailed off. I didn't have the energy for this.

"Ah." He nodded slowly. "I take it both times are my fault, then?"

"If the shoe fits." Satisfied neither car was any worse for wear, I got back in my seat and backed up a few yards to let him out.

He stared at me for a moment through the windshield then did the same.

I let out a frustrated growl. *Fucking guys and fucking cars and fucking people who can't be who you need them to be and do what you need them to do.*

But most of all, fuck me.

Once parked, I slammed the door shut before I set a course for the garage and walked up the stairs. Back in my room, I flung my purse onto the bed and toed off my sneakers. Then I paced. I'd made Joel an alcoholic. Not only had I abandoned him and the kids, but I'd failed to do the bare minimum of due diligence while away. *How did I ever think I could stop being a mother?*

My hands shook when I pulled my cell out and dialed Dr. Samson.

"You're a fucking plague is what you are," I whispered to myself as the call rang through. When it went to voicemail, I kicked the trundle of the bed so hard a blistering flash of pain shot up my leg.

CHAPTER 16

"Holy mother! Fuuuck!" I collapsed on top of the duvet, my hands clasped around my foot. "Ooow."

I pressed my face into the fabric and bit down to stop myself from screaming further. Slowly, a pulsing numbness replaced the pain but only as long as I kept still. I lay there curled up on my side, and once the anger drained away, the tears started. I didn't fight them like I usually did, but just when I was about to set them free, a distant voice called my name from below.

I choked in a sob and listened.

"Annie, is everything all right?" It was Mina at the bottom of the stairs.

I wiped my cheeks and rolled to my back. "Be right there!" I sat up, a new wave of pain radiating up my foot at the movement. I'd have to make it across the floor to talk to her. A low groan rose from my chest.

With the help of various chairs and some clumsy jumping, I reached the top landing and opened the door. Carefully, I lowered myself to sitting and peered downstairs to see Mina's concerned face looking up at me.

"I heard banging and shouting. Everything okay?"

"I think I broke my toe."

"Can you make it down here? I can get you some ice."

Ice sounded amazing, so I scooted on my behind down the long staircase until I reached the floor. By then, cold sweat was making my shirt cling to my back, and the room wasn't entirely steady.

"Hurts that bad, huh?" Mina asked.

I nodded, my lips pressed tightly together.

"Can you take off your sock and put your foot in my lap?" When I hesitated, she added, "I used to be a nurse."

Taking a deep breath to steel myself, I did as asked, revealing a rapidly swelling appendage on my left foot. Mina took one peek and announced I would need to see a doctor.

"I don't think I can drive."

"Of course you can't." She pressed a button on a key fob-like thing that hung on a cord around her neck.

"What's that?"

"I'm calling Wic."

"Oh, no. That's not—"

But she was already wheeling herself back to the kitchen. "He'll call back as soon as he can. That's our agreement. You stay there and put your foot high if you can."

I didn't have much of an option. I was in no state to make it back up the stairs, and to be honest, the rug in the foyer was as fine a place as any to collapse. I rolled onto my back and put my foot up on the stool next to the door—and that was where Wic found me when he returned fifteen minutes later.

MINA MET US IN THE doorway when we got back from the mortifying ordeal that was Wic helping me through the doctor's appointment. Not only had he more or less carried me to his car, but he'd also supplied me with tissues, since I couldn't stop crying. I didn't know where the physical pain ended and the emotional turmoil over Joel took over, but they'd ganged up and kept me a blubbering mess the whole time.

"It's a fracture," Wic told his mom. "Six weeks in a boot."

"Just the big toe?" she asked as I hobbled into the house.

"Yeah," I replied through gritted teeth.

"We need coffee," Wic said. "You go sit on the couch and put your foot up."

I looked longingly at the stairs leading to solitude, but the thought of climbing them made me swallow the objection.

"Thank you," I said instead. "For everything."

"No worries." He smiled over his shoulder. "I'll fill your prescription when I head out later."

"Were you able to reschedule, then?" Mina asked.

"Reschedule what?" I craned my neck to see the two of them exchange a look in the kitchen.

"It's nothing." Wic turned his back to me.

"Not nothing." Mina faced me. "He had a job interview today."

"Still have. John's a good guy."

"What? Wait, you ditched your interview because of my foot?"

He shrugged. "Mom called."

I stared at him with incredulity.

"And anyway, it's only a temporary job. John Hopper down at Millworks Lumber needed someone to fill in for a while. It's not a big deal."

Mina joined me in the family room, giving me a thorough once-over. "You want to tell me how it happened?" She spoke in a low voice, I assumed to keep Wic out of the conversation. Still, I wasn't sure I wanted to share just how messed up my day had been.

"What do you mean?"

She rolled her chair as close to the couch as she could get and parked. As soon as she did, a black-and-white cat I hadn't seen before cautiously approached.

"Ah, there you are Scout," Mina cooed. "She's very shy," she said to me. "Don't take it personally." She made a repeated *tss* sound with her tongue and held out her hand toward the feline. When it was clear Scout wanted nothing to do with us, Mina turned to me again.

"I saw you through the window, and I heard you go upstairs. Something more than that toe broke this morning, no?"

I deflated, resting my head against the pillows. "I had some bad news is all."

"Ah."

"Someone wasn't who I thought they were, and I'm pretty sure that's my fault."

"That makes no sense."

I smiled glumly. "Sorry. I don't want to get into it."

"No need. The skies will clear. You'll see."

Just then Wic entered, balancing the coffee pot and three mugs. "What are you two talking about?"

"The weather," Mina and I said simultaneously.

Wic pursed his lips. "Right." He poured the coffee then sank into the lone armchair in the array of furniture—a maroon corduroy monstrosity with threadbare armrests. A beaded purse decorated one corner of its back. Scout instantly jumped up next to him, playing favorites. "Fine, don't tell me. How's the foot, Annie? Need more ice?"

"I'm good." I picked up my mug. The warm beverage went down smoothly, and sip by sip, I started feeling like myself again. I'd never been in the family room before and took a minute to look around while Wic helped Mina with her drink.

Like the kitchen, the room was dated but homey and clutter-free. The blue and teal curtains had faded from years of sun exposure, and there was no hiding the high traffic paths worn in the carpet, yet it didn't feel run-down. In fact, the carved wooden artwork that decorated the large wall next to the bedroom hallway gave the room an almost stately Northwestern flair. An unusually wide fireplace for such a modest home was situated on the wall facing the front of the house. No doubt, the unique touches had been Wic's dad's design. The mantel was a slab of driftwood, kneaded and polished by decades in the wet. On top of it stood a carved horse sculpture, a few framed photographs, a candle, and a large brass bell. It was easy to picture Mina calling Wic in to dinner with it when he was little.

"What did you go to college for?" I asked after a while, thoughts of a younger Wic having brought the question back to mind. "Shane said you lost your job a while back but not what you did."

"Oh, this should be fun." Mina cocked an eyebrow and waved off Wic's hand when he tried to offer her another drink of coffee.

"Mom."

"What, son? The girl asked you a question. I'm interested in the answer."

The headshake he gave her was almost imperceptible, but I saw both that and how he struggled to put on that pleasant veneer people donned when getting ready to bamboozle you.

He turned to me with a breezy smile. "I majored in fine arts."

I almost spit out my coffee. If he'd said health science, or sales, or even teaching, I could have seen it. Something about him said people-person, and he was certainly good-looking enough to be the face of any gym or company. *But art?* There was still so much I didn't know about him.

"Not a lot of money in that field," Mina filled in as if reading my thoughts. "But he's a fabulous woodworker. Got it from his dad. He made the kitchen table and that one." She pointed at the wall installation. Upon closer inspection, it resembled a flock of geese taking flight, the slant of a log at the base reluctantly releasing them into the air. "And see that horse up on the mantel? That's my favorite. Wic, bring it over."

He did as she asked. His fingers caressed the horse's curves almost tenderly before handing it to me.

"Wow." The dark wood was cool to the touch except where Wic had just held it, and as I ran my fingers over its ridges and planes, turning the equine shape this way and that, I was left speechless. It was so lifelike and animated in its suspension that I could almost hear it neighing. I'd never seen anything like it.

"He looks just like my Opie," Mina said, following my movements with a tender expression.

"Who?"

When she didn't respond, Wic answered for her. "A horse she had when she was little."

"He was my pride, my heart." Mina turned to me as if she hadn't heard Wic. "We didn't have much, but Opie was enough for me. When Wic made that, he'd never even seen a picture. How did he know?"

For a while, we all sat in silence, focused on the sculpted wood until Wic cleared his throat.

"Anyway." He ran a hand through his hair and reached for the horse. "It's been years since I did anything like that. Reality hit pretty hard when I discovered I couldn't exactly make a living doing that stuff."

"So what did you do?" My eyes were still locked on the sculpture and on Wic's hands, holding it so gently.

"Um, a little bit of this. A little bit of that."

"Oh, he was a model," Mina mused. Whatever memories had come over her minutes ago were now gone, her eyes once again bright and clear.

"For God's sake," Wic muttered before returning the horse to its place of honor.

"Quite popular for a bit. Catalogs, ads—you know."

I hummed something noncommittal in response then adjusted the pillows behind my back to hide my rosy complexion.

"In fact, I might have some of them lying around here somewhere." She scanned the room as if about to go dig them out.

"No," Wic and I said at the same time, a bit too loudly. He looked at me in surprise.

"I mean, that's not necessary. I don't want you to trouble yourself on my account." I smiled, hoping the explanation was enough for my reaction.

"And they're old and dated. No one needs to see that," Wic added.

"But you were so handsome and stylish. He even did some underwear—"

"Mom, that's enough."

She giggled, watching him collect our dishes and bring them to the kitchen. "I'll show you sometime," she whispered to me, "when he's not around."

Please don't, I thought, but I kept my smile in place.

"What else have you done for work?" I asked Wic when he helped me upstairs a little later. "Construction, right? And some stuff at the school?"

"Uh-huh." He deposited me on my bed along with my bag of prescription ibuprofen he'd picked up then helped himself to a seat at the table. He looked around the room at the changes I had made—some curtains and pillows to soften the space, a few photo frames. "It's nice. Let me know if you need anything else in here."

"Thanks. And I'm sorry you got laid off."

His chin retracted. "Laid off? I wasn't laid off."

"Oh. But Shane said—I assumed—" I snapped my mouth shut. "Sorry, I'll mind my own business now."

He considered me for a moment. "No, it's fine. I'll tell you what really happened. But you'll have to promise not to judge."

I crossed my heart and kissed my fingers.

He took a deep breath. "I sold weed."

I stared at him. "What do you mean? Like a drug dealer?"

"Uh-huh." He leaned back in the chair and crossed his arms. His biceps strained against the material of his shirt. "But it sounds sordid when you say it like that."

"And it wasn't?"

"Look." He leaned forward, resting his elbows on his thighs. "It was good money, and I only dealt in a harmless recreational drug. Plus, I didn't sell to kids. Olympia's business district was all I needed."

"How long?"

"Five, six years, maybe. Four when I could live off of it."

"And then?"

"Washington legalized marijuana." A self-deprecating little laugh rumbled through his chest. "The irony. Everyone was happy except people like me—the middlemen. My growers got licenses, and that was that. Probably for the best. It's not exactly a career."

"Right."

"For the record, Shane thinks I worked in landscaping. I don't know where he got the idea. Maybe he heard me talk about plants or something. I didn't think it necessary to correct him."

"But your mom knows?"

"Of course. It actually helps a bit with her spasms."

"But you don't sell anymore?"

"Nah. It was a relatively steady income for a while, but I actually like construction stuff. I'm hoping to do more of it, get on a steady crew. It's been hard, though, with Mom." He scrubbed a hand across his face. "You've seen—when she needs me, I have to go. Not many employers are cool with that." A weariness came over him and settled in his shoulders. Facing the window, he drew inward, disappearing into his thoughts.

"Hey," I said, watching him carefully. I wanted him to know I understood.

He glanced up at me. "Maybe I shouldn't have told you. Keep it to yourself, yeah?"

"Of course. And just so you know, I'm not judging. My life's been way more messed up than yours."

He got up. "It's not a competition."

"No, that's not what I—what I meant was, no one is perfect. You did what worked for you."

For a moment, our eyes locked, and I thought he was about to say something else, but then he turned and headed toward the stairs. "Let me know if you need anything else. I'm running out for the interview, but I should be here after that. I'm assuming you're not going anywhere?"

The dinner. *Crap.* I had to call Brandy. "Right. Thanks again!" I hollered after him as he disappeared downstairs. I frowned at my booted foot and reached for the pills.

"Nope. Not going anywhere tonight," I muttered. Just my thoughts and me.

CHAPTER 17

The next afternoon, I was still in bed, my laptop balancing on a pillow, when I was pulled out of work mode by the sound of footsteps climbing the stairs. A light rap on the door followed, and it slid open.

"Hello?" Connor's voice reached me before his head became visible.

"Oh, hi." I tried to keep the surprise out of my voice. I closed the laptop and set it aside.

My heart did a somersault when Grace emerged behind her brother.

"Brandy said you got hurt, so we wanted to stop by," Connor said. "Shane drove us."

"That's a nice surprise. Hi, Grace."

She'd been scrutinizing the room, but now she stopped and turned to me. "Hi."

A joyful rush bubbled through me at seeing them both together in my room. The cool fall sunlight was suddenly brighter, slanting across the floor, and the air in the room crisper.

"How was school?" I asked as any mother would.

"The usual." Connor's posture was cautious when he sat down at the foot of the bed.

At first, I thought he was worried about my injury, but then it dawned on me—Joel and the conversation at the cemetery, how I'd run off.

"Hey." I offered what I hoped was a reassuring smile. "Everything is fine."

"Doesn't look like it." Grace dumped her backpack on the floor before grabbing a chair from the table. "Looks like you have a boot on your foot."

She was talking. My daughter was talking to me.

"Smart-ass," Connor said with a bite.

"Nuh-uh—none of that." I gave the both of them as stern an admonishment as I could, which was an accomplishment, considering my insides were bursting with this new development. *Be as snarky as you want, Grace. But keep talking.*

Connor's expression softened first. "Sorry."

"Do you have anything to eat?" Grace asked. "Lunch was horrible."

"Did you buy school lunch?"

"Brandy always packs us stuff," Connor said. "She says the food they serve in school is pathetic."

"But lentil soup?" Grace rolled her eyes. "Who eats stuff like that?"

"Yeah, I hate beans," I said before I could stop myself. It was one of the few foods that I'd never come to terms with.

"You do?"

"Um, yeah." *Uh oh. This could be treacherous ground.* "But you know, your aunt means well."

"I'd be okay with her meaning a little less well," Grace muttered.

Connor got up and walked over to my bookcase, where I had two photos of them and a couple of binders containing all my teaching stuff. "No books?"

"No, I left them back home—back in Albuquerque, I mean." The alarm in his eyes made me curse my rogue tongue.

"You still have your place there, then?" He kept his back to me.

"I just haven't had time to deal with it yet." In all honesty, it was a bit of a conundrum how I would get my place in New Mexico packed up and cleaned from all the way over here. I assumed there were people you could hire, but I hadn't done my research yet.

Connor and Grace looked at each other, a silent understanding passing between them.

"What?"

Connor squirmed at my probing.

"He was worried," Grace offered. "Yesterday."

"When I told you about Dad, you got so weird. I thought maybe it changed things. That it would make you leave again."

"And you didn't come to dinner." The accusation was sharp on Grace's tongue.

My heart sank. I'd been so preoccupied with my own drama yesterday that I hadn't even stopped to consider them. Some mom I was. Something cold and slithery made its way down my spine. *This is what you do*, it hissed. *You hurt them. You're not fit.*

It took all my willpower to ignore it in favor of the more urgent need to assure and settle.

I put as much gravitas in my voice as I could. "I'm still staying. I'm sorry about yesterday, but it was a shock to learn about your dad. I had thought... I know it's not fair to assume he'd always be that perfect guy, but I kind of counted on it. So to find out that wasn't the case—"

Grace scoffed. "You know what? I think I'll wait outside."

Before I could finish, she stormed off.

Connor raised an eyebrow, and it took a moment for me to register his silent accusation was meant for me. "Dad's a sensitive topic," he said, pursing his lips to the side.

I cursed the boot that stopped me from following her. "But I was about to say it was my mistake, and had I known—oh, damn it." I looked at the door where she'd disappeared. "Will you please tell her I'm sorry?"

"Not sure that'll do anything." Connor shrugged and stood. "But, for what it's worth, she did ask about you when you didn't show last night."

That was something, I supposed. Baby steps.

"Well, Shane told us to be quick, since I'm grounded, so—"

"For skipping church?"

He gave me a crooked smile.

"I can tell them I asked you to meet me at the cemetery if that would help?"

"They wouldn't believe you." His grin widened. "I'm grounded pretty much every Sunday. Church just isn't for me. But it's not too bad. I can still do soccer and drama club, and if I want to see a friend, I can have them over."

I balked. "What kind of toothless punishment is that?"

"You'd do it differently?"

"You bet your skinny-McLaren-behind I would."

We both laughed at that, but Connor quickly grew serious again. "Then why don't you?"

"What do you mean?"

"Why do you live here while we live with Aunt Brandy and Uncle Shane? If you're staying, shouldn't we live with you?"

My breath caught. "Uh, that, ehm..."

His expression hardened, making him seem suddenly much older than his fifteen years. "Got it." He scoffed.

I expelled another sputter, one hand flying to my throat. "No," I managed to say. "No, I don't think you do. Come here." I patted the mattress next to me. Reluctantly, he did as I asked while I tried to find the words that would set things right.

"I *just* got back. I've been away most of your life. Shane and Brandy have been here all along. In a way, they know you better than I do."

He sucked in air as if about to launch an objection.

"Wait. Hear me out." I searched his face for understanding. "I love you. And your sister. All I want is for you to be happy, for you to have everything you need. To be safe. I don't know if I can offer that yet. This is new to all of us. And you're good, right? At Brandy's?"

He stood, then, staring at me as if I'd just slapped him. "That's not the point. We're *your* kids. Seems pretty simple to me."

"Because you're fifteen." Tears were starting to burn their way from behind my eyelids. I didn't want to fight with him, and I didn't understand his sudden shift in attitude. He'd been so reasonable thus far. Maybe too reasonable, all things considered, but I'd lapped it up. The lump in my throat grew. I wanted to ask him to trust me, to believe me when I said I loved him, but before I could form the words, he turned away from me.

"Whatever. Hope your foot feels better."

And he was gone.

The first few sobs sounded like hiccups, loud and dry into the still air around me. I pulled a pillow to my mouth to try to stifle them, but as soon as I heard tires retreating on the gravel outside, the dam broke.

I couldn't do anything right. Not when I was ten, not eight years ago, and not now. Not by my mother, my husband, or my children.

I cried the day into evening, hours passing with me at the mercy of one self-doubt after another, each claiming its pound of flesh. All the pent-up grief and guilt—over the years lost, for Joel, for the unfairness of it all—boiled to the surface in a hot mess of blubber and tears. Maybe I was kidding myself that staying was a good idea after all. The fact that we were already fighting would suggest it.

When my toe started hurting again, I took some more painkillers and tried to get to sleep. While tossing and turning to try to get comfortable, I watched the red lines on my alarm clock take me deeper into the night until 2:51 a.m., when I gave up and turned a light on. Not exactly a number prophesying sleep.

I should have paid better attention. 2:51 did tell a story, albeit one of a different kind.

CHAPTER 18

I woke with a start to the honking of a car and pulled the covers tighter over my face. In the five days since the toe incident, 2:51 a.m. had found company in 3:28, 4:13, and even 5:09 a.m. My days were turned around, sleep not finding me until the rest of the world began to stir, and only with the help of old friends in my head-phones—Handel, Mussorgsky, and last night's Puccini. The third act of *Turandot* still echoed in my memory.

The car honked again, farther away this time.

Ugh.

Still not quite awake, I popped another painkiller. My blinds were drawn, my doors locked, and my phone turned off. Or out of battery, perhaps—I hadn't checked lately. Such a cocoon was one I knew well, and it was a blessing to return to it amidst all the drama I'd stirred up. A blessing both for me and those around me, I was sure.

I tried in vain to go back to sleep, but my stomach soon started rumbling, no doubt asking for another helping of cereal. With a sigh, I gingerly swung my legs out of the bed, reaching into the boot shaft to scratch my skin. I could use a shower, but then again, it wasn't like I was planning on seeing anyone anytime soon. It could wait.

I hobbled to the shelf where I kept my food stash then shook out a handful of cornflakes onto a paper plate I'd used for a sandwich ear-lier. *Yesterday?* I was running low both on bread and cereal, and I'd used up the last of the milk two days ago, but I couldn't go to the store for a refill. It was Friday the fourteenth, which was too calendrically off-center. The mere thought of getting dressed and going out-side was insurmountable.

Maybe tomorrow. Saturday the fifteenth had a better ring to it.

The worst hunger pangs sated, I went to the bathroom and re-filled my water glass. For a brief moment, I forgot to avoid my re-flection and stared in disgust at the specter inside the mirror. She looked like me, but I knew better. I knew who she was just like peo-ple recognized their fifth-grade bully or their freshman-year crush who'd asked their friend to prom instead. No matter how many years passed, their memory was etched into your bones. My ghoul may have been hiding for a while, but I knew what she wanted. She want-ed to come out again, to talk to me, and to whisper her wily words in my ear. *It would be so much easier,* she'd say. *Better for everyone if you...*

I turned away from the mirror, tears I barely noticed streaming down my cheeks. It hurt so much more to see her again because I'd hoped she was gone for good. That I'd turned a corner.

As quickly as the boot allowed, I limped back to the bed and sat down. The picture of Grace and Connor stared at me in silent accu-sation. I flipped it down with a loud sniffle then scooted as far back on the bed as I could, arms wrapped tightly around my middle. It was raining—pouring by the sound of the pattering on the roof—and I shivered in my pajamas. I didn't know what to do.

I thought of stuffing what I could into my backpack, getting in the car, and not looking back, but with that, the pain intensified. I thought of sitting down with my kids, telling them I'd made a mis-take, and begging their forgiveness for not being able to make good on my promise. That made it too hard to breathe. Finally, I pictured staying. Opening the blinds, going outside, and facing them all. But that, too, felt unattainable.

Beyond the doors of my momentary shelter, the world was hazy and uncertain, making it impossible to see what lay beyond. It was hopeless.

I curled up on the bed and pulled the covers high, and I had just reached the quivering in-between before sleep when someone knocked loudly on the door.

"Annie?"

It was Wic, and he sounded pissed. No, not pissed—grim. Like he wanted to beat the door down, but self-restraint kept him at bay.

I sat up, my breath hitching.

"I know you're in there," he said, a little softer this time. "Your car is in the driveway."

I stared at the door.

"Are you sick?" he asked after a long pause. "Do you need anything?"

A new sob built, and I clasped a hand across my mouth.

"Annie?"

There was a scrape on the stairs that led me to think he was going to give up, but then he spoke again. "I'm worried, okay? So, sorry in advance, but I'm coming in."

My gaze flew to the door handle. I should have known he had a spare key.

No, no, no, no.

I was about to object when the lock rattled and the door swung open. I dove under the covers and held them tight to my face, feigning sleep.

"Annie?"

I listened for his footfalls as they crossed the floor. Heard the clatter as he pulled the curtains open. Then there was silence again.

"What's going on?" he asked, closer than I had expected. "Why are you in bed in the middle of the afternoon? Are you sick? Is it the flu?"

I bit my lip. "I'm fine." My voice sounded muffled even to my ears.

"How's your toe?"

"Fine."

"So everything is—"

"Fine. Please, leave me alone."

A chair scraped against the floor. As if he hadn't heard me, he sat down and spoke again. "Connor was here yesterday, and Brandy has called. You haven't talked to anyone the whole week."

Against better judgment, I lowered the comforter just enough to peek out at him. "He was here?"

"Asking for you."

"What did you say?"

Wic shrugged. "What could I say? I haven't seen you all week either." The tendon in his jaw twitched, and he glanced up at the ceiling in what could only be described as an amateurish eye roll. "Can you please come out from under there and talk to me like a normal person?"

I hesitated but did as he asked. Sitting up, I still held on to the bedding, keeping them close as a buffer. "Happy?" I said with a sneer.

He didn't look happy. He looked alarmed, his lips pressing together. Wic caught himself and rubbed the back of his hand across his brow. "Mom said to ask—" He cleared his throat. "To ask if you're taking your meds." He brushed something invisible off his jeans.

"Of course I am. If not, you'd hear me screaming in pain every time I move."

His eyes flicked to mine. "Not those." He gestured to the ibuprofen on my nightstand. "The other ones. Your antidepressants."

I stiffened. "I don't think that's any of your business."

"So you're not?"

"I didn't say that."

"Look." He leaned forward. "We're friends now, right? If you tell me you're taking them, I'll believe you, but something is going on. You can't expect me to believe you're fine when—" He made a gesture to my person that said something to the effect of "I can see you're a mess."

I was grateful he didn't say it out loud.

The fight left me, and that much-too-frequent stinging behind my eyelids kicked in again. "I'm fucking everything up." My voice broke.

"Hey, no." Wic pulled the chair closer to the bed. "No. Don't cry."

"They hate me. I should have never... I should have stayed away." Tears started running down my cheeks, and I wiped at my nose with the back of my arm.

"They don't hate you. I've seen them with you. And they're worried."

"I don't know why I thought I could be a mother again. So fucking stupid."

Wic moved over to the bed and sat down next to me. "It's not stupid. Come on."

I couldn't control it. The monster inside spread through my limbs like a noxious black gas, and I pressed the heels of my hands against my eyes to block it, block everything. The feeling was oh so familiar, the precipice one I'd faced many times before, except for one novel difference. Through the fog, I was vaguely aware of Wic, his hands fluttering across the comforter as if unsure where to settle. When the dams burst, it took no time before he pulled me to him and into his arms.

He held me until my tears subsided then a little longer because I didn't have enough energy to move.

"I'm sorry," I mumbled into his T-shirt. "This is so embarrassing."

He raised his left hand, hesitated, then gently stroked the hair away from my forehead. "Don't be. It's not your fault."

I made myself move away from him and his soothing fingers. "I think I need to call my therapist."

Without responding, he got up and fetched my phone from the dresser.

I turned it on and was greeted by at least a dozen beeps from all the calls and texts I'd missed. I ignored them for the moment.

"I'll... I'm gonna go check on Mom," Wic said. "Back in a bit."

I was about to tell him that wasn't necessary, but the words wouldn't come out. If he wanted to check on me later for his own peace of mind, it wasn't like anything I could say would stop him.

He left, and I dialed Dr. Samson's personal cell. She answered right away.

"Annie, I've been trying to reach you. Where are you at?"

I let out a shaky breath. "About an eight. It's been a rough week."

"Is anyone there with you?"

I looked toward the stairs where Wic had disappeared, knowing he wouldn't be gone long. The thought wasn't nearly as annoying as I thought it would be. "Yeah, someone's here."

"Good." There was a pause on the line and the sound of a door closing. "Then tell me all about it."

AT DR. SAMSON'S URGING, I got off the NSAIDs I'd been taking for my toe. It was possible, she said, that, together with the increased tension in my life and a need to up the dosage of Lexapro, the ibuprofen had stirred up a perfect storm that contributed to the rapid downward spiral I'd ended up in. I felt dumb for not seeing it myself, but then again, I hardly ever took over-the-counter medications, so drug interactions weren't something on the forefront of my mind. I had to come to terms with the pain in my toe for a few days, but with icing and elevation, I got through that too.

Wic watched over me. It was subtle, and if I had called him out on it, he would have probably denied it, but over the next couple of weeks, he was rarely far away. When I was working at home, he popped in for quick chats, and when he was off on a job, he sent me texts to check in. Soon, it became more of a rule than an exception that I had dinner with him and Mina. I even suspected he had a hand in getting Connor to start showing up again. I owed him more than he knew, and without intending to, I started to look forward to his company.

One damp afternoon in late October, on a day when I'd managed a limping walk around the block, a video call with a student, *and* a run to the grocery store without being fazed, I sought him out in his workshop to give him a bag of his favorite chocolate-covered peanuts just because. The high-pitched buzzing of a sander covered my footfalls, so he didn't notice me right away. I stopped in the doorway and took the chance to watch him work. His movements were both determined and gentle, his arms straining against the T-shirt sleeves as he applied pressure, a bare palm caressing the board after each turn. The air was thick with the scent of raw wood.

When he turned off the machine, I finally stepped into the room. "What are you working on?"

He yanked his goggles off and spun around. "Annie! Hey. Didn't see you there."

"Brought you these."

He pulled his mask down, his face lighting up. "You went to the store? How are you feeling?"

"Better every day."

He took off his gloves and didn't waste any time before tearing open the package and helping himself to a handful of treats. While he chewed, I made my way around him to his current project.

"It's a bench for the yard," he said. "Not the right season, but I needed something to do with my time off."

I reached out but hesitated. "Can I touch it? I won't ruin anything?"

"Go ahead." He shook another few pieces of candy into his palm.

The wood was almost white, the surface fuzzy with remaining sawdust. "It's soft."

He let out a short laugh. "Then I've done my job. No one wants splinters up their caboose."

I snorted. "Caboose?"

"'Ass' seemed too crude." He shrugged and grinned at me.

"I promise, I can take it."

He tipped his head to the side. "Yes, somehow I do believe you could." The warmth in his voice sparked a tingle along my spine that I was quick to disregard.

"What else do you have in here?" I walked over to the shelf in the back, where smaller projects sat awaiting completion. A wood carving of a bird caught my attention in particular, and I glanced over my shoulder in question before I picked it up. "You're so good at this," I said, running my fingertips across the ridged feathers.

Wic put the candy bag down on the workbench and approached, shoving his hands in his pockets. "It's what I like to do best, but it doesn't exactly pay the bills. One day, maybe."

I set the bird down. "Definitely." I gave him a decisive nod. "I believe in you."

A boyish grin blossomed on his lips. "You don't think it's a pipe dream and I should settle for a nine-to-five like everyone else?"

"What? No way." I couldn't picture Wic in a cubicle. He would be miserable. "I like that you have a goal that's very you."

"Thanks. Maybe I can show you how sometime? Wood carving, I mean."

I took in the remaining shelves, momentarily tongue-tied by his ability to create detailed curves and realistic movement in such a rigid material. "Yeah, maybe."

He chuckled. "You don't have to sound so enthusiastic."

"Huh?" I shifted my focus back to him. "Oh, sorry. I was just admiring everything. No, I'd like a lesson. I really would."

"Cool."

"Yeah." Our gazes locked briefly before I turned. "Anyway, I should head back upstairs. I've got a couple of assignments that won't grade themselves."

When I was almost to the stairs, he called to me. "It's really good to see you feeling better. And thanks for the candy."

"Don't mention it." I owed him a lot. But I also suspected he didn't see it that way. He was just a good guy. Maybe even a great one.

CHAPTER 19

My mental fog continued to lift, and gradually, I settled at a steady four on Dr. Samson's scale. I was still dealing with the revelation of Joel's alcoholism, and my anxiety acted up any time I thought the kids looked less than content, but at least I was functioning again. All I had to do going forward was make it last.

A few days before Halloween, Connor stopped by after school as he'd been in the habit of doing every few days. We were back to enjoying each other's company in the tentative way of two people who were not quite sure yet what role they should play on the other's stage, but I was also very aware of the elephants in the room—my relapse, our fight, Joel, and our current living arrangements. At least he was there. Grace had yet to speak to me at all since that day.

It was a windy day, and outside my windows, the cedars bowed back and forth while evergreen needles showered the lawn. But inside was warm, and the amber glow from my side lamp made the room cheery enough. I'd lit a candle on the table where Connor was doing his homework, and my legs were snug beneath a knitted throw Mina had lent me from the house.

Connor closed his books. "Hey, Mom?"

I looked up from my screen. "Yeah?"

"Do you like Halloween?"

"Sure. Why?"

"No reason." He tapped the back of his pencil against the table a few times. "Actually, I was wondering if you have plans this year? Me and a friend want to go trick-or-treating for a bit then hand out candy, but Brandy says we can't."

I frowned and pushed my laptop aside. "Why not?"

"She wants us to do the All Saints' Vigil and potluck at the church instead." He scrunched up his nose. "But I'm not going to that. She can't make me. So I was wondering, could we do it here instead?"

"Oh." The full implication of what he was asking sank in. He wanted to go behind Brandy's back, and he wanted me to help. "I don't know. I'd probably have to talk to her."

His face fell. "Do you have to?"

"Look, I'm fine with it. In fact, I think it sounds like a lot of fun. I'm sure Wic and Mina would be on board too. They've already stocked up on enough fun-sized candy to last for three Halloweens. But you live under Brandy's roof."

He looked down. "I wish we didn't."

The skin at my sides went clammy. I couldn't go there. Not yet. "I'll find a way to clear it with her, okay? I'm sure it'll be fine."

He scoffed.

"Hey." I searched his face until he was forced to meet my gaze. "I'll take care of it."

His shoulders slumped, but he reached for a cookie in the pack on the table, which I took as acceptance.

"WHAT DO YOU THINK ABOUT throwing a Halloween party here?" I asked Wic that evening over dinner. "We can make some chili, those who want can dress up, and we'll give out candy."

Mina lit up as she turned to Wic. "We haven't done anything like that since you were little. I think it's a great idea."

"It wouldn't tire you too much, Mom?"

"Tire me? Maybe it would tire you."

As if on cue, Wic yawned. Come to think of it, he did look exhausted. At the moment, he was working three different part-time jobs—driving the school bus in the morning, a two-week construction job demoing an old warehouse, and bartending at a sports bar eight miles down the road in Monroe. He didn't complain, but I knew he was desperate to find something more permanent.

"I'll do everything," I hurried to say. "I'm sure Kara can help me with the food, and it would be super casual. All you have to do is show up. And maybe invite a few people."

Wic finished chewing. "I guess it could be fun."

Mina and I shared a smile.

"Oh, also," I added, feigning indifference. "Could you call Shane and invite them?"

"Why can't you?"

"Long story." I got up from the table and put my dishes in the dishwasher. "Make sure you tell him we need the kids to help handing out candy."

"Because?"

"Because we do."

His eyes narrowed. "Why do I get the feeling there's something you're not telling me?"

"I'm going to call Kara," I said over my shoulder as I hobbled up the stairs. "I'll be down to clean up in a few."

I didn't wait to hear his response. As long as Wic could get Shane to say yes, I would have come through for Connor without getting in Brandy's way. Perhaps it was cowardly of me not to talk to her myself, and part of me felt bad about interfering in her plans, but I also knew there was no way Connor would be at that church function. It didn't matter if she presented it as an only option—I'd long since grasped that Brandy and Shane's religion was a point of contention for my son. I'd rather have him here, then, engaged in some organized fun he'd asked for, perhaps with the whole family gathered. It wouldn't hurt anyone. Surely, Brandy would come around.

ON THE DAY OF THE PARTY, Kara and her son, Connor and his friend Miles, one of Wic's work buddies, and a neighbor couple about Mina's age showed up around half past four. Kara brought cornbread and brownies, but even though she'd offered to do the chili, too, Wic had insisted on cooking it himself. The whole house smelled of cumin and tomatoes, making my mouth water.

"Let's set all the food stuff over there." Mina indicated the peninsula at the end of the kitchen counter. "Drinks can go in the cooler on the deck. Wic, you got them?"

"Sure do."

He and his friend disappeared out back to light up the fire pit, while Mina settled in by the couch, chatting with the neighbors. The rest of us converged at the kitchen table, where a huge bowl full of fun-sized candies awaited their looters.

"Just one for now," Kara told Logan, who already had his arm elbow-deep in the bowl.

"Is Grace coming?" I asked Connor, trying not to sound too eager. I harbored secret hopes tonight would mean a change in the right direction for us. I had given her space, but now that my mind was steady again, I needed to make a move.

"They'll be here after church." Connor adjusted his costume, a foam replica of a piece of peanut butter toast with holes for his arms and legs. Miles was in the corresponding jelly one. It was very difficult to take either of them seriously.

I handed them each a bag of chips and a bowl and told them to set the snacks out, then I joined Wic and his friend outside.

It was a cloudy day, the skies heavy with the promise of rain, but if the forecast held, the trick-or-treaters would stay dry as long as they were back inside by nine o'clock. The fire had taken nicely and was crackling in its steel drum nest, giving off a pleasantly sharp tang of pine embers. Wic pulled one of the folding chairs closer to the heat when he saw me.

"Come take a load off." He held up a bottle of beer in salute.

"Annie, this is Fred—Fred, Annie."

I shook the other man's hand before sitting down.

"I've heard a lot about you," Fred said.

Wic gave a little cough as he handed me a beer.

"Oh?"

Fred looked from me to Wic then took a swig. "Well, that you moved in, and, you know. Yeah, that's about it. You're a teacher, I understand?"

"Online tutoring mostly."

"Gotcha." He rested the bottle on his thigh, which was bobbing up and down. It didn't make for a very steady perch.

"Everything good inside?" Wic asked me.

"Under control."

"I like your hat."

My hand flew to the black witch's hat I'd found at Goodwill. It had a wide purple ribbon near the brim and a giant spider climbing up the side of it. "Thanks. Something for the kids." I smiled.

"You have little ones?" Fred asked.

So he hadn't heard that much about me after all. I wasn't sure if I was relieved or disappointed.

"No, I meant for the ones who come to the house later. But the peanut butter toast inside is mine."

Fred glanced toward the house where Connor and Miles were visible through the window.

"Really? You have a teenager?"

"Two, actually. The other one should be here shortly." Or so I hoped.

Fred pushed forward his lower lip and nodded as if this impressed him.

"You two know each other from work?" I asked.

"That's right." Fred put a boot-clad foot across his knee. "I work in the kitchen at Elna's Pub. Have been for, oh, eight years now. But it turns out our dads actually knew each other way back."

"Really?" I glanced at Wic and found him watching me, a peculiar expression on his face.

"Yeah. Construction. Different crews, but they hung out."

"Small world." I kept my focus on Fred, but I couldn't help but notice Wic's lingering attention. I willed the odd fluttery thrill of something long forgotten to settle down. Maybe he was still admiring the hat.

Fred held up his bottle to Wic. "You got any IPAs?"

"In the fridge inside."

Fred excused himself and disappeared into the house. I checked my watch, but it was only half past five. Probably at least another half hour until Grace showed up. I took another swig of my bottle, watching the flames in front of me dance in a mesmerizing tangle of white, blue, and orange. If I could only get Grace to sit down with me, allow me to explain. If she would open up just a little bit and let me in. But I understood that that was a scary thing for her and not something I'd earned yet.

I glanced at my watch again.

"How are you feeling?" Wic asked out of nowhere. "You seem on edge."

I made a conscious effort to relax before I answered. *Shoulders down, jaw unclenched, legs still.* "No, I'm fine."

"Okay." He looked away, his thumb picking at the label on his beer. The light from the fire cast his down-turned face in a golden hue, the sharp angles of his jaw and cheekbones rendering shadows that animated otherwise still features. His hair was tied back in a ponytail or I was sure its inky mass would have made for a dramatic backdrop to that burnished skin. The blaze made his features more unique and more familiar at the same time, and I couldn't take my eyes off him. The necklace he always wore had fallen outside his collar, and its metal pendant sparkled, a beacon to my attention. I'd noticed it once before, when I'd cried in his arms, but had forgotten to ask about it.

"Nice necklace." *Ugh.* I cursed myself for how dimwitted I sounded. "I mean, it's really different."

He held the sun-shaped pendant out from his body as far as it would go. "It was my grandma's." He reached behind his neck, unclasped the chain, and offered it to me. "Mom gave it to me when Dad died."

I took it from him and ran my thumb across the smooth surface. It was still warm from his skin. "It's pretty."

"I like it. I never met any of my grandparents. From what little I've heard, Mom and Dad met when she was pretty young, maybe just a few years older than Grace. His family came to stay for a short while to do seasonal work in the village where she grew up in Alaska, and she took off with them when they moved on. They got married as soon as she turned eighteen and came out here. She doesn't talk about her childhood much other than to say things were hard."

I handed the necklace back. When he flexed his arms to clasp it behind his neck, I couldn't help but recall what it felt like to lean against his wide chest. I hid behind my bottle, brushing aside the memory.

"Don't take this the wrong way, but should you be drinking?" he asked when the necklace was in place. "I meant to ask you before because I researched it online, and there are a lot of things that can interfere with antidepressants."

I was stumped. *He cares that much?*

When I didn't respond right away, he screwed up his face in an apologetic grimace. "Sorry. None of my business."

"No." I set the bottle down. "You're not wrong. My doctor says a few sips won't do any harm, but considering everything, I probably shouldn't."

"Didn't mean to be a spoilsport." He got up and reached for my bottle. "Here, I'll get you something else from inside."

I wanted to tell him not to go. Urge him to sit back down. Instead, I watched in silence as he pushed open the patio door with his hip then disappeared into the house. It got colder as soon as he was gone.

I HAD JUST FINISHED stirring the chili when the doorbell rang, and Connor announced that the rest of the family had arrived.

I wiped my hands on a paper towel then went to greet my daughter, hoping and pleading with any higher power out there that she would let me.

Shane was first in the door, and he gave me a brief hug. "You look well, Annie."

Grace was right behind him, carrying a plate covered with aluminum foil. She was dressed in all black as usual, but underneath one arm, she carried a rolled-up sheet.

"Hi, Grace." I took the plate from her. "Is that your costume?"

"She's a ghost," Shane filled in, unbidden. "Crafty, this one."

Grace glared at him. "I wanted to be a zombie, but you guys wouldn't let me." She pushed past us into the house, and just then, Brandy stepped over the threshold.

It surprised me, perhaps more than it should have. I wouldn't have put it past her to choose the church potluck over our little soiree. Nevertheless, I put as much enthusiasm into my voice as I could when I said, "I'm glad you decided to join us."

She frowned at my hat. "Well, Wic and Shane insisted, so..."

Shane gave me a nervous smile before turning to his wife. "Come on now. Friends, treats, food and drink."

She made a face at him, her hand unwittingly going to the slight rounding of her belly. "You know I don't drink."

"Yes, how are you feeling?" I asked, trying to steer the conversation to less turbid waters. "You look great."

It worked. She turned her back to Shane and focused solely on me. "I'm better, thank the Lord." She tilted her face toward the heavens. Then she gave me a thorough once-over. "And you? I heard you were sick."

If that euphemism works... Instead of nitpicking her choice of words, I told her I was much better and not to worry. Then, done with the small talk and eager to find Grace again, I pointed my sister- and brother-in-law in the direction of the food. Luckily, Brandy didn't probe further.

After filling a plate in the kitchen, I found Grace in a corner of the living room with her nose in a book. Biscuit was snugly wedged between her leg and the armrest. I paused in the doorway to watch her, my memory conjuring similar images of a smaller girl in a different chair, though still as absorbed by the fictional world du jour.

"I brought you some cornbread." I sat down in the chair next to hers. "It used to be your favorite."

She frowned at it like someone startled into reality in the middle of a nice escape. Then her brow smoothed, and she took the plate. "Thanks." She returned to the book.

"Grace?"

"Mm-hmm."

"Can I talk to you for a sec?" I folded one leg underneath me and took a bite of my brownie.

"What?" Finally, I had her attention.

"Could you put the book away for a little bit?"

She gnawed at the inside of her cheek as if contemplating my request and finding it peculiar. Then, with a sigh, she put her bookmark into the pages and closed the book. She took a big bite of the cornbread and chewed slowly, staring at me. It was as close to an invite as I would get.

"I wanted to say I'm sorry. I did a poor job of explaining why I couldn't come to dinner that night after I hurt my foot. And for how I reacted when I learned about your dad's accident. I understand that I made you and Connor think something had changed. I didn't mean to scare you."

"I know." She licked buttery crumbs off her fingers, waiting for me to continue.

"Okay. It's just seemed like you've been more upset with me since." My hands fluttered about my lap, and I forced them to settle.

Her chin jutted out. "No."

"No?"

"That's what I said."

"But..." I rubbed a finger across my chin. "I've barely seen you since. Connor's been by several times, but you know I'd love to see you too."

"Does it really matter? I mean, it's not like you're going to stick around forever anyway." She picked up her book again and opened it to where she'd left off.

That time, I reached out and took it from her. "What do you mean, I'm not going to stay? I've told you I am."

She tugged at the book. "People say lots of stuff all the time. Doesn't mean shit."

I had to stop myself from calling out her language. There were more important things to focus on. She didn't believe me. And the worst part was, I couldn't blame her. Trust had to be earned, and so far, I'd already broken our budding truce by storming off as soon as things got tough then isolating myself in the aftermath.

"I know," I said in a low voice. "Words don't mean shit."

Her eyes rounded.

"I'm really sorry, Grace. I'm sorry I left, I'm sorry about your dad, I'm sorry to be messing things up right now. But I am staying, and—" I drew in a shaky breath. "I want to be in your life." Saying it out loud was both exhilarating and terrifying.

She scowled at me.

"It's okay for you to be mad at me, and I'm not going to make you do anything you don't want to do. All I'm asking is a little bit of your time." I held my breath, my heart skipping a beat.

"I'll think about it," she said finally.

I patted the couch and stood up. "Thank you." Trying to contain a smile, I turned to head back to the kitchen where Shane, Wic, and Fred were bickering about what level of spiciness was optimal for a "real" chili.

"Um, Annie?"

I turned back to face my daughter. "Yeah?"

She watched me warily, her fingers digging into the book cover. Then she said the best thing I could have hoped for on that particular night.

"Is there any more cornbread?"

CHAPTER 20

I helped Wic tidy the house after everyone left. Hobbling along in my boot, I picked up empty cans, candy wrappers, and paper plates that were strewn about on all flat surfaces. Kara's sister and her family had shown up, as had two more of Connor's friends and a handful of neighbors. The small house had been bursting with laughter and commotion until the little ones passed out on the couch, worn out after going house-to-house with the teenagers and trying to keep up. Now it was approaching eleven at night, and everything was still. Mina had gone to bed as soon as the last person was out the door.

My heart felt fuller than it had in a while, new possibilities within reach. After my talk with Grace, I'd left her alone most of the evening, but she'd taken part in the trick-or-treating, and she'd said good night. It was promising.

As I cleaned, Connor's question a few weeks back about our living situation kept popping into my mind, and while I skirted it, I didn't push it away. Maybe it was possible that, sometime in the future, the kids could live with me. That we might be a family again.

I knew I had just relapsed. I wasn't "cured" and likely never would be. Depression was like a squatter, always waiting for the next opportunity to get back inside. But I'd come through and had been able to keep the darkest thoughts at bay even as I'd flailed. I had no good explanation for this shift, and yet, it was there. True, the voices in my head warning of danger had not yet completely ceased, but after a night like tonight, at least, I might dare to stop listening to them for a while. Sometime soon, I would have to decide if it was worth the risk.

Once done collecting leftover trash, I grabbed a towel and started drying dishes next to Wic. He'd rolled up the sleeves of his Waffle Henley, and suds of soap made it up his muscular forearms. I tried not to stare.

"The party was a good idea," he said when our silence had stretched long enough.

"I didn't expect so many people." I opened one of the upper cabinets to put a bowl away but found I couldn't. The boot didn't allow for tiptoe reaching.

"Here, hold on." Wic quickly wiped his hands on his shirt then took the bowl from me. He was wearing the aftershave I'd sometimes sensed traces of in the bathroom—something crisp and piney, but now it mixed with an earthier tone that was his own. He was so close that our hips touched as he reached above me, and from that point of contact, a burst of heat spread across my skin. I dug my fingers into the towel I was still holding, waiting for him to move away. He did so too soon.

"Thanks." I grabbed another pot to dry. "Can't wait to be done with this boot."

He offered a quick smile that sent my heart racing. Maybe it was time I admitted to myself that some small part of me had never forgotten the photos Kara had shown me. Wic *was* hot. And he was a good guy, pot-dealing notwithstanding, who, as my friend had so helpfully pointed out, was single. Maybe—

"I'm beat. I've got to hit the sack. Gotta get up early." Wic turned off the faucet and yawned big.

Stupid, that was what I was. It had been a fun night, and I was feeling frisky, but making a move on my landlord would have been unbelievably idiotic. For all I knew, he had no interest whatsoever in me. *Close call, Annie.*

"I'll finish up here. Have a good night."

"You too." He ran his hand across the counter and backed up a few steps before he stopped. "Um, Annie?"

"Yeah?"

He shoved both hands into his pockets only to remove them a second later. Our eyes met and held in the dim light, and for a moment, I thought I saw something cross his face—a decision being made, perhaps, or a muster of will. It was in the intensity of his gaze and the set of his shoulder. But just as quickly it retreated.

"Never mind." He offered half a smile. "Not important. I'll see you tomorrow." He strode across the family room and disappeared into the hallway that led to the bedrooms.

I sucked in my lips and took a deep breath. Yeah, I would see him tomorrow. And the day after that and the one after that. I'd better get my stuff in order and focus only on my number-one priority, or I had a feeling I could easily be in trouble where Wic was concerned. I'd let myself become dependent on his company over the past few weeks, but now that I was better, it was time to take a step back. The only problem was, he was around so much in between his jobs.

As I finished wiping down the table and taking out the garbage, my mind churned with the need to come up with a plan. I had to keep renting from Wic yet create distance between us. *But how?* I had coffee with Mina daily and enjoyed her company, but that put me inside their house. Consequently, seeing Wic less might mean I would have to forego Mina's friendship, and I didn't want that.

I tossed and turned for an hour that night before finally sinking into a deep sleep. For once, it helped. As soon as I awoke the next morning, an idea was there, laid out in stark simplicity. Wic wanted a full-time job with regular hours, which was impossible with Mina needing him. I wanted to focus on my kids and making a life in Snohomish without distractions, which was hard with Wic nearby. To get Wic out of the house and into a job, someone else needed to be

Mina's primary caregiver during the day. *I* worked from home and set my own hours.

I was the answer.

Not only would my plan give Wic a chance at a steady paycheck and me a respite from the budding attraction I felt for him, but it would also signal to the kids that I was committed to staying. *A win-win-win!*

I swung my legs out of bed. The doctor had finally approved me sleeping without the brace, but I caught myself before putting my feet on the floor and reached for it. A quick glance at the time told me Wic might be back from his bus route already. I hurried to tighten the Velcro around my ankle and limped with the gait of a pirate to the window. His car was outside.

A quick tango with the toothbrush later, I made my way down the stairs.

I found him asleep on the couch with Mina tucked into the easy chair on his left, watching one of her talk shows. She looked tired, and I hoped having people over hadn't put too much strain on her. She turned when she heard me, and a smile brightened her pallid complexion.

"Good morning," she whispered. "Sleep well?"

I answered with a wave and a nod. "Coffee?" I mouthed.

"Please."

By the time I'd prepped our mugs and brought them back into the family room, Wic was awake. Dark circles marred his complexion, and he blinked repeatedly as if trying hard to focus.

"Here, you take mine." I handed him my coffee. I returned to the kitchen for a replacement before sitting down on the couch next to him. "I have a proposition."

After laying out the details, I added, "It would give you a chance to work a more regular job, and I'm here anyway. I really think it could work. That is, if you'd be okay with me helping out?" I aimed my question at Mina. Perhaps I'd been presumptuous. She and I were friendly, yes, but that didn't necessarily mean she would want me as a personal assistant. Being helpless in front of others was one of the hardest concessions one could make. I knew that.

"I couldn't pay you much," Wic said.

"Oh, you don't have to pay me. I'm here anyway—I can do my work in the house so I'm at hand, and you've already done so much for me. It would be like repaying a favor."

Wic frowned. "You don't owe me anything."

"I know."

"But wouldn't this make it hard for you to get your work done?"

"Like I said, I set my own hours."

"Mom, what do you think?"

Mina tilted her head back in the chair and closed her eyes for a moment before opening them again. "I like it. It has weighed on me that you're stuck here." She reached her good hand out to Wic, and he took it. "I think we should give it a whirl."

"Yeah?" My heart lightened at the feeling of being of help.

"I can call John back," Wic said, more to himself than to us. "Maybe that job is still open, or he has something else." A smile chased the shadows from his face. "I'll have to show you the ropes and where everything is."

"I can talk, you know," Mina interjected.

"The physical therapy is probably the most important part to start with—we do it twice a day." Wic rattled off things I needed to know as if Mina hadn't spoken. I giggled when she rolled her eyes—her good one anyway—in a move that would rival Grace's.

Wic looked at me, an unnatural stillness coming over him as if bracing for the unexpected. "Are you sure? There's nothing in it for you."

Our eyes locked. I allowed myself a momentary lapse of self-control to feel that jolt his gaze caused in my core. *If only he knew.*

"I'm sure. That's what friends are for." With some effort, I turned to offer Mina a reassuring smile and found her watching us with a bemused smirk.

"Wow." Wic expelled a breathy chuckle. "Thanks, Annie." He pulled me into a one-armed hug, and at once, the heat from his body electrified my skin.

Yeah, the sooner I can get him out of the house, the better.

CHAPTER 21

November came with rains that cemented both the wet reputation of the Pacific Northwest and the commencement of the gray doldrums felt by every man, woman, and child in those parts. But despite the less-than-uplifting weather, we settled into a comfortable routine at the house in our new roles.

John offered Wic the job, which he started as soon as the temporary one was up. He quit driving the school bus but stayed on as a bartender at Elna's Pub, since it was decent money, and he enjoyed his coworkers. A few weeks into this new arrangement, I could already see a difference in him—a lightness in his step that hadn't been there before. I imagined it a relief to not always be chasing the next paycheck, and it felt good to have contributed to that.

The new arrangement also changed up my daily schedule. As soon as I heard his car pull away around half past seven in the morning, I headed downstairs to have coffee with Mina. On mornings she slept in, I worked until she called for me. Other mornings, Wic had already gotten her settled in her wheelchair or on the couch, and then she and I would chat while I had breakfast.

In addition to meals and personal care, we did two rounds of physical therapy every day. The exercises focused on tonus and range of motion in the functional parts of her body and preventing muscle atrophy in the rest. No one expected her to recover completely from the paralysis, but she still worked as hard as any gym-goer, often pushing for a few more reps when I told her she was done.

"The bare minimum is for people content with mediocrity," she would say then proceed to tell me about the time she'd biked to Portland or the year she'd taken a daily dip in the lake she'd grown up by even when she'd had to break the ice to reach the water.

One thing was for certain—it was difficult to be bored with Mina around. Ours was an easy rhythm, and between her naps and TV shows, I was able to get all my work done too.

The first couple of weeks, I tried to leave as soon as Wic got home around five, usually using work or the kids as an excuse. The latter was more of a legitimate reason since I'd offered to cook dinner at Brandy's a couple of times per week. She'd started showing more in her pregnancy, and her back wasn't game for the additional weight.

But as the days rolled by, I once again found myself lingering in the house well into the evening whenever I wasn't needed at the Hemingways'. Connor often stopped by after school anyway, and a few times, Grace had joined us, too, so it was the best of both worlds. In letting the kids set the pace for our deepening relationship, I was able to relax a bit into simply *being* in the world. Kara's words about me not needing anyone's permission to enjoy the little things finally settled like a puzzle piece in one of the holes in my soul. For so long, I'd been shackled by unspoken limits, but it had never occurred to me that, since I was the jailer, I also held the key to release. I could just let myself out. It was such an obvious yet novel idea. Such a relief.

I enjoyed listening to Wic's stories of the various worksites he was at, of the camaraderie between the guys, and the plans he was making for Mina's house. With his new paycheck, he could start on the repairs that he had put off, and he wanted them all specked out before spring. One was replacing the roof—for the time being, a tarp ensured the southern corner of the living room didn't leak—and the other, updating the bathroom. Being in the midst of the wet season, there was no hiding the musty smell from behind the old tile in the shower. While air fresheners did their part, renovating would be healthier for everyone.

Admittedly, I also liked watching him—to see the new, relaxed version of Wic move about, banter with his mom, and throw easy smiles around. Some people possessed an almost innate ability to steady the air about them with nothing other than their presence. Wic was like that. When he laughed, the sound wrapped itself around me like a comforting blanket, and when he looked directly at me, his gaze alone settled me. It took every ounce of effort not to look back.

THE MORNING AFTER ONE such pleasant evening when we'd had dinner and talked well past nine o'clock, I found Mina pulled up to the kitchen table when I came downstairs. She was working on a Sudoku puzzle that Wic had weighed down for her with a pan so the paper wouldn't move, but she put the pencil down as soon as she saw me.

"I have questions." She pinned me with a squinted gaze.

"Good morning to you too." I set my phone on the table and poured myself a cup of coffee. "How's the puzzle coming?"

She didn't take her eyes off me. "I'm working on it." She waited until I sat down before she continued. "Help me understand something. You were gone eight years, came back to check on the kids after Joel died, decided to stay, and now you live here."

I put the cup against my lips to drink but thought better of it when the steam from the brew reached my skin. "I guess that sums it up."

"And is that it?"

"Is what it?"

"This." She glared as if I was a nitwit for not understanding what she was getting at. "Is there a next step?"

A nervous twitch started in my left eyelid. I rubbed at it absent-mindedly. "Um, I don't know. Aren't you happy with our arrangement?"

"Psh, that's not what I meant."

I brought the cup to my mouth again and swallowed a big gulp of the scalding beverage. My tongue stung.

"What about the kids? Are they going to stay with Shane and Brandy? Wic tells me you still have your place in Albuquerque."

"Only because of logistics."

"Right."

My teeth dug into the inside of my cheek. I wanted to tell her it was none of her business. Just because I lived in her house and was her caretaker didn't mean she could barge in demanding access to my soul. My voice came out clipped when I spoke. "It's complicated, okay? The kids are fine. I'm fine."

"Everyone is fine?"

I nodded decisively.

"No need to change what's working so well?"

I ignored the sarcasm in her tone and got up to place my cup in the sink.

"If you ask me, you're still not all here," Mina said behind me.

"I didn't ask."

She was quiet for a moment. "I've seen how you look at him, you know."

I froze, my hand halfway to the faucet. "Who?"

"Santa Claus. Who do you think? My son."

I turned the water on to rinse the dishes and put them to dry. "I don't. Look at him, I mean." I returned to the table.

She chuckled. "And I could win the Boston Marathon tomorrow. Don't worry. Your secret's safe with me. But for the record, he looks at you too."

My eyes bolted to her shrewd ones.

"Ah," she said as if I'd somehow offered an explanation. "What are you afraid would happen?"

"I didn't say anything."

"You didn't have to."

"Isn't *Ellen* on or something?"

"All caught up." She patted the table a couple of times. "Talk to me, Annie. Indulge an old crone. You're seeing the kids more. Even Grace seems to be warming up a bit."

It was true. Grace had shown up twice with Connor to visit in the weeks since the party. She was monosyllabic at best, but that was fine with me. I just wanted to see her.

"What do you want?" Mina asked.

I looked out the rain-streaked pane of the window toward the street. Someone was walking their dog at a brisk pace, a hood pulled up for protection. No doubt they were in a hurry to get home. *Home.*

"I want the kids back." The words slipped out. Hearing them was different from thinking them. They grew bigger somehow.

"Now we're getting somewhere." Mina sounded pleased.

"But it's not that simple."

"Because Shane and Brandy are their guardians?"

I hadn't even thought of that. Legally, I suspected formal rights were still on my side as their mother, but that was something I would have to research further.

"No, because of me." I scrambled for a way to explain. "It's like if you bury a landmine in your backyard, wouldn't you warn people you care about to keep their distance so they don't get caught in the blast?"

"I take it you're the explosive in this scenario?"

"What if I hurt them?"

"What if you don't?" She leveled me with her gaze. "They're in your life now. You're in theirs."

"At a relatively safe distance. If something happened, there would be a buffer." I flattened my palms to the tabletop. "I didn't have a normal childhood, didn't do playdates after school or sleepovers. I hurried home at the end of each and every day—first, second, third grade—to make sure my mom had gotten out of bed, and if she hadn't, I did my homework on the floor next to her. My dad didn't talk about it. He said 'thank you' when I made dinner, and he gave me money if I needed something from the store, but that was it." I sighed. "I loved my parents, okay? But I'd never wish that situation on anyone. Especially not my children."

She reached out a hand for me, and I took it. "I'm sorry," she said. "That sounds very hard. But like I said once before, you are not your mother."

I started to protest, but she squeezed my hand with as much strength as she could muster.

"I've never told anyone this, but when I met Wic's dad, I almost let him slip between my fingers." She released her grip and sat back. "You see, my father was a mean drunk. He ruled our house with an iron fist, so we were always vigilant, always aware. It made it difficult to plan for later. And then Charles came along." She fell silent, a dreamy air coming over her.

"What happened?"

Mina smiled. "My mother helped me run away with him. I was only fifteen, but she packed me a bag and told me if I didn't leave then, I'd never get out. That she loved me and would miss me."

"But that's not the same. She was protecting you from someone else. I'm protecting Grace and Connor from myself."

"You're missing the point. Motherhood is full of difficult choices. You never know if they're going to work out—if the sum of your decisions will be positive in the end. When I left, I thought I'd never see her again, but a few years later she showed up on our doorstep, bags in hand. She stayed with us for the last two years of her life. As it turned out, her sending me away was what ultimately allowed her to leave too." Her eyes bore into me, gentle but firm. "All that to say, the future is hypothetical. Nothing is set in stone. If you want the kids with you, don't let the risk of hurting them outweigh your desire to be here for them or the chance to be the mother they need. That desire can scale mountains."

One of the raindrops rushed down the glass, merging with others, swelling until it reached the sill and splattered. The possibility of actually being there for Grace and Connor boggled my mind.

"Besides, you might be fine with things as they are, but do the kids feel the same?" Mina started wheeling herself away from the table. "Something to consider. Now come on. Let's get some exercise."

I looked after her as she disappeared into the family room, the memory of Connor asking why they weren't living with me front and center. As much as I didn't want to admit it to myself, I already had the answer to her question.

CHAPTER 22

"What are you doing for Thanksgiving?" Kara asked a few days later as the credits to *The Breakfast Club* rolled on her TV. "You want to come here for dinner?"

I screwed up my face. "Can't. Brandy's hosting. They've invited Mina and Wic too."

Kara smirked at me. "Whoa there. Curb your enthusiasm."

In a moment of weakness, I had told her what Mina had said about Wic, and I'd lived to regret it ever since.

"Wic the Dick is into you," she'd said, elbowing me in the shoulder. "Saw it coming a mile away." Of course, I'd blushed with a fury.

Now, for the umpteenth time in the days since, she wiggled her eyebrows and sighed with the exaggerated flair of a teenager swooning over her favorite pop star. "Those abs, though. I don't know what's wrong with you. Just go for it. I'm living vicariously here."

"No reconciliation on the horizon, then?" For a while, it had seemed she and her husband might patch things up, but she was back to not talking about him.

"Ugh, no. I found out he's been staying with that girl at work I thought he was flirting with. I mean, seriously, even if it's completely innocent, why go there? No, fuck him. I deserve better."

"Good for you. We don't need men."

"Ha! Nice try. I don't, but you most certainly do."

I threw a pillow at her. "I think that's my cue to leave."

"Aw, don't be like that."

"No, it's getting late anyway. See you tomorrow?"

We made tentative plans for Monday dinner to celebrate my
boot coming off, then I headed back to Wic's. The lights were still on
in the kitchen when I pulled into the driveway, but I ignored them
and went straight up to my room. I'd only seen Wic in passing since
Mina's comments, and that was how I needed to keep it. Maintain
the perimeter. It was best for everyone.

I had just brushed my teeth when my phone chimed with a text.
I reached for it, expecting it to be more of Kara's badgering. Instead,
Wic's name shone at me from the screen.

*Saw you come home. All good? Tacos tomorrow after work, want to
join?*

I stared at his words for a long time, allowing that fizzy warmth
to bubble up inside against my better judgment. My thumbs hovered
over the keyboard as I considered my response. Kara would hardly
fault me for standing her up if I chose to accept Wic's offer. As much
as I'd protested her insinuations, I missed his company, missed how
light I felt when he smiled at me, and the soothing cadence of his
voice. Now he was reaching out, wanting me there.

I moved my finger closer to the *Y* but hesitated. The fact that I
wanted to accept Wic's invitation as much as I did was precisely the
reason I shouldn't. I didn't want to make promises I couldn't keep.
Didn't want to hurt him. Besides, I'd made a deal with myself to focus solely on the kids.

Sorry, tomorrow doesn't work. Raincheck? I typed, biting my lip. I
waited to see if the three moving dots would appear, but they didn't.
Just as well.

I turned the phone off and crawled under the covers. Somewhere
outside, an owl hooted in the night, but the only response it received
was that of the wind howling. The sounds gradually lulled me to
sleep but not before my mutinous brain conjured up another image
of a smiling twenty-something Wic with his smooth skin, ridiculous

abs, and arms to wrap myself in on a stormy night. I rolled over on my side with a groan. *Damn that Kara.*

AS IT TURNED OUT, KARA stood me up the next evening because Logan was sick. Having lost my excuse for skipping dinner, I considered hiding out in my room under the pretense of having a headache, but knowing Wic, he would be up to check on me faster than I could say "acetaminophen." My heart softened at the thought but only for the short amount of time it took me to drum up a better resolve. It wasn't sweet—it was overbearing. I was a grown woman, for God's sake. I *had* to leave the house when he got home, at least for a few hours.

By the time five o'clock rolled around, the wind and rain had picked up again, the tall pines in the neighbor's yard swaying with a menacing pitch against pewter skies. Mina and I both jumped when my cell rang.

"It's Wic," I told her after glancing at the screen. "Hello?"

"Hey, Annie, you guys all right over there?" The background noise was loud on his end.

"Yeah. You?"

"Bit of a problem. There's a tree down at the end of this guy's driveway, and if we want to get the trucks out, we'll have to help move it. I know you had plans, but is there any chance you can stay with Mom until I get there?"

"Tree down," I whispered to Mina. "He's running late." She nodded and returned her attention to the book she was reading.

"Yeah, sure. I can do that," I said to Wic.

He exhaled sharply. "Thanks. You're the best. I'll be there as soon as I can."

A warm pulse swelled high in my chest. *The best.*

I hung up then turned to Mina. "Sounds like it's just us for dinner."

I HAD JUST PUT OUR dishes away when the telltale sound of tires on gravel announced Wic's arrival. He was soaked to the bone and shook like a wet dog upon entering, but he was in good spirits. He hugged his mother when she reached for him, though she quickly pushed him off with an exaggerated shiver.

"Go get dry, you," she said.

"Don't have to ask me twice." He grinned and shed his dripping parka.

"Are you hungry?" Mina turned to me. "Do we have something to heat up, Annie?"

"Oh, I can do that myself," Wic said.

"Yeah, I should probably..." I nodded toward the stairs.

Wic's eyes met mine, and for a moment, I thought I saw disappointment in them. Then he blinked and smiled again. "Of course. But thanks for staying. You really helped in a bind."

The rain was louder in my room, but I curled up in bed and opened my email. Soon, I was deeply engrossed in my own world.

The first drop fell just before ten and landed behind my left ear. I startled as if someone had tapped me on the shoulder. The lowest branch of the fir tree behind the garage kept brushing against the building, but other than that, I heard nothing but wind and rain.

The second drop fell on the small of my back, where my T-shirt had hiked up. It felt like a needle prick and made me let out a shriek as I jumped out of bed. Above me, a shadow moved where the walls met the ceiling, undulating like a gray flame until it grew enough to release drop number three and four in quick succession. The roof was leaking.

Just then, the lamp on my dresser flickered twice, and everything went dark.

For a long minute, I stood frozen in place, my brain scrambling. I tried to remember the last place I'd seen a bucket but to no avail. I didn't have a flashlight either. They were all downstairs in the laundry room.

I came to life again when Wic called from downstairs. "You all right, Annie? Need a light?"

I spun and banged my knee into the chair at the table and promptly let out a string of curses. That would leave a mark. "Yeah!" I called back, rubbing the tender spot. I needed to be more careful—I'd just gotten out of the boot.

I listened to his footsteps up the stairs, afraid to move from my spot in the middle of the room. The beam from his flashlight danced across the landing.

"I'm over here." I shaded my eyes when the bright searchlight struck me.

"Oops, sorry." He diverted the light. "Here's a lantern you can use. Hopefully, the power comes back on again soon."

"Thanks."

He started to leave, but then I remembered why I was out of bed in the first place.

"Actually, the roof is leaking." I held up the lantern as high as I could. "Above the bed. It was dripping on me."

Wic shone on the spot above where I'd been sitting. "Oh, jeez."

"Do you have a bucket?"

He cracked his neck and sighed. "Damn it!"

"Sorry."

"Not your fault." He let out an exasperated noise. "Yeah, I'll go get one."

While he was gone, I unplugged all electronics within a three-yard radius from the leak and pulled the bedding off the bed.

"You'll have to sleep downstairs tonight," Wic said when he returned. "I'll put a tarp up tomorrow. I'm really sorry."

He sounded so genuinely upset that it tugged at something within me. "It's not a problem."

"You could take my bed," he offered as we made our way down the stairs. "It's more comfortable."

There was a thought. His sheets crumpled around me, placing my head on a pillow that normally held his stubbled cheek, his clothes on the chair by the window, and his scent lingering in the air. I shook my head rapidly to rid myself of the image. "The couch is totally fine. But if I could borrow a pillow, that would be great. Mine got wet."

"I'm on it."

In the family room, another lantern on the coffee table lit up a plate with a half-eaten sandwich. I snuggled up in one corner of the couch, listening to the storm outside while Wic found a bucket and some towels for upstairs then got me a new pillow.

When he returned, he reached for the plate. "I'll get this out of your way."

I looked at him in the faint light of the lantern. His arm was close enough that I could have reached out and touched it. And I wanted to. "You can eat here. I'm not tired yet."

"Yeah?"

"Pretty late dinner." I nodded at the plate.

"I helped Mom first. My dad had his heart attack in a thunderstorm, so she always gets a bit frazzled in weather like this." He sat down, and the couch shifted under his weight.

"Oh?" I pulled my legs up under me.

He took a big bite of the sandwich and washed it down with half a glass of milk. Every movement made the light dance across his skin.

"How old were you when he died?"

"Seventeen. Is your dad still around? I just realized I don't know."

I shook my head. "He passed when Connor was a baby. Early-on-set Alzheimer's. He was in a home for two years."

"I'm so sorry. It must have made things even harder for you."

I was about to object, but the words stuck on my tongue. I'd never thought about it that way. By the time he'd passed, he was already long-lost to me, so I'd told myself it was for the best. I was pregnant and had a toddler to worry about, and my own demons were starting to take over—I'd had no headspace for more grief.

"Maybe," I said. I didn't want to dwell on that, though. "Were you close with your dad?"

He seemed to weigh what was left of the sandwich in his hand before putting it into his mouth and leaning back in his seat.

"I was always closer with Mom. Dad was a quiet guy, and Mom and I are talkers."

"Really? I hadn't noticed."

A brief smile lit up his features.

"Sorry." I struggled to keep my lips from curling up. If there was ever a topic not appropriate for joking, it was this, but the new giddiness sparked by his proximity had thrown me off.

"It's fine." He drained what was left in his glass and set it on the side table. "It was a long time ago."

"Some things stay recent."

"True." He bobbed his head up and down twice, then he looked at me. His mouth opened, but it took a while for him to ask his question. "Is that what it's like for you? With your mom? Does it feel like it just happened?"

The memory flashed before me. How I'd let myself into the house after school. The silence. Dishes sitting in the sink. My muted steps on the carpet in the hallway. It was a scratchy beige material that made dents on my skin when I crawled on it with bare knees. No one in the bedroom, the door to the bathroom closed. My hand on the brass doorknob, hesitating. I had a Minnie Mouse Band-Aid on my pinkie because annoying Dylan T. had chased me on the playground, and I'd gotten a splinter from the jungle gym. I knew I should have knocked, but I was ten, and I wanted to tell Mom that Mrs. Colbert had read my poem aloud in class.

There was so much blood.

"I might as well have found her yesterday," I whispered. A shiver rushed through me.

"Hey." Wic moved closer and took my hand. He squeezed it, the warmth of his palm sending a countering wave of comfort up my arm and down my spine. I threaded my fingers with his and closed my eyes.

"I'm so sorry. I shouldn't have asked." His thumb rubbed circles across the back of my hand.

My inner focus was locked on our connection, our touch the only thing keeping my mind from teetering. "Talk about something else." I swallowed, my tongue like sandpaper, and willed the cold sweat to retreat. "Anything, please."

He told me about his childhood in Snohomish, their move to Tacoma when he was twelve, and how the kids had tried to pick on him when he'd first started but thought better of it when the loudest of the bullies showed up after recess with a split lip. He'd dated his first girlfriend for two years in high school, but it ended when she graduated a year ahead of him. His second girlfriend had been a fellow art student in college—she was into yarn bombing and experimental haircuts, and they'd lived together for a brief time.

"It didn't work out. She thought I was too much of a 'conformist.'" He made bunny ears in the air with his free hand. I was still clinging to the other.

"Anyway, I graduated, moved to Olympia with a buddy, tried to get life going, and—" He shrugged. "That's about it. You know the rest."

"No other girlfriends?"

"Um." He scratched his head. "One."

"Uh-oh. You're looking very serious all of a sudden." I shouldn't have asked. I wasn't sure I wanted to hear what he was about to tell me.

"Linda. We dated for a couple of years, and I kind of thought she was the one."

Linda. I already didn't like the sound of her. "What happened?"

He squinted. "I guess I wasn't marriage material. Not 'career minded' enough." Bunny ears again.

"Ouch. Sorry."

"No need. Long over that. She wanted me to be someone I'm not—better, then, to wait for the right person to come along."

Outside, the rain picked up, its hammering consuming our sudden silence. Wic's grip tightened around my fingers.

"I saw one of your modeling photos," I blurted, wishing instantly I hadn't. I chalked it up to the charged atmosphere surrounding us, the darkness, my hand in his, our legs touching. *How did we end up so close together?*

He was quiet for a beat. "And? What did you think?"

A nervous flutter stirred inside me as I willed myself to meet his gaze. It was dark enough in the room that there was no telling where his pupils ended and the irises began, but the reflection of the lantern light in them was mesmerizing. When his free hand joined his other one to caress mine, my lips parted on a short gasp.

"I-I liked it." I wondered briefly if I was tugging him closer or if that was an illusion. I wanted to pull him to me and nestle in, disappearing completely in his embrace.

His lips curved up, and he pursed them as if trying to contain the smile. "I'm glad." His warm fingers trailed up and around my wrist, teasing the entrance of my sleeve.

I was melting. It took every ounce of effort to keep my breathing under control. I wanted him so badly.

That was when the power decided to come back on.

One moment, we were inches apart, and the next, I'd yanked my hand away and scrambled back to my corner of the couch. Blinking against the light, I pulled the blanket to me and clutched it tight. "I'm sorry. I don't know what... Sorry."

His hands were still resting on his thigh, cradling the specter of my hand. He looked down at them then slowly brushed his palms against his jeans and stood. "Don't be. It's fine." The slump in his shoulders contradicted his words.

What was my problem?

"I guess I should—" He hiked his thumb in the direction of the bedrooms then started walking away. When he reached the hallway, he paused as if about to speak.

I held my breath as the silence stretched on.

When he disappeared into his room without another word, I told myself it was relief, not disappointment, that I felt. Nevertheless, I lay awake listening for him until well past midnight, hoping for something. Anything. But what exactly, I didn't know.

CHAPTER 23

Flurries drifted through the air when I picked up the pecan caramel pie from the store on Thanksgiving morning. I burrowed my chin deeper into the scarf Kara had gifted me from her overflowing closet and unlocked the car with stiff fingers. Contrary to popular belief, New Mexico did have winters, but I hadn't brought any of my warm clothes with me. I needed to deal with my place there pretty soon. It was overdue.

At three o'clock sharp, I rang the doorbell at the Hemingways. Wic had offered to drive, but I'd declined. I didn't trust myself in his presence. Saying I was attracted to him was an understatement. I wanted him more than I'd wanted anyone since my early days with Joel. But that was not the deal. My priority was the kids. More than once since the power outage, I'd wished I could tell him that without sounding presumptuous.

Connor opened the door, wearing a smart button-down shirt with rolled-up sleeves and skinny jeans. Very *GQ*.

"You know you can just walk right in, right?" he said, taking the pie from me.

Not sure Brandy agrees. I gave him a one-armed hug. "Smells great in here."

"I made the stuffing. The turkey is enormous, so I hope you're hungry."

"Annie!" Shane came into the hallway, arms stretched wide as if he hadn't seen me in a long time. "Good to see you. Blessings and happy Thanksgiving!"

I couldn't help but smile at his exuberance, which made sense when he showed me the cup in his hand. "You've got to try some of this spiced apple cider." He lowered his voice conspiratorially. "There's bourbon in it, but don't tell Bee."

"She wouldn't approve?"

"She'd be jealous." He made a gesture with his hand to indicate a round belly.

"Ah." I smiled. "She still doing all right?"

His face grew even more radiant. "Never better!" He hooked an arm through mine and led me into the kitchen.

"There you are." Brandy came around the counter, wiping her hands on her checkered apron. Her face was glowing, though I suspected that had more to do with the temperature in the room than the pregnancy. "Happy Thanksgiving." She embraced me and, to my surprise, kissed both my cheeks.

"Happy Thanksgiving. Need help with anything?"

She scanned the various items on the counter. "No, don't think so."

"Everything looks delicious."

Shane handed me a cup. "Here. Try it." He watched me, eyes sparkling as I put it to my lips. It was way too strong for me.

"Mm, delicious." I nodded.

"Hon, can you take out the garbage?" Brandy asked him. "And then put this platter in the dining room?"

He gave her a peck on the lips. "Of course, my dear."

The two of them were certainly in a good mood today. I wondered what had brought it on—if it was just the pregnancy entering a safer phase or something else.

"Where's Grace?" I asked after Shane had gone outside.

Brandy's face soured. "Probably still upstairs. Actually, if you want to go get her, that would be great. Maybe she'll listen to you."

I very much doubted that, but I was eager as always to see my daughter, so I bounded up the stairs and down the hallway to her room. The faint sound of an orchestra with a violin solo dancing high above seeped out from underneath her closed door, and I paused to listen before knocking. It sounded familiar, yet I couldn't quite put my finger on what it was.

"Yeah?" she replied to my knock.

"It's Annie. Can I come in?"

The music stopped, and I heard her close a drawer. A moment later, she opened the door. "Hi." She'd mixed up her all-black wardrobe today in favor of dark-blue leggings and a black-and-blue-striped sweater. Her hair was pulled back in a ponytail, but I suspected that might work against her once Brandy spotted the heavy smears of purple eye shadow.

"You look... nice," I said.

"Don't start." She sat down at her desk and opened a small jewelry box.

I followed her inside, eagerly scanning the walls of her room, where posters of her favorite bands and singers mixed with pictures of adorable baby animals. *Straddling two worlds.*

"I snuck mascara once in sixth grade." I leaned closer to the mirror next to the window to view the photos she had stuck to it with tape. "I found it among Mom's old things a couple of years after she died, and I put it on right before I had to run to the bus so Dad wouldn't see. He didn't want me in her stuff, and he definitely didn't want his twelve-year-old wearing makeup."

Grace still had her back to me, but I could tell she was listening because her hand rested idly on the box.

"It was raining sideways that day, but I didn't think twice about it—rain is hardly newsworthy here, right? But anyway, classes started, and I thought maybe more people than usual stared at me in the hallway. I figured—hey, they're appreciating this new cooler me." I picked up a heart-shaped necklace with gears stuck in resin from the nightstand, weighed it in my hand, then put it back. "Well, I get to third-period social studies, and Mrs. Lowell took one look at me and said 'oh my, aren't we pretty today?' At first, I thought she was complimenting me, but when several of the other kids started laughing, I excused myself to go to the bathroom and—"

"Let me guess, it had run?" Grace turned, a small smile on her lips.

"They called me 'Raccoonie' the rest of the semester."

She giggled, and the sound warmed me more than any spiked cider could.

"Lucky for me, another kid returned from Christmas break with two broken legs—skiing accident—and they forgot all about *moi*."

"I would die."

"Well, it did force me to get better at doing makeup. I can help you if you want." I glanced her way before resuming studying her wall décor.

"You're not going to tell me to take it off?"

I wrinkled my nose as if thinking about it. "Nah. Makeup is fun. And we're just family tonight. School's another thing, but I'll leave that to your aunt and uncle."

Together, we wiped off the purple and set a new base. Where I needed two different concealers to hide my dark circles, her skin was dewy and plump. I limited the application to two small dots in the inner corners of her eyes, more to make her feel like we were doing real makeup than to conceal anything. I relished every bit of showing her how to apply the colors correctly, the blending, where on the lid the shades should go, and how to accentuate with liner. It had been a while, but it came back to me quickly.

"A little goes a long way," I told her. "You never want it to be the first thing people see when they meet you." I spun her toward the mirror. "There. What do you think?"

My work was more discreet than what she'd managed on her own, and I kept my fingers crossed that she wouldn't hate it. I wasn't stupid. I understood that part of what she was after was shock value, but I hoped she would see that makeup could be put to better use.

She leaned closer to the mirror, angling her head from side to side. Finally, a wide grin spread across her lips. "You're really good at this."

"Yeah?"

"It's so different."

"Is it too much?"

"Ha, no." She rolled her eyes, but unlike previous times, there was nothing catty about it. "I love it. Thanks."

"Wic and Mina are here!" Connor hollered from the stairs.

Grace and I looked at each other. My brain scrambled for something else to say but came up short.

"I'm not going to hug you or anything," Grace said with a crooked smile. "You can go downstairs."

It was so *her* that I couldn't help but chuckle. "Right. You coming?"

"I need earrings."

"But then you'll—"

"Yes, yes. I'll be there."

I may or may not have done a fist bump to myself walking down the hallway.

"Well?" Brandy asked when I entered the kitchen.

"She'll be down in a few."

"Looking decent?"

"Of course." I frowned, defenses going up on Grace's behalf.

"Good. Here, can you do me a favor and strain these potatoes? The pot is too heavy for me." She placed a gentle hand on her baby bump.

I grabbed the oven mitts and reached for the pot. "How are you feeling? Nausea completely gone?"

"Yeah, I'm great. Cautiously optimistic, but you know, God willing." She touched the crucifix around her neck. "You've got to hold a finger on the lid or the potatoes will go in the sink."

"Got it."

She watched anxiously as if a mishap was inevitable.

"I can mash them, too, if you want. Why don't you go sit for a bit?"

She hesitated.

"I've made mashed potatoes before, you know."

"Of course. There's butter and sour cream in the fridge. But don't make it too runny. I can't stand that. And no clumps."

"Table, chair, sit." I pointed at the corner where Shane and Connor were already relaxing.

Brandy threw up her hands with an upbeat "I'm going."

It was nice to glimpse the old version of my sister-in-law—a little more relaxed, her smile not buried quite so deep inside. I got that she was a sterner guardian than I'd been, but perhaps, as she became a mother herself, she would ease up a bit on Grace and Connor as well. One could hope.

"Hey." Wic pulled me out of my thoughts as I worked the masher in the pot. "Need a hand?"

"Hi. No, I've got it."

"Haven't seen you much this week." He took a swig of his beer.

I gave him a cursory smile. "It's been a busy one."

"So it's got nothing to do with that night, then?"

I almost dropped the masher. Right to it. "What night?"

He scoffed and muttered something that sounded like "whatever" then turned to lean against the sink.

I mashed and mashed and mashed and mashed. If Brandy wanted no clumps, she'd get no clumps. Without looking at him, I walked past Wic to the butter and milk then added them to the potatoes. I should have known my pulling away wouldn't go unnoticed by him.

"Can you hand me the salt and pepper?" I asked. "In the cabinet above your head."

He reached for them, allowing me a covert glance as he turned away. He wore a maroon, shawl-collar sweater that clung to him in all the right ways. He smelled good, too, and I had to force my attention back to the food prep at hand.

He set the spices down next to me with a loud *clank*. "Here you go."

"Thanks."

He let out a sharp exhale. "I don't get it. Are you mad at me or something? I've been wracking my brain about it, but I don't think I did anything to offend you."

I put the wooden spoon down and massaged the fingertips on my right hand. "No, I'm not mad." I gnawed at my lip. "It's just..."

"What?" He shifted from one foot to the other. "What is it?"

I made myself face him. "It's not why I'm here," I mumbled.

His eyes narrowed. "What's not why you're here?"

My cheeks heated. Was he really going to make me spell it out? *I'm not here to fall for you. I'm not here to break your heart. You deserve someone better.*

"Nothing. Forget it." I picked up the spoon again and returned to stirring. "I need to finish this, or Brandy will be pissed."

As if saying her name had summoned her from across the room, Brandy's voice suddenly rose above the others. "But I told you to wash it off before coming downstairs!"

I glanced over my shoulder to find her leaning into Grace, blatant disapproval on her face. Grace looked equally displeased, arms crossed over her stomach.

"Hold this." I shoved the spoon into Wic's hand, then I hurried through the kitchen to where the standoff was taking place.

"What's going on?" I asked in my most placating voice. "Potatoes are done, so should we maybe call everyone to the table?"

"She's wearing makeup." Brandy stared at Grace with her lips pursed. "I don't know how many times I have to tell you—"

"I helped her put it on," I said, interrupting the tirade. "It's my fault—I should have checked with you first. I figured we're not going anywhere, so what's the harm? Come on. I think it looks great."

Brandy's glare could have frozen a pot of boiling habanero chili. "My house, my rules. She's thirteen for goodness sake. It looks cheap."

My chin jerked back. "It's tasteful, and she's at home. Besides, you and I are both wearing makeup."

"That's different, and you know it."

Grace was watching the two of us as if we were in a Ping-Pong match.

I straightened to get my full two inches over Brandy and lowered my voice. "Even if that's the case—and I'm not saying I agree—is it worth fighting over right now? It's Thanksgiving, and dinner is ready. Everyone's gathered. Can we save this for another day?"

Brandy's mouth opened as if she was about to object, but then she inhaled deeply. "Fine." To Grace, she said, "We'll talk about this tomorrow," then she stormed past me to the stove.

"Don't worry about it." I touched Grace's arm gently.

She shrugged me off. "Easy for you to say. You're not the one who has to live here." She turned her back to me, setting a course for the dining room.

At least the turkey looked delicious.

Shane said grace, and everybody dug in. The air resounded with spirited exclamations on the quality of the food and how their taste buds were celebrating. Connor was on my left and Grace on my right. Wic and Mina sat across from us. Mina was unusually quiet, and I told her as much, expecting a snappy response in return.

"I haven't been sleeping well for a few nights," she said instead and left it at that.

I knew that wasn't true—I still spent every day with her, and she'd never mentioned it before. She'd seemed perfectly fine yesterday. When I looked to Wic for an explanation, what I found instead was a deep crease between his eyebrows that was not normally there. Something else was going on.

A half hour into the meal, Grace collapsed against the backrest of her chair with a contented sigh. "I'm stuffed." The tension from her argument with Brandy had rolled off her incrementally with each bite.

"Maybe if you didn't inhale your food," Connor said, which awarded him a half-hearted glare from his sister. He ignored it and looked back at me. "I swear, she eats as if it's the last meal she'll ever have."

"Okay, that's enough," I said lightly. "You're both growing. And besides, I'm full as well. How I'm going to fit any pie at all in here is a mystery." I poked myself in the belly.

"Did you like my stuffing?" Connor asked.

"Best I ever had."

He shoveled another spoonful of potatoes and gravy into his mouth with a contented grin. "I made cookies for rehearsal the other day, and they devoured them. Said I should bring treats every day."

"He would if I let him into the kitchen," Brandy said.

"Yeah, but I don't have time. I can't believe next week is tech week."

The drama club's performance of *A Christmas Carol* was coming up, and if Brandy was to be believed, they'd hardly seen Connor at the house for the past few weeks.

"I can't wait." I rubbed circles on my distended midsection. "Do you feel ready?"

"So ready." He nodded eagerly. "Pass the rolls, please." He accepted the breadbasket from Wic across the table. "But I only play Bob Cratchit. You should see Miles. He's amazing as Scrooge."

"I heard the district superintendent will be in the audience too," Shane said. "It'll be a treat. Oh, and speaking of treats, guess who just won the company raffle?" He held out his wine glass as if proposing a toast.

"Doesn't take a genius to figure out you did," Mina grumbled from her seat.

Something was definitely going on with her.

Shane beamed. "I sure did. A two-week all-expenses paid trip to the Bahamas."

"Wow, man. Congrats." Wic raised his glass to Shane's, and I joined them in the felicitations.

"Have you thought about when you'll go?" Wic continued.

"Well, we'd like to go before the baby comes, so we were thinking of trying for New Year's if possible."

"Can you imagine getting out of this rain for a bit? Heavenly." Brandy sighed.

"But of course," Shane continued, glancing my way, "that also depends on... other things."

Wic was watching me, the same frown lines still etched in his forehead. I got the distinct feeling that those "other things" had to do with me and that he was in the know. Even though I couldn't manage one more bite, I reached for another roll and started buttering it.

Grace had been following the conversation quietly so far, but now her voice filled the space left by Shane's ambiguous statement. "And where would we be? Would we go too?"

Shane exchanged a look with his wife. "Well, that is—" He pressed his lips together as if waiting for someone else to fill in his sentence.

Out of the corner of my eye, I noticed Brandy glance at me before she cleared her voice. "Maybe it's not a good idea after all," she said to Shane. "We could wait a bit, maybe."

"Couldn't you stay here with us?" Connor asked me suddenly.

And there was the million-dollar question.

CHAPTER 24

Staying with the kids for two full weeks. Breakfasts, lunches, dinners. Good mornings and good nights. No perimeter. As terrifying as it sounded, it could be a good place to start. "Yeah. I mean, that would be... um... up to Shane and Brandy, I would think."

Across from me, Wic leaned back, folding his arms over his chest. I willed Mina to look my way—she knew what this chance meant—but she was the only one not staring at me.

I tried my best to sit up straight and remain calm despite every fiber of my body twisting into frazzled coils. It seemed unlikely that Brandy would be okay with me watching the kids for that long.

"Why don't we talk about it tomorrow?" she asked at last.

I breathed a small sigh of relief at the reprieve.

"Wouldn't that be great?" Connor said to me between bites as the conversation resumed around other, safer topics.

I shoved the roll in my mouth and nodded to hide how his excitement made me worry I'd never be able to live up to his expectations.

Wic and Mina left right after dessert, and a heavy weight lifted off my shoulders. He only bid me a cursory good night before heading out the door, and while his new disapproval was a bit unsettling, I decided not to let it get to me. It was a blessing, actually—better for the both of us if he avoided my company.

After cleaning up, everyone gathered in front of the TV to watch rerun footage of that morning's Macy's parade.

"Are you coming with us to pick out the Christmas tree tomorrow?" Grace asked once we'd settled on the couch.

"You should," Shane said. "The weather is supposed to be nice. It's a fun little outing."

"Dad used to take us," Connor added. "We'd spend hours finding the perfect one before he cut it down."

"Remember that time it almost fell on top of him?" Grace asked. "He was lucky that big stone was there."

"Aaah! Help me! There's a branch in my ear." Connor playacted the scene from memory, and they both laughed. It was the first time I'd heard the kids talk about Joel so freely.

"He had a cat when we met," I said. "A scrawny thing named Babe Ruth. She loved Christmas trees as if they were made of catnip. For two years straight, we had to keep it plain—no ornaments or anything—or she'd shove them all off the branches. She was a real holiday terror."

"I never knew Dad had a cat," Grace said.

"He got it with his college roommate, who turned out to be allergic."

Connor turned to me. "Tell us something else."

I nestled deeper into the couch, reveling in the temporary sphere of familiarity that unexpectedly surrounded us. Grace sat so close to me that our arms almost touched.

"Hm, let me think."

"He was terrified of the Easter Bunny when we were kids," Brandy said, shifting focus to her. "And he didn't learn to swim until he was eleven."

Connor and Grace both latched on to this new information and started peppering Brandy with questions. The elation I'd initially felt shrank as I listened to their back-and-forth. The further down memory lane they went, the more I felt like a fifth wheel. But perhaps that was to be expected. At least for the time being.

I left shortly thereafter with a promise to touch base in the morning about tree shopping.

WIC WAS STILL UP WHEN I got home close to midnight—or so I assumed based on the light coming from the house. I tried to ignore that awareness as I headed upstairs, but no sooner had I reached my room than a knock sounded on my door.

I bought a few seconds, setting my purse on the table and shrugging out of my jacket before responding. "Come in."

Wic had taken off his sweater and was in a dark short-sleeved T-shirt in defiance of the sinking temperatures outside.

"Hey." He closed the door behind him. "Did you have a good night?"

I watched him suspiciously. Polite small talk was quite the contrast from earlier in the night. "Yeah, it was good. I'm beat. And so full."

He let out a low humming noise in agreement. "Can we talk?"

"Is Mina all right? She was quiet tonight."

"Yeah. It's not about Mom."

Red alerts started blaring in my head. "It's pretty late. Maybe tomorrow would be—"

"I'll be quick." His eyes locked on mine. He wasn't going to take no for an answer.

I took a seat at the table and gestured for him to join me. "What's going on?"

He sat down, elbows on the table, mouth against the thumbs of his steepled hands. "Okay," he said as if bracing himself. He lowered his hands. "I've been thinking, and I know what you're doing."

I reclined away from him. "What's that?"

"It means I'm on to you and this whole... act."

"Act?" I worked to keep my voice level.

"I get that your life has been hard, that you've been through things. But you came back, right? You're here now." He shifted and raked a hand through his tresses. They shimmered in the overhead light. "Did you see the look on Connor's face tonight at your reaction to staying with them over the holidays? Or Grace's relief when you came to her defense about the whole makeup thing? It's obvious they want you here. That they need *you*."

"I want the same. I said I'd do it. Maybe you didn't hear."

"What I heard was far from a commitment. You're pretending not to care when I *know* you care a lot."

I sucked in my cheeks and bit down until I tasted blood. *How dare he be so presumptuous?* I would move out tomorrow, find another place. Our lives had become too enmeshed if he thought I would let this slide. I was about to tell him as much when he spoke again, more softly this time.

"I know you're scared. I get that. And maybe living alone for so many years makes it hard to, I don't know, be mindful of other people—"

"Mindful?" The word came out with a snap. "Who do you think you are? Everything I do revolves around being mindful. I love them. They are everything. To see them again is—" My voice broke, and I pressed my fingers to my throat to halt the growing lump. "But I can't rush this. I have to be careful."

"Why? They're fine. All they want is to spend more time with you."

"I know!" I howled, failing to keep my voice under control. "Why don't you understand? I'm getting there. I'm trying!"

Wic stared at me in silence for a long moment. "Are you trying with me too? Or is this"—he gestured between us—"not worth your effort?"

"Please don't." I turned from him and walked to the window. *So that's what this was really about? Not the kids and me but him and me?* My breath fogged the glass while my heart drummed ever faster against my ribs.

"Why not? Why can't we talk about this? I know I'm not imagining things." His chair scraped against the floor. "You can't deny you've avoided me ever since the power outage." He was getting closer. "If I said I wanted to spend more time with you, what would you do?"

I could see his face behind me in the glass, feel the energy emanating from him. *I'd be thrilled.* "That's a bad idea."

"Would you run? Move out?"

I swallowed, shaken by how well he knew my thoughts. "It's too complicated. *I'm* too complicated. You don't need that in your life."

"And I don't get a say in that? Why can't you trust that you're worth it to us? That we can deal? Let your guard down just a little. What's the worst thing that could happen?"

I spun. "You know the answer to that."

"I don't think even you believe that anymore." He reached for me, but I shrugged him off. "Come on, Annie. Give yourself a chance."

A sob rose in my throat. "I'm not sure I deserve one."

"But you do." He reached for me again, and this time, I didn't pull away. "I know you've been hurting, and I know it's not easy, but something's got to give here. There are people who care about you. Let them." His thumb stroked my cheek. "Let me."

"I'll mess up your life too," I whispered, even as I felt my body yielding to his.

"No, you won't."

My hands clutched the thin material of his shirt, and for a suspended moment, our breaths mingled with each labored intake of air I managed. Then I kissed him.

The first one was little more than a peck, my lips making only the briefest contact with his. But as I reveled in the soft yield of the plump skin, it set off a firestorm inside me. It rose from my toes, raging up my legs and spine, its flames licking every nerve ending I'd kept on ice for years until my very core quivered with the need for him. I pulled him down to me at the same time one of his hands snaked into my hair to tilt my face up, this new all-consuming drive to get closer seeming to strike us both simultaneously.

We came together with a sharp gasp, the second kiss a fury of softness and warmth, of lips and tongue, of arms trailing and air shared. It overwhelmed me, yet I couldn't get close enough.

"You don't have to," he managed over the panting. "Are you sure we—"

I silenced him with more kisses and tore at his shirt, pulling it up and off. Even if I'd been able to form a conscious thought, I doubted it would have made a difference. It was only him and me, his hands burning a trail on my skin, his breath echoing against my neck with the same urgency that spurred me onward.

It felt so damn good I think I might have climbed him.

CHAPTER 25

The room was cloaked in the dim light of early dawn when I woke up the next morning. It was raining, the staccato droplets amplified by the tarp now covering my corner of the roof, and I curled up under my duvet, pulling it tighter around me. I felt heavy as if I'd worked out really hard or—*oh!*

My eyes sprang open as my mind flooded with titillating images. The room slowly came into focus. My purse lay toppled on the table, one of the chairs sat askew several feet away from it, and by the window was a bundle of fabric that could only be my shirt.

I covered my head with the pillow and searched for the guilt I knew should be rearing its ugly head any minute. I'd done exactly the opposite of what I'd promised myself—I'd had sex with Wic. Repeatedly and thoroughly.

To my surprise, my inner voices remained silent. Instead, as in the aftermath of a bomb blast going off nearby, what remained was the residual hum of impact reverberating inside my skull. Memories of the night we'd just spent together flashed before me, colorful like a stained-glass window. His hand trailing my hip, raising goosebumps in its wake. The solid weight of him hovering above me. The heat of his skin against my lips. I knew at once I did not want it undone. The feeling was wholly new to me.

I didn't remember Wic leaving, but considering the pangs of soreness echoing in places both exposed and hidden, perhaps being alone was for the best.

I pulled myself up and propped a pillow behind my back. The morning air was cool and damp as always, so I cocooned myself in the duvet until nothing but my head stuck out. The faintest trace of Wic's aftershave still lingered on the fabric, proof I hadn't imagined everything between us. A smile tugged at my lips.

What's he doing now? Sleeping back in his own room? My thoughts strayed to what would happen once I went downstairs. Late to the party, the butterflies in my stomach awoke with a vengeance. In the bright light of day, he could be regretting last night. He *had* initially tried to slow us down, though in my defense, he hadn't exactly needed a lot of convincing otherwise. But he'd also been upset with me.

A soft knock on the door interrupted my thoughts and forced me to peek out from the safety of my cave.

Wic entered bearing two steaming cups and an adorably sheepish smile. "Coffee?"

I lowered the covers to my chin and nodded. He was in dark sweats and a white T-shirt, and his hair hung in damp tresses down his back. It was hardly fair that he'd had time to freshen up.

"I couldn't sleep." He set down my cup on the nightstand then stood for a moment as if unsure what to do with himself.

I scooted over and patted the bed.

He sat, facing me. "I kept thinking..." He turned the cup in his hands. "Ah, never mind."

"What?" I willed him to look at me, and when he did, I tried my best not to let on how scared I was of what exactly had been going through his mind.

"I guess I wasn't sure what to expect. If you'd freak out."

I assumed an expression of mock indignation. "I never freak out."

The corner of his mouth quivered. "Right. Yeah, that's what I told myself—Annie never freaks out." He laughed quietly, and I joined in.

"But seriously, I'm not." The truth of my words left a warm glow inside me. I freed one arm from the burrito I was in and let it rest idly between us. "Are you?"

He set his cup down and took my hand, his palm gliding across mine before settling. "Not a bit. It was overdue, but you're worth the wait."

Fireworks flashed up my arm as much from his words as from his touch. That ex of his had definitely failed to see the quality of the man in front of her. *Thank you, Linda.*

He scooted closer so that his hip nudged mine. Even through all the layers of blankets, I was instantly aware of him.

"What if I kiss you now? Would *that* freak you out?" His right hand reached for my cheek then lightly trailed my jawbone.

My lips parted even as I fought the impulse to close my eyes and lean into his hand. "I told you—I never freak out," I whispered.

"Good."

IT WAS FULL DAYLIGHT outside by the time we drew apart long enough to notice our surroundings. Wic had stayed on top of the covers—a chaste concession to kissing that had been anything but. As much as being so close to him set me on fire, I still appreciated the attempt at slowing things down, whether intentional or not.

He propped himself up on his elbow, his left hand trailing the curves of my face with fingertips as light as feathers. I exhaled, giggling when he traced beneath my chin.

"Look at me," he said, coaxing.

I did, and the notion of drowning in someone's eyes was instantly less silly. He let his fingers trail down the side of my neck, across my shoulder, then down the goosefleshed skin of my bare arms. When he reached my hand, he lifted it and pressed his lips to the pulse point on the inside of my wrist.

"Your heart's beating pretty fast there, Wolff." His mouth curved up against my skin. "I hope it wasn't something I did."

I swatted him with my free hand and tried to wiggle free, but he kept his fingers around my arm and laid it down carefully on the covers before stroking it gently. By the time the alarm in my head sounded, it was already too late.

He adjusted his weight and leaned back slightly as if to get a better view. "What are these?" His fingers played across skin where thin white lines marred my complexion.

I pulled my arms away from him and hid them under the covers. "It's nothing."

Wic sat up. "They're scars, aren't they?"

I nodded. I couldn't lie to him. Not anymore. And he'd said he could deal. I willed my voice to be casual. "They're old. I don't do it anymore."

"Good." With slow movements, he folded the blanket down enough so that he could extract my left arm again. I let him. "They don't look like cuts," he said, more to himself than to me.

I swallowed. "They're burn marks."

His fingers stilled for a split second then took up their light dance again.

"From what?"

"An iron." I studied his face carefully as I admitted a secret I'd only ever told Dr. Samson.

His jaw twitched, but he didn't recoil in disgust or horror. Instead, he leaned forward and kissed those constant reminders of my darkest hours. "I'm so sorry. I can't imagine. I hate that you felt bad enough to do that."

I wasn't sure what to say, so I leaned into him and let him hold me, reveling in the strength of his body around mine.

"If you ever feel yourself going that way again," he said into my hair, "I want you to know I'm here for you. I'll help in any way I can."

I lifted my face to his. "You mean that, don't you?"

He nodded. "But I believe in you. Good things are coming. You're not going to actually need me, so it's an easy promise to make." His tongue-in-cheek quip was followed by a wink.

A smile breached my lips. There I was in his arms, with an opportunity to spend more time with the kids right in front of me—not to mention I'd made it through my last dip relatively unscathed. Maybe it was time to start believing good things were on their way.

CHAPTER 26

"You're in a great mood today," Brandy said as we trailed behind Shane and the kids through rows and rows of Christmas tree prospects later that day. Wic had reluctantly gotten out of my bed around half past nine to go check on Mina, but we'd made plans to eat dinner together that evening. The raincheck on the taco night I'd avoided what seemed like a lifetime ago.

"It's the sun." I hoped my scarf covered enough of my face so that she wouldn't see me blushing.

"Yes. It's nice, isn't it?" She tilted her head skyward and closed her eyes briefly. "I'll take cold and sunny any day. I've lived here all my life, but I don't think I'll ever get used to the rainy season."

"Me neither."

"Is that why you chose Albuquerque?"

Her question came as a surprise, and it took me a moment to form a response. "Not really. I mean, it's true that there's not a lot of rain there, but they do have seasons. The winters can be pretty cold, actually."

"So why there?"

The ground crunched with dry pine needles beneath our feet as we walked deeper into the field. "I didn't really know where to go when I left. Or what to do. I basically just drove as far as I could get. I had some money saved up, and at the time, I didn't expect to, um, be around long enough to need an income, so I stayed at a motel. Then as the weeks passed, I realized I wasn't ready yet."

Brandy looked confused, so I continued. "It's hard to explain. Depression is cyclical in many ways, with ups and downs. As it entered the more manageable phase, I decided to rent a place. Bide my time. I found a sublet I could rent month to month and stayed."

"Huh."

We walked to the end of the row in silence. Shane, Grace, and Connor were deep into the prickly greenery, weighing the merits of each tree they passed.

"Bee," I said after we'd turned and walked halfway back down the row over. "I'm really not going back there. I know my coming back has caused some commotion in your lives, and I want you to know I'm sorry for that. But I'm not going away."

She kept her gaze steady on the path in front of us. "You'll have to forgive me if I don't take that at face value. But so far so good, I guess."

I reached out and touched her arm, making her stop. "I think you should go on that trip. I'd be happy to stay with the kids. It could be a first step."

"First step to what?"

"I'm their mom. You and Shane are having a baby of your own. In time, I'm hoping they'll live with me again."

Brandy resumed walking. "That's out of left field, don't you think?"

"I'm not saying now."

"I should hope not."

My steps faltered.

"Found it!" Connor yelled from somewhere on our left.

I let Brandy continue alone while I veered in among the trees. I wanted her on my side, but there were two other people whose approval mattered infinitely more to me, and they were currently somewhere inside the green maze.

"Coming!" It took a minute of searching, but eventually, I found the right row. "Wow, that's a beauty."

"Right?" Connor gripped its branches as if staking a claim.

"Shane's going to think it's too big," Grace said from behind the tree.

"I think it will fit," I said.

Just then, Shane emerged from between the green. "All right. What do we have?"

Connor beamed at him. "The perfect tree."

Shane circled it. "Don't you think it's a little on the tall side?"

"Called it," Grace whispered.

The disappointment on Connor's face made my heart ache. "But we'd have to cut a chunk off the trunk, right?" I asked. "And you have nine-foot ceilings in the family room."

I took a few steps back and squinted at the full fir. "Look here." I waved Shane to me. "Can't you just picture it, full of lights and ornaments? That antique gold star at the top?"

"It broke. We use an angel now."

"Or that." I nodded enthusiastically. "Presents underneath, the scent of pine needles throughout the house."

Over Shane's shoulder, Connor gave me a discreet thumbs-up.

"It *is* a very good find," Shane conceded. "All right. What the heck? Let's get it."

"Yes." Connor did a fist pump, and even Grace found the win worthy of a smile.

My mission for the day was complete.

Getting the tree strapped to the roof of the car was a joint effort, but eventually, it was secure enough that we could enjoy a hot cocoa from the sales booth and congratulate one another on a job well done.

"So, what's the next step?" I asked. "Do we decorate today?"

"It needs to be warmed up slowly." Shane cradled his drink close to his face. "I usually leave it in the garage overnight and then drill some holes in the bottom of the trunk tomorrow before bringing it in."

"Why?" Connor asked. "Dad always brought it in right away."

"And by Christmas, was it still lush and green or a bit tired?"

Connor and Grace looked at each other and said in unison, "Tired."

"You don't want to shock it with indoor heat right away, and drilling holes gives it a larger surface to absorb water. I told Joel many times, but he didn't want to listen."

Brandy chuckled quietly. "He always had his way of doing things." Noticing the kids watching her, she added, "Not that there's anything wrong with that."

"Okay, so we decorate tomorrow," I said, steering the conversation back on track. "Would you mind if I helped? We could bake some gingersnaps too."

Connor's face lit up. "Oh, I love gingersnaps!"

"Baking?" Grace frowned.

"What? You used to love it when you were—" I was going to say "little" but stopped myself. *People change. Focus on who she is now.*

Shane came to my rescue. "That's okay. You can help me with the lights instead."

We finished our drinks and crammed into the car. About halfway home, Grace broke away from the window and turned to me. "Did we use to bake together? Some kind of cookie with jam on top?"

I smiled. "Thumbprint cookies. Yeah. You remember?"

"I think so." The crease between her brows deepened. "What else did we do together? All the time, I mean?"

"Well, the park."

"The blue one?"

A rush of nostalgia washed over me. I'd forgotten Connor and Grace always referred to the various neighborhood parks by the color of the jungle gym structures. It used to confuse the heck out of Joel and me. "Among others."

"Do you remember when I climbed up to the crossbar on the swing set?" Connor asked from my other side.

"Sure do. That was the worst. You were too scared to come down. What did we end up doing?"

"I think I jumped."

"No. I would never have let you do that."

Connor shrugged.

"I don't remember that." Grace's voice was short. "What else?"

I returned my attention to her. "Hmm, let's see. You loved feeding the ducks by the river. And reading books."

"Nerd," Connor whispered to my right, and I needled him with my elbow.

"*The Napping House*," Grace said to herself. "I loved that one."

"We must have read it a thousand times."

She nodded and turned back to the window. The conversation was over.

Memories. Soon, we might make new ones.

Shane's eyes met mine in the mirror before he took Brandy's hand and gave it a squeeze. They exchanged a silent question before glancing my way again, making clear their understanding had something to do with me. That served as a harsh reminder any future memory making depended upon them allowing it.

CHAPTER 27

Wic browned the beef while I cut up veggies for dinner that night. The fan's noise paired with his spatula scraping and my knife snapping left little room for conversation. Instead, we moved around each other in a silent dance, hips bumping, arms grazing in passing, gazes stolen, and smiles barely concealed.

Mina was at the table behind us, doing a crossword puzzle. I didn't know if Wic had told her what had happened between us, but just in case he hadn't, I wanted to be as discreet as possible. It was a wasted effort.

"There's more sexual tension in here than at an eighth-grade prom," Mina announced shortly after Wic used his body to scoot me sideways to reach a spoon in the drawer bank. "I may be half-lame, but I see just fine."

I waited to see how Wic would react. Maybe he wanted to keep it a secret. He tapped the spoon against the pan a couple of times then pulled me to him. "Well, thank God for that." He stole a quick kiss that made my lips tingle.

"About time." Mina chuckled.

I allowed myself an unabashed grin in response. "Clearly, I was a moron before."

"You could say that again," she muttered. "Ah, *moron*—foolish, dimwitted person." She scribbled the word into her puzzle. "Thank you!"

Tacos weren't exactly date food, but Wic had seen me at my worst, so I doubted salsa dribbling down my chin would make any difference. We ate, we talked, and we laughed, and even Mina was in good spirits. I had meant to ask Wic about her odd demeanor on Thanksgiving but decided not to press the issue with her around.

Throughout the meal, Wic and I were in constant contact—if not our feet, our knees, and if not our knees, our hands. Mina was right. The tension was palpable, and it made it hard to concentrate. Perhaps I needed to play a bit harder to get, but then again, the proverbial cat was already out of the bag.

"Join me outside for a puff?" Mina asked me when the food was gone. "Wic will do the dishes."

I looked at Wic. "Do you mind?"

"No, you go ahead." He started clearing the plates.

I wheeled Mina out onto the deck and helped her light up her pipe. As usual, the smoke stung my lungs, and I waved it away from my face. Mina ignored me, inhaling deeply.

"You seem to be doing pretty well." Something told me she wasn't referring to me handling the marijuana smoke.

"I am."

"Good. Good. I like you and Wic together." She paused, her gaze boring into me. "So no plans to off yourself currently, then?"

I stared at her.

She blinked twice then held out the carved wooden shaft for me to take. "Want some?"

What the heck? Why not? I attempted a drag but instantly started coughing.

"Newbie." Mina chuckled.

It had been years since I'd last smoked pot, but I immediately recognized the slight tingle in my cheeks. I pulled one of the chairs closer so I could sit down, ignoring how the chill of the seat attacked the back of my thighs.

"No, no plans of that nature at present." I tucked my hands into my armpits. *I'm at a* two *right now*, I thought. I hadn't ever been a two since Dr. Samson and I started using the scale.

"He really cares about you, you know."

"I know."

"He's a good man."

A smile I couldn't control tugged at my lips. "I know that too."

Mina took another puff and showed me a toothy grin. "You're a good match."

"Thanks." Her complete acceptance made me want to cry.

She shrugged, tapped the bowl on her armrest once, then covered the opening of the pipe with two fingers—to put it out, I assumed.

"That'll do," she said, confirming my suspicion. "Colder than a witch's tit out here."

I took hold of the wheelchair and steered her toward the door. "It'll get colder before it turns, I'm sure."

"That's why they call it winter. Isn't it funny that on the other side of the world it's summer now? Summer in November. Summer for Christmas. And it's completely normal. 'It's Christmas break—let's go to the beach!' And poor Santa—he has to wear his red suit in that heat."

She kept talking as I got her settled in front of the TV. By now I was used to her impromptu monologues after she partook, but I always found them entertaining. When her show started, I returned to the kitchen, where Wic was just finishing wiping off the table.

"She good?" he asked.

"Happy as a clam." I sidled up to him by the sink as he wrung out the rag. I wrapped my arms around him, rested my cheek against his back, and closed my eyes. His usual scent was tinged with taco seasoning. I inhaled deeply while his heart drummed solid beats beneath my palm.

He turned off the faucet and spun around to face me, a smile blooming. "You had some, too, didn't you?"

"Only one drag."

He brushed a strand of my hair away from my face and tucked it behind my ear, then he leaned forward so his evening scruff tickled my temple. "Do you want to go upstairs for a bit?" he whispered, ending with a soft kiss to my jaw.

My breath quivered. *Yes, please.* "What about your mom?"

He peeked into the living room. "Her show just started. We have time."

I ran my hands up his chest and tilted my head back. "Well, in that case..."

Neither one of us needed more convincing.

"YOU DID NOT." KARA stopped her rummaging through the closet in the hallway and stared at me. I had just finished regaling her with everything that had happened between Wic and me.

"Yeah, and I kissed him first. Though in all honesty, he might have kissed me anyway if I hadn't."

"Wow." Her mouth hung open. "I don't... I'm not sure what to say. Good for you."

She pulled out a duffel bag from the closet floor and opened it. "Aha! I knew it was here somewhere." With a triumphant grin, she withdrew a long gray Velcro strip about four inches wide. "This saved my life when I was pregnant with Logan. Tell Brandy she can keep it."

She'd run into my sister-in-law in town just before Thanksgiving, and Brandy had not held back when Kara asked about her pregnancy.

"What do you do with it?"

"Wrap it around your hips, like this." She demonstrated. "It holds your pelvis together so walking doesn't feel like torture."

"Very attractive."

"Like I said, a lifesaver. But back to Wic and this fling of yours. You didn't think you'd get away that easily, did you?" A teasing gleam entered her eyes. "What I really want to know is does he or does he not live up to his nickname?"

"Oh, come on." I stuffed the Velcro strip in my purse and started pulling on my jacket. "Ready to go?"

"Please. Pretty please."

"Nope."

She followed me out the door. "Nope, he doesn't, or—"

"Nope, as in I'm not going to tell. Now let's get this over with."

The mission of the day was Christmas shopping. I had enlisted Kara's help as soon as I realized that Christmas would be real for me for the first time in years, not something I only noticed because of the sappy holiday movies on TV 24/7. I desperately needed a festivity crash course. Gift Giving for Mothers 101.

"Fine, but don't think for a moment I'm dropping this for good."

I didn't. In fact, I kind of counted on her dogging me about Wic's and my budding relationship, because whatever was going on between us, I suspected talking about it would make it feel more real, more official. Not her question about his body, obviously, but the mushy stuff. I just wasn't ready to go there yet. Baby steps. We would all go to Connor's play together next weekend, and perhaps that would be a start.

Later that evening, I marveled at how normal wrapping the presents felt. Today, I'd bought Christmas gifts that I would deliver in person at a family holiday party, surrounded by people I cared for. In a week's time, I was going to my son's play with my daughter and my—*do I dare say it?*—boyfriend. Over New Year's, I would be living with my children for the first time in over eight years.

I admired the large bow on Wic's gift. For the first time, I could visualize a future that held none of the darkness I'd always pictured.

"I am not my mother," I whispered into the silence of my room. "My life is worth living."

CHAPTER 28

We arrived at the high school on performance night only ten minutes before call time. Together, Wic, Mina, Kara, Logan, Grace, Shane, Brandy, and I made quite the entourage as we moved en masse through the theater to find our seats. I had struggled to decide whether to sit with Wic and Mina by the handicap seats where her wheelchair would fit, or with the others, but Grace was the deciding factor. I snuck a quick squeeze of Wic's hand before we parted ways. Not a seat was empty, and anticipation was high.

"I'm nervous for him," Grace whispered when the lights dimmed. "He's never been onstage like this before."

Shane patted her arm. "He'll be fine."

The curtains opened, and the play began. As Connor had told us, Miles was fantastic as Scrooge. He struck exactly the right chord between pitiful and comic, and it was hard to believe a sixteen-year-old was hiding beneath the makeup and costume.

Connor had downplayed his part severely. Yes, poor Bob Cratchit was not a huge role, but he was onstage enough and delivered his lines with conviction. I found myself on the edge of my seat whenever it was Connor's turn, so much so that Grace pulled at me to sit back.

"Sorry," I whispered. "He's so good."

She didn't respond, but I could tell she was as captivated as me.

The standing ovation never wanted to end. The kids on stage took bow after bow with the drama teacher in their midst. Finally, to the audience's great delight, the cast dropped their flowers and hoisted her up in the air.

When we exited to the lobby, Wic and Mina were waiting for us.

"What did you think?" I asked.

"Best play I ever saw," Mina said, color high in her cheeks.

"I can't believe these are kids." Wic shook his head. "They were so professional."

"I know." I had lost my words a while back, reeling from the sudden epiphany that Connor had this talent I'd never known about, that he was old enough to pursue something like acting independently. That he was becoming an adult.

"I told him to meet us out here after," Brandy said. Turning to me, she asked, "You're still coming with us to dinner?"

"I think we all are, right?" I raised my brow in question to Wic, and he nodded.

Brandy looked from me to Wic, her lips tightening. "Hopefully they can accommodate us all," she said under her breath.

"I can sit it out if it's inconvenient," Wic said. "Don't want to impose."

Shane clapped him on the shoulder. "Nonsense. What's two more people? We're celebrating. Let's just wait for our star, and we'll head out."

Grace rolled her neck. "What's taking so long? I'm starving."

"I'll go find him," I offered. "Be right back."

Making it through the throngs of people, I pushed open the backstage door and headed into the hallway behind the stage. The floor and walls were a dark gray, the dim light reminiscent of that moment when regret and anticipation mixed upon entering a haunted house. I nodded to the kids I met on the way then peeked my head through a few doors and out on stage, but I couldn't find Connor anywhere.

"Can I help you?" Ms. Dale, the drama teacher, stepped out from a doorway.

"Oh, hi. I was just looking for Connor." I stuck my hand out. "I'm his mom."

Her face brightened. "I remember you. My brother was in your year in high school. I'm two years younger so you wouldn't remember me. He told me you were back."

Ah, small-town gossip. "Yep. Yes, I am." I forced my lips together in what I hoped was a smile. Something about the way she was studying me made me feel like a curious artifact. "You've done a great job with them. Fantastic show."

She lit up. "Thanks. It's all them. Best group I ever had. Connor has made huge strides since our first class."

"Have you seen him by chance? The family is waiting and..."

She circled past me. "Check the makeup room—last door to the left. It was nice meeting you."

"You too."

We hurried our separate ways, and I made my way to the rooms stage right. It was quiet over there with fewer kids milling about, but I could hear low voices where Ms. Dale had suggested Connor might be. The door was ajar, so I pushed it open and stuck my head in. "Connor, you here?"

He and Miles jumped away from each other. "Mom!"

I blinked at them a few times, my brain struggling to process what I'd just seen. *Were they holding hands?* My mouth opened, even though I had no idea what words would come out. Maybe I'd just imagined it.

"Um, awesome play. Really terrific. Ah... Connor, everyone's waiting—we're heading to the restaurant, remember? You ready?"

He looked down at his shoes then at the door next to me. "Sure, let me grab my stuff."

My teeth dug into my lower lip, my eyes darting between the two boys. "Right. Well, I'll be outside. Nice to see you again Miles. Loved your Scrooge." I backed away as quickly as I could and all but ran back down the hallway. *Are Connor and Miles...?* Memories of all the occasions I'd seen them together played like a reel on repeat in my mind. It was possible, I conceded. *But how did I not know?*

I rejoined the rest of the family right before Connor burst through the door to everyone's cheers and congratulations. He took care to avoid me, and I stayed to the side with Wic and Mina.

"You okay? You're a bit pale," Wic said.

"Yeah, I'm fine."

Connor laughed at one of Shane's comments.

Should I talk to Connor about this? That seemed like what a parent would do. I took a step closer to Wic, drawing strength from his warmth.

IF I'D QUESTIONED WHAT I'd seen backstage before, I was certain I'd been right by the time the waiter brought our check. Connor still refused to give me more than a cursory glance, and every time I opened my mouth to speak, he froze up at the head of the table. Something had to be done. I understood well enough that I'd stumbled upon his greatest secret—one that might be especially delicate considering with whom he currently lived—but I would not let the situation drag out unnecessarily. We needed to talk.

I caught up to him on the way out to the cars and hooked my arm through his.

"How about I take you out for ice cream after the final show tomorrow? Just you and me."

He tensed again and didn't respond right away, perhaps stalling to come up with an excuse.

"It'll be a good way to celebrate, and also I think we should talk. About earlier."

He flinched. "Shh. Fine, we'll go. Just..." He glared at me and pulled his arm free, his posture still emanating stress.

"Don't worry, bud. It's all good. I'll meet you outside the school, okay?"

His brow was set in a skeptical frown, but he gave me a curt nod before he stalked off.

"You're going tomorrow too?" Grace asked.

"No, just taking him out after."

"Can I come?" She looked at me with those velvety eyes I remembered well from morning cuddles and bedtime stories. That evening, her face was free of artificial color, her hair pulled back with a simple hairband. My Grace.

I made an apologetic grimace. "Sorry, not this time. But how would you like to go to the movies next weekend? Just you and me."

Brandy cleared her throat next to us. "They have a curfew at nine, just so you know."

"So we'll do an early show. Maybe a matinee. And dinner after." I winked at Grace, who was smiling again.

"I'd like that. Can we get Thai food?"

Take no chances, win nothing, I thought and put my arm around her shoulders. "Of course."

She smiled up at me as we kept walking, and the chilly December air instantly dispersed.

THE FOLLOWING AFTERNOON, I waited for Connor in the parking lot outside the school. The air was heavy with the crisp damp of impending snow, the skies leaden, and the trees unnaturally still. I pulled my jacket tighter around me. Unbeknownst to him, I'd actually snuck in for an encore of the performance. I didn't want to make him more self-conscious than he already was. It was a full house again, and some scenes were even tighter than the night before. The professional actors in the version of *Death of a Salesman* I'd been forced to sit through in high school could learn something from Connor's cast.

Today Connor was one of the first kids outside, though he shuffled his feet as if he were headed to his own funeral and not for a sweet treat.

"Nice job today," I said when he was close enough to hear. "Congrats on a great run."

His hair was getting longer, and he pushed the strands falling across his forehead back. "Thanks. You watched?"

"I did."

"I missed a cue near the end."

"I didn't notice." It was the truth, but I could tell he didn't believe me.

We started walking through the parking lot. "I'm over there. Where do you want to go?"

Connor sighed. "Doesn't matter."

I stopped. "Hey. I'm not mad at you or anything. You know that, right?"

He straightened slightly, finally looking straight at me. "You're not?"

"No. Of course not. Like I said yesterday—it's all good. Now what are you in the mood for? Ice cream?"

His hands unclenched the backpack straps he'd been clinging to. After a moment's consideration, he asked, "Can we get pie?"

I unlocked the car with a flourish and a loud beep. "Pie it is."

It was a short drive downtown, and I scored a spot right outside the Snohomish Pie Company. The scent of warm pastries wafted into the street, making my mouth water. Joel and I had frequented the place a lot when I was pregnant with Connor. For a fleeting moment, I wondered if that was why he favored it.

Only to-go orders were ahead of us, so the line moved quickly. After we ordered slices of apple-berry crumble for me and marion-berry for Connor, we chose one of the empty tables by the windows. I steeped a bag of tea, and Connor took a swig of orange pop while we waited for our plates. Warm with a side of vanilla ice cream—that was the way to go.

"So," I said after letting the first few mouthfuls melt on my tongue.

Connor stabbed his pie with intense focus.

"You and Miles?"

His fork stilled before resuming its butchery of the innocent dessert.

When he didn't respond, I reached out and put my hand on his. "Bud, look at me."

Reluctantly, he put his fork down and did as I asked.

"I get that this is an uncomfortable conversation for you, and I'm very sorry I walked in on you yesterday, but please talk to me."

He faced the window. "I don't know what you want me to say."

"Are you two, like, an item?"

In the bleak light of the receding afternoon, his skin was almost translucent even as his cheeks flushed red. "I think so. Maybe." He shrugged. "I don't know. I guess."

His shoulders curved inward like on a small child being repri-manded, and I had to force down the urge to pull him into my arms. Oh, the arduous days of adolescence, going to battle for oneself with-out the slightest shred of armor. That was parenting, I reminded my-self—powerlessly looking on as one's children were put through the wringer of life.

"I like Miles. He seems like a really nice guy. And I could care less if you're in love with a boy or a girl—I just want you to be happy."

Connor's chin began to tremble, and his nostrils turned red. A solitary tear spilled over, but he wiped it away before it got very far. He glanced up. "Really?" he said, his voice thick. "You're fine with it?"

I leaned as close to him as I could across the table. "Of course."

Something akin to a sob escaped him. "But you seemed so shocked last night."

"Only because to me, you're still my little Connor. Trust me, I'd have reacted the same if it had been a girl. It's weird thinking of you having a relationship with anyone."

He wiped at his face again then inhaled a shaky breath that was followed by a tentative smile. "I'll be sixteen soon."

"Ugh, I know."

He chuckled, the sound filling every dark and empty corner inside me with the reassurance that our precarious journey was worth it. I'd done it. I'd seen him, reached him, and made him feel safe enough to reveal his true self to me.

To me alone.

I speared a piece of pie crust with my fork and swirled it around the melting ice cream on my plate. "So, how long have you two been together? If you don't mind my asking."

"Couple of months." He took a long drink of his bottle.

"Is that why you joined drama club?"

"Maybe."

"But why didn't you tell me?"

He arched an eyebrow. "Sure. Hi, Mom who I haven't seen since I was seven. By the way, I'm gay."

"No, that makes sense. Sorry." I kept forgetting it had only been a few months. In many ways, it was starting to feel like I'd never left. "Does anyone else know?"

"No," he said in a hurry. "And you can't tell anyone. Promise."

"But why? It's really not that big a deal anymore. Not like when I was your age."

He scoffed. "You've clearly never seen Brandy watch TV when anything remotely queer comes on."

"Oh."

"Yeah. The Catholic Church isn't exactly super pro."

"That's why you don't want to go to Mass with them?"

"That, and I just don't believe in that religious stuff. It's so obviously something people made up to explain things they didn't understand way back. There's no way the Pope is right and everyone else is wrong."

"Strong words."

"Dad believed the same thing."

"I know."

"What about you?"

I considered his question for a moment. God had never played a great part in my life, yet there'd been times I'd wondered. If the course of my life was staked out the way I'd always believed it to be, what logically followed was that someone must do the staking. At the same time, the thought of listening to someone else orate about guilt and shame for hours when I was so good at that speech myself was less than appealing.

"I'm probably leaning more toward you and Joel these days." I scraped up the last of my pie. "Though I do believe in the Golden Rule."

Connor drained his pop. "That's not religion. That's common sense."

I chuckled. "How did you get to be so clever, Mr. Smartypants?"

"Genes?"

"Ha! Sure, let's say that." I waited for him to finish up then reached for his empty plate. "You'll have to tell them sooner or later. You know that, right?"

He shrugged on his jacket. "Maybe."

"Brandy may be many things, but she's not easily fooled. You can't hide it forever."

Connor sighed. "I know. But not yet."

I nodded then went to put our dishes away. It was his life and his decision. All I could do was be there for him. And I intended to.

IT STARTED SNOWING when I pulled into the Hemingways' driveway. Large fluffy flakes drifted lazily from low clouds. They settled on the evergreens and the mossy lawns, coating them in a sheer-white blanket.

"Maybe you'll have a snow day tomorrow," I said to Connor as I walked him to the door.

"No way. It'll never stick."

"You never know."

Brandy met us in the foyer as soon as we got inside. "How did it go? Everyone remember their lines? Are you glad it's over?"

Connor and I exchanged a look. "It was fine. And sure, it'll be good to have a bit of a break. We're starting a different play in January, though."

"That'll be exciting," I said.

Connor's smile suggested he felt the same way. "I'm going to head up to wash off the rest of this stage makeup. Thanks for the pie. And everything." He gave me a tight hug before starting up the stairs.

"I'll talk to you later this week!" I called after him. Then I turned back to Brandy. She was wearing Kara's gray support belt, which accentuated her growing curves in a muffin sort of way. "Is it working?"

She tightened the strap with a loud rip of the Velcro. "Yes, it really is a blessing. Tell Kara thanks again."

"I will." I reached for the door, but Brandy cleared her throat and took a step closer to me, making me pause.

"It might not be any of my business, but..."

I froze. *Please don't ask about Connor.* It was one thing to keep his secret by omission but another one entirely to flatout lie. Not that I wouldn't.

"Is there something between you and Wic?"

I let out a breath of relief. That I could handle.

"I could be wrong, but I was watching you two yesterday, and it seemed—I don't know."

Like I'd told Connor—not easily fooled.

"Um, yeah. But it's very new. Not official in any way."

"I see." Her lips pressed together into a tight white line. "Well, you know I care for him in general, him being Shane's cousin and all, but are you sure this is a good idea? There may be things you don't know about him. Things that make him less than suitable."

I squared my shoulders. "Such as?"

Brandy looked around as if to make sure no one was eavesdropping. Then she whispered, "He used to be a drug dealer. But you didn't hear it from me."

"Oh. He told me already."

A deep crease formed across her forehead. "He did? And you're still with him?"

"He sold pot. Which is now a legal substance. Hardly a *Breaking Bad* situation."

"A what?"

"Never mind." I sighed. "He's a good guy."

"Perhaps we define 'good' differently."

My lips pursed. "Clearly. I should be off."

"I meant no offense, you know."

"And yet, somehow I'm offended." I reached for the door.

"You have to understand—my concern is for the kids. Would he be a good influence?"

I spun on her, itching to throw that right back in her face. After the conversation I'd just had with Connor, I could ask the same of her. "Really?"

"No need to bite my head off."

"He moved back in with his mom when she took ill, and even the school district approved him to work for them. If he was a bad influence, they would have never."

"I doubt they know what I know."

My mouth opened for a rebuttal, but I closed it again. She had a point. I still failed to see how his past was in any way a flaw on his current character, though.

"I think I'm going to leave now. Thanks for your concern. It's duly noted." I stomped out to my car then slammed the door closed around me.

My breath stood like a cloud of smoke before me in the chilly cabin. *The nerve of her.* Well, she wasn't the one dating him. I forced the car into reverse and hit the gas pedal. Everyone had a past, but people changed. That was what I should have reminded her of—that she was no longer Florida-spring-break Brandy. I groaned. *Why do good comebacks only strike you in hindsight?*

I huffed and puffed until I pulled onto the street that was my destination. I was so preoccupied with my indignation that the distant red strobe lights illuminating the snow took me by surprise. I squinted through the windshield. No, it wasn't a snowplow. I drove slowly down the cul-de-sac, my pulse quickening with the growing intensity of the red glare.

In Wic's driveway, an ambulance waited, its rear doors open.

CHAPTER 29

I ran into the house, not bothering to grab my purse from the car. "Wic? What's going on?"

Two medics were kneeling by the couch in front of Mina, who sat watching their every move with a distant gaze. Her mouth was slightly ajar, her face pale.

Wic sidestepped over to where I'd frozen in place. I grabbed hold of his arm, my eyes still fixed on Mina. "What happened?"

"We'd just had a cup of coffee, and she started saying strange things. They made no sense—it was like she was doing a crossword puzzle out loud, and when I asked her about it, she couldn't answer."

"What are the medics saying?"

"Nothing yet. They got here five minutes before you." He pressed the knuckles of his left hand to his lips. "I've never had to call 911 before. This isn't happening."

"We're going to need to bring her in so the doctors can check her out," the medic closest to us said. "I'm thinking Everett Providence."

Wic broke free of my hold. "I'd like to come with. Is that okay?"

"Of course."

"I'll take the car and follow," I said. "Should I bring anything?"

Wic frowned like he didn't understand the question. I'd never seen him so freaked out.

"Hey." I took his hand again. "She'll be fine. They're taking care of her."

He nodded stiffly.

"Better get the stretcher," the second medic said to the first one. "The wheelchair is no help in this snow." He turned to Mina. "We're going to take you to the hospital now, ma'am. Your son is coming with us. You're in good hands."

Mina kept on staring straight ahead.

I FOUND WIC SEATED in the waiting area with an unopened magazine in his lap and one leg bouncing. It had taken me twice as long as it usually did to get to Everett. No one knew how to drive in winter weather.

I handed him his jacket, which he'd left without, and sat down next to him. "What are they saying?"

"It's probably another stroke. They took her for a CT scan a minute ago."

"Oh, Wic. I'm so sorry."

He hung his head. "She was completely fine earlier. Then all of a sudden—"

"You did the right thing. She's here now."

I threaded my fingers through his, and together, we sat there waiting for the hour-long minutes to pass. We didn't speak much, mostly because few words seemed safe in our current state of limbo. When a nurse finally called for Wic, we both sprang to our feet.

"You're the son?" The nurse asked.

Wic nodded.

"She's fine. I'll take you to her now. The doctor will explain everything in detail." She held the door for us and led us through an open office-looking landscape where curtained doorways lined the perimeter. Treatment rooms, I guessed.

Mina was in a room with a real door, propped up in a bed underneath a gray waffle blanket. A man about my age dressed in scrubs was checking the monitor that beeped and whirred at her side.

"You can have a seat," the first nurse said. "Doctor Erickson will be right in."

Wic ignored her and walked up to the bed. "Hi, Mom."

Mina turned to him, and a faint smile spread across her lips. "There you are."

"How are you feeling?"

"A little tired. Can we go home soon?"

"Maybe in a bit. Let's meet the doctor first, all right?"

There was a cheerful knock on the door, and a bespectacled older woman entered. "Hi, I'm Dr. Erickson, your mother's neurologist," she said in a Southern accent, extending a hand to Wic. She placed a gentle hand on Mina's shoulder. "How are you doing, Mrs. Dubray? I heard you charmed the techs upstairs."

"What did the CT show? Is it a stroke?" Wic asked.

Dr. Erickson briefly pressed her lips together. "Yes. We did see some clotting. These small ones—we call them TIAs—often resolve on their own, but we'd rather not chance it given her history. Since she came in so quickly, we've given her some medication that should take care of it for now, and we'll admit her so we can monitor the condition closely."

"If that means a sleepover, I'll need an extra blanket," Mina said, her voice now stronger. "I get very cold at night."

Dr. Erickson smiled. "We'll see to it. Don't you worry." She turned to Wic. "See? She's coming around already."

The doctor took leave of us with a promise to check in later, and soon after, the male nurse also left.

The light outside the window had dwindled, and I was surprised to see it was already seven o'clock at night. Mina slept on and off, while Wic and I watched old sitcom reruns on his phone. I leaned my head against his shoulder. At some point, we would head home, but I didn't have the heart to ask when that would be. I suspected he would want to stay until they kicked him out.

The credits on our fourth episode started rolling, and I yawned widely. Wic kissed my forehead. "Tired?"

"Busy weekend."

He turned off his phone and tucked it into his jacket pocket. For a while, he sat watching Mina sleep. "I think I always knew this day would come at some point. When she had the big one, that's what the doctors told us. Risk factors and all that. But then the years went by, and she was fine—or at least as fine as she could be. I didn't see it coming." His voice broke on the last word, and he buried his face in his hands.

I wrapped an arm around his shoulders and held him as he cried. "Hey, she'll get through this. She's okay."

He sniffled and straightened in his seat. "But for how long? There'll be another one. And another one after that until—"

"Maybe." I took hold of his hand and covered it in both of mine. "Not for sure."

"But chances aren't great. Her brain is laced with weaknesses—faults that could kill her any moment."

I looked at Mina, who seemed so much smaller tucked in like a child in the bed. "She's stronger than you think. It's not set in stone."

"So, do you only believe in predestination when it comes to yourself? You're doomed but not Mom, even though she has actual medical reasons why she might not have a future?"

I dropped him like he'd burned me. "And I don't?" I stared at him. I knew he was upset about Mina, but his dismissive tone grated on me. "I realize you're hurting right now, and I'll probably forgive you later, but for the record, clinical depression is also a medical condition. Also 'faults' in the brain. It's not something imagined that people magically can snap out of or treat with prayers and herbal creams."

His expression softened. "No, I know. I'm sorry, I didn't mean—"

"And you *know* I'm working on myself and reevaluating my defeatist outlook on life. Perhaps you should do the same. Use the evidence in front of you regarding your mom. It's been seven years since her big stroke. Relapse free all these years. She's almost seventy and could live well into her eighties with the right medications and lifestyle. To me, that *is* 'being okay.'"

"You're right." Wic scrubbed a hand across his face. "I'm being a jerk. I'm just—there's no excuse." He reached for me. "Forgive me? I'm not making light of your situation, I promise. And I'm glad you no longer believe there's only one possible outcome to your life."

"Me too," Mina said from the bed.

We both spun, having been too busy arguing to notice she'd woken up.

Wic jumped to his feet. "Sorry, Mom. We didn't mean to be loud."

"I have better things to do than sleep," she said. "Got to make sure you don't step in it apparently."

"I apologized," Wic said, looking to me for backup.

"Men," Mina said to me. "They tread about as light-footed as a hippo on a freshly frozen pond. Don't mind him. He's rambling because he's scared." She turned her head to face Wic again. "And she's right, you know. I intend to live many years yet, whether you think me capable or not."

"Of course. But I... I just—"

"But I, but I." She squinted at him. "No, *not* you. If Annie says she's going to live, she will. If I say I'm going to live, I will."

"Yes, ma'am."

"Good. That's settled, then. Now get out of here, the both of you. I'm tired. And I don't want to watch you make up."

At that, a reluctant smile crept onto Wic's features, which grew wider as our eyes met. I'd been right. I couldn't stay mad at him for long.

"We'll come get you in the morning." I leaned over Mina to kiss her forehead. "I'll be outside."

When Wic emerged a few minutes later, he didn't say anything. He took my hand, squeezed it tight, and didn't let go.

DECEMBER GREW DARKER, damper, and colder, but inside, we made quite a nice and cheerful gathering. Mina was released after one night in the hospital, none the worse for wear. She was in good spirits, and if she was in any way worried about her health, she didn't let on. In turn, her resilience placated Wic's concerns as well, and we were back to a routine that worked.

For me, Christmas came early. A week before the actual holiday, the truck bearing my boxed-up stuff from Albuquerque arrived. The landlord had agreed to let the movers in to pack as long as I faxed over a signed affidavit stating I accepted sole responsibility for anything damaged. I had nothing to lose. Everything that mattered to me was already in Snohomish.

Wic helped me carry the boxes upstairs and kept me company while I dug through the remainders of a life that now felt so far away—kitchen utensils, bedsheets, and a toaster that probably should have stayed with the apartment. I didn't want any of it aside from my clothes and books.

I leaned forward and picked up a childhood edition of *The Secret Garden*. It was one of few things I'd brought with me when I'd left back then. It reminded me of days when my mom was still smiling, of strawberry picking and long flowy skirts.

I flipped through the pages, put my nose to them. Inhaled. Books made a home. And now I had books. It seemed almost possible—another move, another future. The kids and me together. A house—not a big one but one we could make our own. Three bedrooms, a nice kitchen, and a family room where we'd hang out in the evenings, talking about our days. I no longer had the rent in Albuquerque, and I could pick up more classes to teach online or find something local. Maybe.

"Earth to Annie," Wic said from over on the sofa bed. "Penny for your thoughts."

I put the book down. "Just thinking of the future. I told Brandy I want the kids to live with me one day."

"Makes sense to me. What did she say?"

"She was skeptical."

"She'll come around. They're starting a family of their own, and you've gotten closer to the kids. Even Grace is warming up. There's definitely a bond between you that they don't have with Brandy. You get them. I mean, the whole thing with Grace's makeup and trying to force Connor to go to church all the time... Brandy wants a mini version of herself, but your kids aren't that."

"Connor is gay." It slipped off my tongue before I could stop myself. I knew I shouldn't have, but Wic was the least judgmental person I'd met, and I needed to confide in someone about it.

He didn't miss a beat. "I'm not surprised. Something about how he and that friend of his—Miles—were together when we went trick-or-treating. I wondered."

"You didn't say anything."

"Wasn't my place."

I nodded. "He thinks Brandy and Shane wouldn't approve."

"Do you think he's wrong?"

"No." I counted and recounted the four boxes still on the floor, the numbers a calming mantra. "We'll see how things go when I stay with the kids after Christmas. They would need a say in their future too. They're old enough."

"Of course. And there's no hurry."

"Right." I pulled another stack of books closer. *Alice's Adventures in Wonderland* was next. After my return to Snohomish, I could relate to that feeling of being thrust into the unknown. The colors on the cover had faded and the frayed binding tickled my fingertips as I traced the corners of the book.

I could leave the past behind. Build something new, start over. People had done it since the beginning of time. Tear down, build up. Strive forward.

I got up and put the book in my bookcase. If things worked out, the coming weeks would show me which direction to take.

CHAPTER 30

It rained on Christmas Day. Sheets of icy droplets pounded the car roof as we drove through a cheerfully decorated Snohomish to celebrate one of my least favorite holidays. Not wanting to come off as a Grinch, I hadn't mentioned to anyone that Christmas held no special place in my heart. The pressure of "being in the holiday spirit" had often had the opposite effect on my mother when I was growing up. That, in turn, had aggravated my father, which, in the end, made for a rather bleak event all around. I got presents, but I'd have much rather opened them in my parents' company. Instead, they'd avoided each other and me in the aftermath of the traditional Christmas Eve row.

An old-timey rendition of "White Christmas" played over the car radio, agitating my already prevalent sense of impending doom. I reached for Wic's hand across the console to shake it off, and it did help a bit. He awarded me a bright smile and a wink that made his eyes sparkle like black diamonds in the darkness. My mouth twitched up at the corners. Suddenly, Bing Crosby's dreaming seemed almost reasonable.

Shane, Brandy, Connor, and Grace were all in the kitchen when we arrived. The house smelled of cinnamon and fir, the light from the decorated tree glowed like a beacon from the corner of the family room, and everyone wore their finest. Grace's red top made me happier than I could explain.

We added our wrapped gifts to the piles already stacked underneath the lowest branches then accepted offers of drinks from our hosts.

"Can't wait to escape this weather," Shane said. "Two more days. You ready, Annie?"

I was nowhere near ready, but that was to be expected. "Looking forward to it."

"I've made up the guest room already," Grace said. "And I put extra pillows in the closet in case you need more."

"That's so nice." I put my arm around her. "Thank you. Any specific plans for break I should know about? Playdates and the like?"

Connor shook his head. "Mom, no one calls them playdates anymore."

I wrinkled my nose. "Of course. Sorry."

"I'm leaving you a list of their chores and responsibilities so you can keep that up while we're gone," Brandy said. "Continuity is important."

Connor and Grace exchanged a look.

"I'm sure we'll be fine." I didn't intend for a minute to take over her role as drill sergeant when I moved in. The coming week was important in more ways than one. I'd spend 24/7 with the kids. We would get closer, I hoped. We'd laugh, talk, feel each other out. If there was indeed a future where the kids and I could live together permanently as a family, we would have to find our new roles in *that* threesome based on what worked for us. While Brandy had every right to mother the way she saw fit, over the next two weeks, *I* would be the parent.

When I was little, our Christmas dinners had mainly consisted of store-bought ham and some variation of frozen potatoes and veggies as a side. The one concession to homemade goodies had been my dad's snickerdoodle cookies. It was the only time a year I saw him in the kitchen, and I used to love helping him. My job was to gather all the bowls and utensils he might need—possibly because he didn't know his way around in there—and set the timer on the oven. Every year, I'd watched the timer tick down for that first batch, the sugary-cinnamon warmth emanating from within the oven spreading like a jolly cloud throughout the room, making my mouth water.

The Hemingway approach to Christmas was very different. Brussel sprouts and carrots were roasting in the oven. On the covered deck outside, a rack of lamb sat on the grill, filling the damp air with scents of garlic, thyme, and cumin. The scalloped potatoes were ready and needed only another ten minutes to warm up once the veggies were done, and on the stove simmered a thick gravy. The desserts had been set up on a side table in the dining room—a spread of caramels, chocolate chip cookies, fudge, and peppermint bark that would later be crowned by an eggnog cheesecake, Connor had promised. My stomach growled just thinking about it, and I decided then and there to stop comparing Christmases going forward. The past was the past.

When no one could eat another bite, we filed into the family room, a moaning, sighing, belly-rubbing bunch barely able to carry on a conversation for a good half hour. Dishes were piled high in the kitchen, and I had promised I would help with them later, which, for once, Brandy didn't take issue with. She was normally the clean-as-you-go type, but either the holiday cheer or possibly the pregnancy had made her a little wild and crazy.

"It can wait," she said. "Let's go sit down." It was as close to spring-break Brandy as I'd seen of late.

Slowly but surely, we came back to life. After a comment here, a laugh there, Grace couldn't wait a minute longer and announced it was present time. Her first gift was for Mina—a thoughtful gesture that surprised everyone. One look at Brandy revealed she had no idea what was in the tubular wrapping.

"For me?" Mina exclaimed. "Oh, sweet girl, you shouldn't have."

Grace beamed at the attention and held the gift still while Mina tore at the paper. "It's a whole magazine with crossword puzzles. I thought of you when I saw it at the store one day. It's not a big deal."

But Mina held the periodical to her chest and beamed at Grace. "It's the perfect thing, and it is a big deal." She reached for Grace to hug her. "What a gem you've got here," she said to me once they'd separated.

Grace's cheeks blossomed pink in the light from the tree.

"I do, don't I?"

"Yes, that was very thoughtful, Grace," came Brandy's voice to my left. "Your dad would be proud."

Perhaps she hadn't meant it as a reminder of how little Grace's upbringing had to do with me, but the comment stung nevertheless.

Shane cleared his throat. "How about something from us, honey? Connor, that big red one over there is for you."

The pile of gifts under the tree shrank one by one until only a few remained. From me, Grace got some clothes, nail polish, a curling iron like the one I had—I'd caught her admiring it once when she was over—and the next book in the series she was reading. Connor had been trickier. His wish list was full of boring things like shin guards and expensive things like an Xbox, and none of them really screamed "thoughtful gift from newly committed Mom." In the end, I'd settled for a behind-the-scenes book on the making of his favorite musical, *Hamilton*, and a soccer jersey. I also gave him an IOU for a show or concert downtown. He was old enough that he might enjoy experiences as much as things.

Grace still sat with the book I gave her in her lap, flipping through the pages. Connor insisted he knew just the play we should see as long as I could wait until June. He said it with a hint of uncertainty, and I assured him June would be just fine. My gifts were nowhere near as expensive as what Shane and Brandy gave them, but the kids still genuinely appreciated them. I felt for Brandy, who'd also gifted Grace a book but one she'd already read.

"I could have sworn this was the one you wanted," she kept saying until Shane politely asked her to move on.

The last present under the tree was for me. It was a rectangular box about two feet long, wrapped in brown butcher paper and tied with a white bow. I had opened others during the course of the evening—an emerald sweater from Shane and Brandy, which she insisted would do wonders for my colors, a book on the power of now from Mina, candy and a framed picture of all of us at opening night from Connor, and a chart-topping novel from Grace. The one remaining was from Wic.

He sat down next to me after handing me the gift, his eyes bright with anticipation.

"What did you do?" I asked in a low voice.

"You'll see."

I tore at the paper, glancing up at him quickly before opening the lid to the box and folding back the tissue paper. My fingers touched smooth wood stained a deep walnut color. I lifted the sign into my lap and stared at it. "You made this?"

He grinned. "It's not a big deal. Do you like it?"

The sign was beautiful, the carved letters made up of intricate curves and hollows, but more than the obvious craftsmanship, it was the sentiment that made me well up.

"Welcome to Wolff-McLaren," Grace read. "It's our names."

I nodded, not sure my voice would carry.

"Is it, like, for a house?" Connor asked. "Are we going to live together?"

The confusion on both his and Grace's faces was laced with enthusiasm, and that made the tears come in earnest.

Wic believed in me so much that he'd carved it in the proverbial stone.

"Thank you," I said, flinging myself into his arms. "It's perfect."

He let out a surprised "Oh" and patted my back.

I reached up and rested my hand on his cheek. "It's the best gift. Truly."

"Um, Annie," he mumbled.

Somewhere in the room, someone let out a discreet cough that jolted me out of the moment. I looked up, finding five pairs of eyes locked on us, their expressions ranging from apprehension—Brandy—to bewilderment—Shane and Grace—to indignation—Connor. Only Mina smiled serenely.

I'd completely forgotten where we were. *Shit.*

Grace came to my rescue. "So are we? Going to live with you?"

Brandy's voice came down like a crisp snap. "That's not something we need to talk about this minute. Right, Annie?"

I looked from Grace to Connor, who was still staring at Wic and me, a frown on his face. "No, we don't have to talk about it now." I took a deep breath, drawing on Wic's proximity for strength. "But it is something I'm hoping for. I think that should be said."

Brandy huffed and pushed herself off the couch, smoothing the blouse over her bump as she did so. "I think it's time we clean up the kitchen. Join me, Annie." It was not a request.

The earlier sense of calm that had bolstered us through dinner scattered, chased away by the electrical current of unrest that came with words unspoken.

"I can help too," Grace offered, not picking up on the charged atmosphere.

Shane placed a hand on her arm. "That's okay. They've got it. Why don't we play a game or something? How about Yahtzee?"

Connor scoffed. "I'll be in my room." He stalked off, refusing to look my way.

My heart sank. One moment, we'd been having a great time, and the next, everything was in turmoil because of me. I got up and braced myself for what was sure to come.

Now this *is Christmas.*

Brandy was waiting for me when I entered the kitchen. She leaned against the counter, arms crossed, lips tight.

"I didn't know he was going to give me that," I said. "He didn't mean to upset anyone."

"But you're going for it, then? Taking the kids?"

I balked. "Going for? Taking? You make it sound—I already told you before, it's something I'm hoping for. It's the logical progression of things. I'm forming a relationship with them. We're getting closer. It's only natural that eventually, they live with me again. You're starting your own family."

Her gaze dropped from mine, and she deflated. Without responding, she turned and started stacking plates in the sink. The silverware rattled against the enamel, loudly at first, then gradually with a more measured timbre. I went to her side and reached for the larger serving platters. The leftovers needed to be transferred to plastic bins. For a while, we worked side by side in silence.

"I've gotten used to having them here," she said eventually. "I like having them here." She put a hand up to stop me from interrupting. "They've been through so much, and I just feel like I can protect them from more heartache. Watch over them."

I clutched the towel I'd been using to wipe wine glasses. "I'm sure you could. And you'll be a great mom, I have no doubt. I also know I want to be Connor's and Grace's mom again."

"But for how long? I'll be honest with you—I'm worried that you think you know what you're doing, but the minute things get tough, you'll be off again. They couldn't take that. We'd be left to pick up the pieces."

"Totally get it, but things did get tough, remember? And I stayed. I'm not the same person anymore, not even the same person who came back. I want what you want for them, and I think I can provide it. We don't need to rush it. Maybe when the baby comes."

"If it comes."

I reached out and placed my hand on her arm. "It will."

"God willing."

"Sure." I gave her arm a quick squeeze. "Look, it's Christmas, and we still have a whole table full of desserts out there. I don't want to fight. What do you say?"

She offered half a smile. "Yeah, me neither. Let's finish up with these. We can talk about everything after we get back from the trip."

I agreed, and soon, we were back in the cheery cocoon that was the family room.

"Everything okay?" Wic whispered to me when I sat down next to him.

I let my foot slide up to his under the coffee table. "No worries. I love it. She'll come around."

Connor returned with a board game that he set in the middle of the table with an unnecessary bang. "Pictionary," he said. "Me, Grace, and Mom against the others."

"I'll be judge," Mina piped up. "My drawing skills are not what they used to be."

"Wic, Bee, and I will whoop your behinds, son," Shane blustered.

"Bring it." Instead of looking at Shane when he said it, Connor kept his gaze fixed on Wic. "I think you'll find our team unbeatable."

I'd never seen him so competitive, not even on the soccer field. The set of his jaw made me wonder if he intended something more than a good-natured competition. Before I could figure it out, Wic cracked his knuckles with a rumbling laugh. "Is that so? Well, give me a pencil, and I'll show you how a real man does it."

Connor's eyes darkened, but he didn't respond. I turned to Grace for an explanation, but she merely shrugged.

"Okay, let's do this." I picked a sharp pencil out of the stack. "Whoever wins gets first pick of desserts."

"Lame." A glint of a younger version of Shane showed for a moment. "Let's make it a bit more interesting." He ran into the kitchen and returned with a can of whipped cream that he held triumphantly above his head.

"No." Brandy cocked her head decisively, though the corner of her mouth twitched.

"Oh, yes, honey. Whoever wins gets to give someone on the losing team a Santa beard with this."

"I like this already," Mina said. "Let the game begin."

COURTESY OF MY SON, Wic still had whipped cream behind his ears when I kissed him good night later that evening. It made us both laugh, but I should have known even such an innocent revenge was a sign of things to come.

CHAPTER 31

I had my very first sleepover with a friend when I was nine. Her name was Julie, and we were in the same class in fourth grade until her family moved away. Dad walked me to her house, a pillow underneath one arm, a sleeping bag that also held my toothbrush and whatever stuffed animal I favored at the time in the other. The apprehension I felt was laced with something sweeter that I couldn't put my finger on until Dad said goodbye. Then I realized my parents wouldn't know if I went to bed at nine like I was supposed to. The new and exhilarating sense of freedom had mixed with the innate danger of being away from their watchful eyes.

Loading a duffel bag and driving myself to Brandy's on the morning of the twenty-seventh felt much the same way. I wanted so desperately to have a good time—to have a couple of good weeks with the kids—that my stomach had been in knots long before I went to bed the night before. Sleep was restless at best, and not even Wic's steady breathing beside me had worked to settle my mind.

"I can do this," I told myself, turning onto their street. I had activities prepared both for staying indoors and for going places, but I wasn't about to enter the kids' domain a dictator, demanding their every moment. I would let them decide what they wanted to do. I hoped they would want to spend time with me, but they were teenagers, and I wasn't kidding myself. Certainly, there would be closed doors and unfamiliar music playing behind them too. It was a give-and-take, and I would be fine entertaining myself if it came to that, even if I hoped it wouldn't.

"She's here!" Grace called over her shoulder after opening the door for me. "Is that all you brought?"

I looked down at my paltry duffel. "I can always stop at home and pick up more if needed."

"I guess."

Shane trudged down the stairs, two large, heavy suitcases in his hands. That explained Grace thinking my packing inadequate.

"Wait!" Brandy hollered from the second-floor landing. "I forgot to pack the hairdryer."

Shane stopped, wobbling precariously three steps from the bottom. "They have them at the hotel."

"But mine is much better."

I stifled a smile as Shane tried out Grace's favorite expression—eyes rolled skyward.

"I'm telling you, you won't need it, honey. Now let's go, or we'll miss our flight."

Brandy considered his words, rushed back to her bedroom, then joined us downstairs. Without speaking, Shane set the suitcases down on the floor, ready to accept the hairdryer with impressive equanimity.

"I put all the numbers you might need on the counter, Annie—doctor, dentist, school, friends' parents." Brandy counted them off on one hand. "Garbage pickup is Thursday, there are some leftovers from Christmas dinner in the freezer, and don't forget to bring in the mail."

Shane returned from loading up the car. "Bee, we've got to go."

"I'm coming." She turned to me. "If you think of any questions, just text me." She hugged Grace goodbye and hollered up the stairs, "Bye, Connor!"

I held the door for her, and she gave me a peck on the cheek before shaking her head. "He's been moody since the holidays. Up and down. Teenagers."

"I'm sure we'll be fine."

She stopped then and really looked at me for the first time since I'd stepped into the house. "Take care." Two simple, everyday words said casually at many departures. But her cadence held a deeper context, censored, I was sure, for Grace's ears. The true sentiment was clear in my mind. *Don't screw this up. Or else.*

Then it was just the kids and me. The door had closed around us, and a new silence permeated the air. I faced the innards of the house and inhaled deeply. "So," I said to Grace. "What do we do now?"

Her lips quirked into a smile. "Let's bake some cookies."

"Right away?"

"Yeah."

I carried my duffel to the bottom of the stairs and set it down. "I suppose the sooner we bake them, the sooner we can eat them."

She beamed at me. "Exactly!"

I didn't have to do much as we made our way through a recipe for white-chocolate-chip, macadamia-nut cookies. I helped stir the batter and portion it out onto the cookie sheet, but other than that, I mostly watched. Soon, the scent of vanilla and melting sugar wafted through the air. The first batch of golden discs came out of the oven then the next.

"Should I make some cocoa to go with them?" I asked.

Grace pushed the last tray into the heat. "Perfect, yeah."

"What's smelling so good?" Connor had come downstairs and was standing in the doorway. His hair was on end, and he was still in his pajama pants. I decided to let slide the fact that he hadn't bothered to say "hi" to me.

"We're making cookies," Grace said. "Want some?"

"I didn't have breakfast yet." The question was clear on his face.

"Oh, I don't think cookies for breakfast will kill you this once. As long as we don't make it a habit."

He pushed off the door jamb and entered. "Sweet. Thanks."

"Got any plans today?" I set a plate of treats and our mugs on the table before taking a seat.

"I was going to play some video games."

"Can I play too?" Grace asked.

"No, I'm teaming up with Zach and Miles."

"They're coming over?" I popped another piece of cookie in my mouth. The white chocolate melted like velvet on my tongue.

"No, it's an online thing. We just log on and stuff."

"But I want to play too. It's not fair for you to hog the Xbox the whole day."

"I called it first."

"It's not yours."

"Okay, okay." I leaned forward across the table to get their attention. "No need for that. You can take turns. Connor, what time are your friends on?"

"Not sure. I'll find out."

"Then Grace can play while you figure that stuff out. Right?"

They both nodded. A swell of pride washed over me. I'd mediated. Parented. No fighting on my watch.

"But she has to get off when it's time." Connor reached for another cookie and got up.

Grace stuck her tongue out at him.

At least they were comfortable enough to be themselves around me nowadays. That was a good thing. Everything else would soon fall in place.

"I THOUGHT WE COULD go see a movie later today, since it's raining," I said the next morning over a breakfast of waffles and bacon—slightly healthier than the day before. "Maybe the new *Star Wars* one?"

Connor helped himself to more food. "I'm not really into sci-fi. Is there anything else?"

"I want to see *The Sound of Music*," Grace said.

Connor stuffed half a waffle into his mouth. "Kid movie," he muttered, speech garbled.

"It's a classic, and the theater only shows it at Christmas."

"What's the name of that new Broadway adaptation that won all those awards? How about that one?" I suggested. "Compromise? If you don't like it, I'll take you to see Julie Andrews another day, Grace."

She appeared fine with that and finished off the last piece of bacon.

Connor swallowed and pushed the other half of his waffle around in the syrup on his plate. "Um, I know Miles really wants to see it too. Would it be okay if he came with?" He glanced up at me from beneath floppy bangs. The boy needed a haircut badly.

"I guess, sure."

He smiled, a more genuine expression than I'd seen since Christmas Day. "Cool. I'll let him know."

"I thought movies were family time," Grace said. "That's what Brandy says."

Connor scowled. "Well, she's not here now, is she? Mom can do things her way."

I wasn't used to this constant back and forth, the tension, the always present annoyance. I would have to ask Kara the next time I saw her if this was par for the course with all siblings.

Grace was about to rebut so I intervened. "I know I'm not what you're used to, and Connor is right—I may do things a little differently. That doesn't mean it's wrong or bad, though, right?" I looked at both of them in earnest. "I'm really glad to be here, and I want us to have a good time, get to know each other even better. Of course, you should tell me if things are just too weird, but I hope, in time, it won't seem that way."

They were quiet for a moment, then Grace said, "I guess Miles can come. Can I bring a friend too?"

I told her yes, and she went off to make phone calls. In the end, she didn't find anyone who was available, so we ended up as a party of four at the movies that night.

THE KIDS CHATTED ANIMATEDLY as we exited the theater. Grace had been a bit sulky about going alone when Connor had Miles at first, but the lead actor had managed to snap her out of it. The boys were already talking about seeing it a second time, caught up in the cinematography, the ending that hadn't gone the way they'd wanted it to, and the music. I was on the fence. For me, it hadn't quite lived up to its hype.

"Pizza for dinner?" I asked once we'd dropped off Miles. "We can pick one up on the way home."

"Don't you cook at all?" Grace asked.

Connor turned around and slapped her on the leg.

"Ouch!"

"Come on, don't hit your sister."

"She's being rude."

"No, you're rude." Grace's eyes narrowed as she glared at him.

"Pepperoni okay?" I pulled into the strip mall parking lot that housed our favorite place.

"Fine with me," Connor said.

Grace didn't respond.

We placed our order and sat down on the vinyl bench by the window to wait. It wasn't a busy night, since it was the middle of the week, but a couple of people came to pick up their orders while we sat there. The third time the bell jingled, I didn't even turn. I was lost in thought pondering the movie, what it might be like to be in a musical like that. The production of it. Once when we were seniors, Kara had talked her mom into letting her be an extra at the set of *Ten Things I Hate About You* when they'd filmed in Seattle. I hadn't gone, and I regretted it. *What else did I miss out on?*

"Annie?" A shadow fell across my lap. There was Wic, beaming down at me. "Great minds think alike, eh?"

"Hi." I didn't know why, but it felt like ages since I'd seen him and not just a day and a half. Without thinking, I stood and wrapped my arms around him. Not until I sensed him tensing underneath my hands did I realize my faux pas. I released him and took a step back.

"Hi there, kids."

Grace and Connor stared at him, Grace with some confusion, Connor with open hostility.

"Pizzas for Annie!" the cashier called out.

Grateful for the excuse, I hurried to the counter and paid. Connor was already outside when I turned.

"I'll talk to you later, okay?" I said to Wic in a low voice as I passed him.

"Sorry," he mouthed, scrunching up his face.

The ride home was quiet. I had hoped to keep Wic and me on the down low a little bit longer, and now I'd messed that up. Gone were the days of eating, sleeping, and working with no one to mind. No one to mind me. Parenting was complicated stuff.

"Can I eat in my room?" Connor asked as soon as we got inside. At least he was polite enough to ask permission.

"I'd like to talk to you both. Let's eat in the kitchen."

He sighed but didn't argue.

Is this why Brandy turned to religion? Because God grant me the strength...

CHAPTER 32

Only Grace and I remained in the kitchen, picking at our food. One mention of Wic as something more than a friend and Connor had stormed off up the stairs. I would deal with him and his door slamming later. He liked Wic—he'd said so himself a while back. I was unclear on why *me* liking him was such an issue.

"Is Wic, like, your boyfriend, then?" Grace asked.

"It's a little early to say. Would it bother you if he was?"

"If we went to live with you, would he be there too?"

I almost choked on my pizza. "Oh. Um, no. That's *way* early."

"Then I'm fine with it." She took her plate to the sink and rinsed it.

I cleared my throat. *Should I, or shouldn't I?* The blue numbers on the microwave clock said 6:36. *Yes.*

"Grace? How *would* you feel about living with me? Sometime in the future, I mean. I know it's been a bit hard on you, me coming back and everything." She had seemed less volatile lately, but I'd be foolish to make assumptions.

She frowned. "You're asking me?"

"Of course."

"Why?"

"You're thirteen. It's your life too. I don't want to force you into something you have no interest in. If you wanted to stay here, and Shane and Brandy agreed, I wouldn't get in the way."

Her eyes were round and clear, perfect windows to her beautiful soul, as she took this in. "Can I show you something?" she asked after a moment.

"Sure."

She darted upstairs, returning a minute later with a photo album clutched in her arms. "Brandy gave it to me for Christmas. They keep some of Dad's stuff in the attic. I never knew he had these." She took a seat next to me and opened the red pleather cover.

I already knew what was inside, since I'd once put it together, but I let Grace set the pace.

"It's me." She glanced up at me. "When I was first born."

There I was in my hospital bed, twenty-three, exhausted, and with a newborn in my arms. Twenty-four, with one hand on a stroller handle, the other holding Connor by the jacket. He was always on the go—I couldn't let my guard down for two seconds. Twenty-five, overseeing Grace blowing out the two candles on her cake. My hair was shorter then. So much of it had fallen out while I'd breastfed that I kept it shoulder length to offer at least the illusion of fullness. A rare shot of the four of us on a blanket by the lake. *What year was that?* It must have been later when I'd stopped smiling altogether.

Grace's finger traced the outline of the photo. "I didn't really remember you. I know I cried when you were gone, but then somehow, it was normal. Whenever I asked Dad, he'd get all quiet, so I stopped. It was almost easier to pretend I didn't have a mom."

"And then I came back."

She flipped the page and chewed at her lower lip. She was on Joel's shoulders as he ran through the sprinkler in the backyard. I remembered that day. We'd fought in the morning—over something stupid like him wanting to take the kids to the zoo and me wanting to stay home. I always wanted to stay home. I'd compromised by bringing out the sprinkler and settling into a chair on the deck while he entertained Connor and Grace. Man, I'd been a terrible wife to him.

"Then you came back," she said pensively.

"If there are things you want to say to me, I can take it. You have every right to be mad, and you have every right not to trust me."

"I guess—" She turned her face to me. "I guess I still don't understand how you could leave if you loved us."

The weight of her question stung as I reached for her hand. "I did love you. I still do. Very much. But my mind wasn't clear at the time. I thought I was bad for you. I really believed leaving you was the only way I could do right by that love."

She frowned. "That doesn't make any sense."

"I know."

She turned back to the album as if the explanation could be found there among glossy colors and freeze frames. "I've remembered more after seeing these," she said after a while. "Enough to know you were there. You used to read to me, and I liked when you played that little buzzy thing."

"The harmonica."

"Yeah." She turned another page. The photo at the top was of Connor offering Grace a spoonful of his ice cream. They both looked like they'd rubbed their faces in it. "I guess I wouldn't mind."

"Wouldn't mind what?"

"Living with you."

My chest inflated. "Really?" I couldn't stifle the face-tingling smile bursting on my lips. "You have no idea how happy that makes me."

She shrugged her teenaged shrug, but she was smiling, too, even as we continued leafing through the rest of the album.

I knocked on Connor's door a little later. Grace and I had cleaned up the kitchen and watered the tree before she'd retired to the couch to watch some sitcom with an obnoxious laugh track.

"Connor? It's me. Can I come in?"

Music played inside as usual, and light seeped from underneath the door, but I got no response.

"I just want to talk for a bit." I knocked again and opened the door. The room was empty.

I took in the space then retraced my steps to the hallway bathroom to see if perhaps he was in there, and I'd just missed it. But no, the bathroom door was open, the lights off.

"Connor?" I called. I checked Grace's room, Shane and Brandy's room, and the guest room. All empty. He wasn't there.

"Hey, Grace!" I called, jogging down the stairs. "Do you know if your brother had plans tonight?"

She answered without taking her eyes off the screen. "Don't think so. But he never tells me stuff."

"Huh." I put my hands on my hips. My fingers started tingling. *What should I do?*

"Why?" Grace looked up.

"He's not in his room."

She lowered the volume. "He's not?"

"No."

She let out a shocked little laugh. "Like, he snuck out? Connor?"

My face flushed hot. *Great job, Mom.* Brandy would kill me. "Seems like it."

"I'll text him." She jumped off the couch and went to retrieve her phone from the charging station in the kitchen where they were required to keep them while home. Her thumbs flashed against the screen when she returned.

I still stood frozen in the middle of the hallway. I had no idea what the protocol was for runaway children. Whether I should take the car to go look for him or call the numbers on the list Brandy had left. *Maybe the police?*

My heart raced toward panic, but before I could succumb, Grace's phone chirped with an incoming message. "It's him," she announced. "He's at Miles's house."

Relief and something a bit sharper jarred me back.

"He asks if you're pissed. What should I say?"

"Don't worry. I'll handle it." I retrieved my phone from the kitchen and considered my message. *What the fuck*, I wanted to type. *Get back here right this minute, or you're grounded forever.* But that wouldn't do. I just wanted to understand.

I was worried, I typed instead. *Wish you'd told me you were going out.*

There was a long pause before his message came through. *It's no big deal.*

"Does he do stuff like this all the time?" I asked Grace.

"Ha. No."

Are Miles's parents there? I typed next.

Yes.

I could call them, I supposed. Make sure he was telling the truth.

We're playing video games. I'll be home before 9 tomorrow morning. They're going skiing.

I took a deep breath. Maybe he was right. Maybe it wasn't such a big deal. He was at a friend's house—no, *boyfriend's*, I corrected myself. That was something to consider.

You're staying over?

As if he knew what I was getting at, he responded, *In the guest room.* There was an eye roll emoji at the end.

Without knowing it, I'd paced around the whole first floor while messaging. I'd ended up in the hallway outside the home office, where Brandy and Shane's wedding collage adorned the wall. She would definitely not approve. She'd let him have sleepovers before, of course, but she didn't know what I did. And then there was the whole taking off without permission. On the other hand, he would be home before I knew it. We could talk then. No need to embarrass him when something had already disturbed the balance.

Tomorrow, I decided. I would find out what was going on, I'd be understanding, listen, and he would make a change. This was a one-time thing and a small one at that.

OK, I typed. *See you tomorrow.*

He didn't respond.

I DIDN'T SLEEP WELL. New bed, new room, new noises. The comforter was too warm, the pillow too soft, and I kept dreaming of cars going down winding mountain roads with no guard rails. At six, I gave up and went downstairs to make coffee. I grabbed a magazine from Brandy's stash of *Good Housekeeping* and curled up on the couch under a blanket. I was still sitting there when Connor snuck in the front door at eight. I debated putting off the inevitable confrontation, but in the end, I called out for him and asked him to join me.

"Did you sleep?"

He stopped in the doorway and scrubbed a hand across his face. "Yup."

"They give you a ride over? I thought I heard a car."

"Mm-hmm." He kept his eyes on the floor.

I set my coffee mug down on the side table next to me and waited. "You have nothing more to say?"

Finally, he glanced up at me. "Like what?"

"How about 'sorry for sneaking out'?"

"Sorry." He shifted his stance.

"Are you?"

"I just said. Can I go upstairs now?"

We stared at each other. I had no idea what was going on with him. He was a completely different kid than the one who'd come to see me that day at Kara's house. My relationship with my son had been the one easy thing in all of this until, suddenly, it wasn't.

"What's this really about?" I asked. "What's changed? Are you upset Shane and Brandy are gone? That I'm here? Is it Wic?"

Connor flinched when I said Wic's name.

So that's the raw nerve. "I thought you liked Wic."

"Never said I didn't."

"Well, clearly you're upset. What did he do?"

"Nothing."

"Come sit."

Connor hesitated at first, but then he pushed off the wall and complied.

"Why did you sneak out without telling me?"

He shrugged. "I wanted to see Miles. I figured you'd understand."

"Understand what?"

"I told you." He squirmed in his seat.

"Well, first of all, having a boyfriend—or girlfriend—is no reason to run off in the middle of the night. Anything could have happened. I didn't know where you were."

"I'm not a little kid anymore."

"I'm aware. So don't act like one."

His head jerked up. "Why do you care? You probably don't even want to be here now that you have Wic."

The anger that had been building up inside me shriveled. He was jealous. That was what this was. "Connor, no," I started. "That's not true at all. Where is this coming from?"

"I have eyes. It's obvious."

"Well, whatever you think you're seeing, I'm telling you, you're wrong."

"Sure."

"I mean it. I just talked to Grace about this last night. I want us to be a family again."

"With Wic."

"No, not with Wic. The three of us. Yeah, I like him, and we're... exploring things. But it's not why I'm here. You have to believe me." I scooted over on the couch to get closer to his chair. "I came back for you and Grace—to make sure you were taken care of. I'm staying for you and Grace because I've come to believe I'm the one to do that. That wouldn't change if Wic wasn't here. I'm not staying for him. He's a bonus. You guys come first, he comes second, and he knows that."

Connor's nose turned pink, and his shoulders settled as I spoke. He slumped back in his seat and tilted his face to the ceiling. "Fine," he said eventually. "Can I go upstairs now? I need to sleep some more."

I wasn't done talking, and he hadn't truly apologized, but judging from his expression, that would have to wait. If he had somehow convinced himself that Wic was his competition for my attention, I would have to work harder to assure him that wasn't the case. Heck, if it came to that, I'd even take a step back from Wic. I didn't want to, but if I had to choose, I would.

"Sure." I offered a small smile. "Sleep tight."

After he'd gone, I picked up my coffee again, finding it cold. I grimaced and put it away, reaching instead for a box of hazelnut-covered chocolates left out after Christmas. If the kids came to live with me one day, there would surely be more conflict, more quicksand to navigate. The questions mounted as I considered a future of which I'd so far only had a small taste.

Will I hold up? Or will I crumble?

CHAPTER 33

Wic and Mina invited us over for New Year's Eve. I longed for him more than I'd thought I would. I didn't realize how much I'd taken his closeness for granted. But with Connor's worries fresh in my mind, no matter how unfounded, I wasn't sure dinner together was a good idea. I brought it up the night before when Grace asked if we were shooting off any fireworks.

"I'm not really comfortable doing it myself," I said. "But we could go over to the Dubrays'. They've asked us." Looking at Connor, I added, "It's completely up to you, though."

"Wic's doing fireworks?" he asked.

"If we're there, yeah. I was thinking I could ask Kara and Logan to join us too." A buffer might help alleviate the tension.

"I want to go. I want to see the kitties," Grace said. "And we can play games. It's more fun with a group."

"I'll be just as happy hanging out the three of us." I focused my attention on Connor. "I agree with Grace—it's more festive with more people, but like I said—*you* are my priority. And I never frown upon getting takeout and watching movies either."

"Come on, Con," Grace pleaded.

"Yeah, okay," he said. "We can go. But he'd better have some cool bombs."

I smiled. "I'll make sure. Hey, what if we made some treats to bring for dessert. Didn't you say you had a cheesecake recipe you wanted to try?"

Connor lit up. "I'll need blueberries, though. And more cream cheese. Can we go to the store?"

"Now?" I laughed. "It's dark out."

"It needs to chill overnight."

That settled it. If Connor had even the smallest ounce of excitement at the prospect of going over to Wic's, I wasn't about to stifle it. I wanted the two of them to get along.

I called Kara the first chance I got, and she was all for it, especially after hearing how Connor felt about Wic.

"Better than sitting home, and I'm happy to be your chaperone."

"Wasn't that long ago you were playing matchmaker."

"Jill-of-all-trades, what can I say?" She paused. "But seriously, how's it going?"

"With Wic?"

"No, with the kids. I already know you and lover boy can't keep your hands off each other."

"Whatever."

"It's totally understandable with the drought you've lived through. Just saying. Anyway, the kids. Spill."

"Oh, the kids are—" *Challenging, complicated, soul-stirring.* "They're fine."

"Fine? My oatmeal this morning was fine. My ten-year-old Toyota is fine. You and your kids living together? Nope. I demand a different adjective."

I sighed. "What do you want me to say? That it's hard?" I lowered my voice. "Connor actually snuck out of the house the other night. And they snap at each other any chance they get. I think the three of us have only eaten a whole meal together twice."

"Normal, normal, and normal."

"At least Grace seems to be happy I'm here. But I'm worried it won't last. It's like I have to be conscious of everything I do and say all the time so I don't accidentally set them off. It's exhausting. Also totally worth it of course," I hurried to add.

"Well, welcome to parenting. It's hell, and I love it."

"Thanks, that actually makes me feel a little better." I pulled a blanket over my legs on the bed in the guest room. "But in all seriousness, it feels pretty good. I talked to Dr. Samson last night. I'm keeping on top of the meds and trying to be mindful of not letting my brain run amok with catastrophic scenarios. I'm handling it."

Kara's voice softened. "That's great, Annie. Really great. And you know you can call anytime."

"I do. Thanks."

We agreed on who would bring what to the New Year's celebration, then we hung up.

"TEN. NINE. EIGHT. SEVEN. Six. Five. Four. Three. Two. One! Happy New Year!"

On the TV, the people in Times Square threw their hats in the air for what must have been the fourth rerun of the night. Time differences and all that. Kara had taken Logan home before ten o'clock, and Mina had gone to bed shortly after, but Wic, my kids, and I hoisted our glasses with non-alcoholic bubbly high and clanged them together, broad smiles all around. It had been a surprisingly pleasant evening with great food, several rounds of Codenames, which Connor and I aced, and an impressive array of amateur pyrotechnics.

"Worth it," Connor said as we returned to the warm comfort of indoors. High praise indeed.

I kept my distance from Wic all evening. I'd given him a heads-up on what was going on with Connor, but now it was midnight, and all of New York was kissing.

Not very stealthily, Wic made his way around the coffee table to me. To his credit, he addressed Connor first, asking, "Do you mind? It *is* New Year's Eve."

Connor considered us both. "Yeah, yeah. Whatever. I'm getting more chips." He spun and disappeared to the kitchen.

"Me too." Grace followed him.

Progress.

Wic didn't waste any time. He pulled me to him and nuzzled his cheek to mine. "I've missed you," he whispered, his breath warm on my ear. All the hairs down my left arm rose as he kissed me slowly and sweetly before pulling away. "Happy New Year." He kept his voice low before giving me another quick peck. "To be continued."

I didn't realize I was grabbing his shirt until he tried to step back and found he couldn't. I glanced toward the kitchen, willing the kids to take their time with the snacks. "Nuh-uh." I molded into him, inhaling. "One more. Please."

Wic looked over his shoulder as if he didn't trust my evaluation of the kids' whereabouts. Then he slid his hands around my waist and under the hem of my shirt, finding the soft skin at the small of my back. I wrapped my arms around his neck and pressed even closer. We were playing with fire. The kiss that followed was deeper—needier—and I felt it all the way to my core. His cheek was scruffy beneath my palm, his long hair loose and tickling my skin. It was only with the most herculean effort that I managed to take a step back. Touching my fingers to my tingling lips, I struggled to catch my breath.

"Can we have another pop?" Grace called from the kitchen.

Eyes still locked on Wic's, I called back, "Sure!"

Wic adjusted himself—his jeans had turned a bit restrictive—then gave me a crooked smile. He took a seat in the armchair where the kids wouldn't be right upon him. I supposed he needed a moment.

"Can I get you anything else?" I asked in my most seductive voice.

His mouth quirked. "Oh, don't even."

"What? I meant something to drink. Get your mind out of the gutter." I winked.

The kids returned, balancing a bowl of chips, another bowl with popcorn, a plate of cookies, and their drinks. They plopped down on the couch.

"Wow. You'd think it wasn't past midnight," I said.

"I'm not tired." Connor reached for the remote. "We can hang out for a bit, right? Watch a movie or something?"

I aimed a questioning brow at Wic, who nodded. "I don't have to be up early tomorrow. Be my guest."

"Cool."

It was a relief to have Connor once more at ease around Wic. Maybe all that had been needed to assuage his illogical fears was my explicit reassurance and for him to see for himself that I was first and foremost his mom, even when Wic was around.

I stretched, releasing the leftover tension in my neck, and yawned. Gone were the days where midnight was a time for beginnings. My day was over. Except it wasn't. "Don't mind me if I fall asleep." I curled up in the corner closest to Wic's chair. "Just wake me when you're ready to go home."

"Lame-o." Connor threw a piece of popcorn at me.

"Agreed." Wic chuckled.

If that was what it took for them to unite, that was fine by me.

FOR THE NEXT HOUR OR so, I drifted in and out of a half sleep punctuated by Judy Garland's rich vibrato. Grace had picked *The Wizard of Oz* from the rather paltry offerings in Wic's basic cable package, and I'd seen it enough to feel as though I was watching with them as I dozed. Glinda's sparkly dress morphed into the Cowardly Lion's mane, which drifted into a sea of poppies. When the end credits finally rolled, I swore I'd just dreamed of flying monkeys.

Wic was snoring softly in his chair, mouth half-open, but Grace and Connor were still wide awake, if somewhat owl eyed.

"You guys ready to go?" Reluctantly, I set my sleep-tingly legs on the floor.

They both nodded and gathered their dishes and garbage.

"Hey." I shook Wic's arms gently. "We're heading out."

He jumped, searching the room frantically. "What? Huh?"

"You were sleeping. We're going now."

He strained to focus on me. "Oh." He rubbed his face with both hands. "Okay. I'll walk you out."

We put on our coats, grabbed the empty springform pan that had held the most delicious blueberry cheesecake I'd ever eaten, and braced ourselves for the chill outside.

"Thanks for tonight." I kissed Wic quickly on the cheek. "I'll talk to you later today, I guess."

"Thanks, Wic." Grace gave him a hug.

"Hey, maybe—" Wic paused. "Maybe we can all do something together one day before school starts? A museum or a movie or something?"

I had to hand it to him—he wasn't afraid to put himself out there. But it wasn't the time, and I was about to say as much, in less specific terms, when Connor beat me to it.

"I have plans. But tonight was all right."

"I want to do something," Grace said. "You don't have plans, Connor."

"Yeah, I'm seeing Miles tomorrow when he gets back."

"That's okay," I said, attempting to nip the looming argument in its bud. "Grace, we can still find something to do."

"Or you can bring Miles," Wic said. "I'm totally fine with, you know, everything."

I froze. *He didn't.*

I glanced quickly at Connor to see if he'd caught the sentiment and was met by such a dumbfounded stare that I wished I could have rewound the evening and left earlier, rewound the day, even, and never have come there.

Wic must have realized his slipup. As soon as it was out of his mouth, he started prattling on about the various museums downtown he hadn't been to in years, the panic in his eyes building with each passing second.

I forced myself out of my stupor and opened the door, welcoming the cold blast of air on my hot face. "We really should go," I said to no one in particular. "I'll talk to you later."

Fuck.

CHAPTER 34

I awoke with a vain hope that if I acted as if Wic's slip of the tongue had never happened, it would go away. That if I didn't make a big deal out of it, Connor would follow my lead.

Clearly, I didn't know teenagers.

Connor didn't award me even a cursory glance when he came downstairs close to noon. Surprisingly, I had slept despite my inner turmoil and felt optimistic and ready for anything he could throw my way, so I greeted him with a cheerful "Good morning."

He poured himself a glass of milk and grabbed a string cheese from the fridge.

"Sleep good?"

He pushed two frozen waffles in the toaster and stood watching them cook, keeping his back to me until they popped up.

My optimism dwindled, so I tried a different angle instead. "Can you believe Grace is still asleep? I guess we did make it a pretty late night."

He stacked the waffles on a plate, doused them with syrup, grabbed a banana from the fruit bowl, and then, balancing everything in his hands, he walked back upstairs without a word.

Correction—I had been ready for anything but silence. Silence was like quicksilver. It surrounded you and coursed over your skin but never settled. There was no capturing it. The overwhelming nothingness of silence made its recipient doubt their very existence.

A lump formed in my throat, making swallowing painful. I rinsed the bread down with lukewarm green tea that made my tongue curl. It was supposed to be good for you—antioxidants and stuff—but like too many other healthy things, it was disgusting. To distract from the threatening tears, I put on a pot of coffee instead and had a Girl Scout cookie from Brandy's not-so-secret stash in the freezer.

I knew I had to make amends and explain myself to Connor. Be the grown-up, the mom. Problem was, I was a coward.

THREE, FOUR, THEN FIVE days passed, and still, I hadn't managed to bring myself to talk to my son. He was avoiding me—made easier by school starting again—and I didn't put up much of a fight. If Grace wondered why our meals were so quiet, she didn't say so. She'd been more attached to her phone since her friend Chrissy had gotten back from vacation and was testier than usual about giving it up when she walked in the door. Consequently, I had my hands full on that front too. All she would tell me was that someone had a new boyfriend and someone else was upset about it. Although I knew I shouldn't, I let Brandy's rules about electronics slide a little. It was easier for everyone that way.

That Friday, Grace got home before Connor, who had drama club after school. I had spent the morning at Mina's to let Wic get some work done and had walked in the door only ten minutes earlier. I was taking stock of the ingredients in the fridge when I heard the front door open and close.

"I'm in here!" I hollered, putting my list down. "How was your day?"

Grace didn't answer, and when I entered the hallway, she kept her back to me as she pulled off her boots.

"Happy Friday."

She threw her left boot onto the shoe rack, ignoring the dirty water dripping on the shoes underneath.

"Could you put that in nicely, please?"

She tossed the right one in too.

"Something wrong, Grace?"

She spun. "I don't want to talk about it. Leave me alone."

Whoa. "Did something happen today?"

She got to her feet. "I said, don't talk to me." She stormed up the stairs, and a few seconds later, the door to her room slammed shut.

I stared after her, considering my options. If I was thirteen, I would probably need a few minutes to calm down and to wallow, but I would still want to know someone cared. I decided to finish the grocery list then go check on her. With any luck, she would be in a better place by then, and I could find out what had set her off.

"GRACE?" I KNOCKED BEFORE turning the door handle only to find it stuck. The bedroom doors didn't lock, but she had found a way to jam it shut. The fine hairs on the back of my neck rose as I pushed on it with my shoulder. "Grace, open the door, please."

"Just a minute."

I heard a drawer open and close, and other rustles of her scuttling about in there, then the door opened. She jumped onto the bed and pulled a pillow into her lap as I entered. It was clear she'd been crying.

"What were you doing?" I asked, scanning the room. "Why did you bar the door?"

She picked at a hangnail. "Just wanted some privacy. Is that a crime now?"

I lifted a pile of her clothes off the desk chair then sat down. "I take it the first week back hasn't been awesome?"

She let out a sad little scoff. "Lucy is being a bitch."

"Come on. Language. What did she do?"

"She's having friends over tomorrow night, and I'm not—" Grace's chin trembled, and big tears swelled and started running down her cheeks. She sniffled. "I mean, I know we're not *best* friends or anything, but I would invite her."

"Is she the girl who pierced her own nose?"

"Yeah."

"I thought you said you don't like her very much."

Grace's face contorted even more. "You don't get it." She wiped her nose with the back of her sleeve-covered hand. "No one told me about it. Not even Chrissy, and we hang out all the time. Or we used to anyway."

Damn middle-school girls. There was no one crueler. My heart broke for Grace. Whether or not it mattered in the long run was not the point—she'd been left on the outside at a time in her life when all that mattered was being on the inside. It could change at any given time, but today, her pain was real, and I felt it.

I moved to the bed. "I'm so sorry. That bites."

"What if this is how it will be now?" she sobbed. "What if no one wants to hang out with me?"

"It's only one day. I'm sure next week will be better. These things, they go up and down. Here." I reached for the tissues on her night-stand and handed her one.

She blew her nose and wiped her cheeks. "I hate school. I wish I could quit."

I took the discarded tissues from her and threw them in the bin. "How about I make us some hot chocolate? We can play UNO if you want. It'll take your mind off things." Whether the age was thirteen or three, distraction was the best way to disarm hyperbolic drama.

"I have homework."

"It can wait."

She thought for a moment, her eyes finally dry if still red rimmed. "Okay."

"I'll see you downstairs in a minute? Don't think about this any-more. They're not worth it."

She nodded, hugging the pillow in her lap closer. "Thanks, Mom."

The word hit me right in my solar plexus. I had been nothing but "Annie" to her all this time. Suddenly, I'd broken through the barrier. I took the steps downstairs two at a time, the lightness inside buoy-ing me out of sight, where I could finally release my smile. I caught my reflection in the window, a grinning maniacal lunatic to be sure, but with good reason. I had never thought a title could mean that much, but there I was. Grace's mom.

I paused with the milk in my hand. Connor's too.

Connor.

The thought of him dampened my smile somewhat. *If not one, then the other.* I could only hope that his day had been better, because tonight, I needed him to let me in the way Grace had. I needed to apologize, and I needed him to listen. One of these days, I vowed to have both my kids amenable at the same time. Surely, that wasn't too much to ask.

GRACE HAD GONE TO BED, but the light in Connor's room was still on when I finished cleaning the kitchen that evening. I'd taken out the garbage, sorted the mail by importance, and vacuumed up all the pine needles for the second time that day. I wouldn't want Brandy to come back to the mess she no doubt expected.

Connor had greeted me when he came home, so I was cautiously optimistic as I knocked on his door. *Now or never.* Soon I'd be back in my room above the garage.

"Come in."

He was at his desk, doing math.

"You're not staying up too late, are you?" I asked. "You need your sleep."

"I'm almost done." He kept writing.

I sat down at the end of his bed and looked at the clock on his nightstand: 11:01 p.m. Not as good as 11:11 but also not bad. "Take a break for a bit?"

His shoulders tensed, but he put the pen down and spun in his chair. "I'd really like to finish this."

"It won't take long." I took a deep breath. "You've been avoiding me."

"I'm talking to you now."

"Come on, you know what I mean."

He turned his head away. The seconds dragged. "I just can't believe you told him." His voice was so quiet, I could barely hear him. When he looked back at me, his gaze was hard. "You promised."

"I know." I leaned forward, resting my elbows on my legs. "And I'm so sorry."

"Like, how can I trust you now?"

I swallowed. "You can, Connor, I promise—"

He cut me off with a short laugh, bitter beyond his years. It made me feel like a kid again, powerless to fight the disapproval I had provoked. Our trust had been paper-thin to begin with, and I had to wonder if the new rift was even mendable.

"Wic won't say anything if you're worried about that."

"That's not the point." Connor's voice rose as he spoke. "I thought you were different, that you had my back. That I could tell you anything. But maybe I was right before, and *he's* more important."

"You know that's not true."

"Then why? It was between us." His voice broke. "It's no one else's business."

"You're right. And I won't fight you on that. I will apologize for as long as it takes. I made a mistake. It slipped out. I can't excuse it. But please don't let this ruin everything. And for what it's worth, I'm proud of you. You know that. I don't want you to be ashamed."

His head jerked up, nostrils flaring. "I'm not ashamed. There's a difference between not wanting to tell everyone you're gay and not wanting to be gay. I'm fine with it, and when I move out, I don't care who knows. But for right now..."

"Okay." I wished I could reach for him. "Do Miles's parents know?"

"No."

"No one else?"

"No."

In spite of myself, a flash of pride surged through me. He'd confided in me out of all the people in his life. That had to count for something.

He turned halfway back to his desk. "I really need to finish this homework now."

I stood. "And where does that leave us?"

He gave a little shrug. "I don't know."

"Will you forgive me?"

He picked up his pencil, spun it once around a finger. "I don't know."

My heart sank. *This can't be it.* There had to be a way I could prove I was worthy of his trust again. The few weeks of me staying with the kids should have been a time where we set the tone for our future—a future together. Instead, our delicate status quo was crumbling.

CHAPTER 35

After four more days of little sleep and lingering tension, Shane and Brandy came home relaxed and tan, full of stories about the "silver mafia," as they called the cluster of retired elderly couples staying at their hotel. I was happy for them and secretly relieved to retreat to my own place for a bit, away from the frosty silence that followed Connor around wherever he went.

There was no denying I'd messed up big time. With no solution in sight, not even a Xanax had managed to settle the jumble of thoughts in my head, and it was taking its toll. A few days apart would be good for us both to get some perspective, I told myself. Then I would fix things.

I kept in touch with Grace via text, my fingers crossed that the drama at school would also settle. Wednesday had been all right—I could only hope things would continue that way.

Mina was eager to chat when I got up Thursday morning to fix her breakfast. She'd missed my coffee-making skills, she said. Wic didn't make it as strong. He had already left for the day. While I'd stayed with the kids, he had once again pulled a heavier load at home, and he had some catching up to do if he and his crew were to get their current project done on time.

It was closing in on noon when my cell rang where I'd left it on the table. Mina was watching TV, and I was in the middle of entering the rubric for the next assignment in my Beginner German course, so it took a while for the sound to register. By the time I'd moved the laptop aside and gotten out of the comfy chair, I'd missed the call.

The screen informed me it had been Brandy. I was about to call her back when it started ringing again.

"Hello."

"You should really keep the phone closer." Her voice was edgy, the words coming like rapid fire. "I tried calling once already."

"Sorry I was in the other room. Is something wrong?"

"Yes, that's the question, isn't it?" She scoffed. "The school called. I'm at urgent care with Grace."

"Oh my God. What happened?" *And why does she sound so angry?*

"She's broken a finger, it seems. PE. Why they have to do all these ball sports is beyond me. But that's neither here nor there."

While she spoke, I rummaged through the room for my purse and keys, wondering if Mina would be all right if I left. "Where are you exactly? I'll be there as soon as I can."

Brandy was silent for a moment. "Yes, I suppose maybe you should come. There are some things we need to discuss." She gave me the address and hung up.

If my thoughts hadn't been so preoccupied with Grace, how much pain she must be in, how worried she might be about how this injury would affect her violin playing, maybe I'd have wondered more about Brandy's demeanor on the phone. Later, I realized she had not called to inform and assure as one might in a situation like that. She'd been ready for battle, riled up.

"I came as fast as I could," I said, rushing through the door to the doctor's office, still oblivious. "Where's Grace? Is she okay?"

Brandy and the doctor both looked up at me, one with an expression of practiced neutrality, the other like a bull taunted by a red cape. I didn't dare meet Brandy's glare for long, so instead, I turned to the physician.

"You must be Mrs. McLaren," he said.

I sat down. "It's Ms. Wolff, actually. Or you can call me Annie."

"Very well." He rested his hands in front of him and deferred to Brandy.

"What's going on?" I asked.

Brandy's lips were set in a grimace as if I'd brought some kind of stench with me inside, but she didn't say a thing.

"Where's Grace? What aren't you telling me? Is it more than a broken finger? Did she hit her head?" Their silence had me on edge, but perhaps that was what Brandy wanted.

Finally, her lips parted, and she spoke with visible restraint as if underneath the surface, something trembled that was loath to be contained. "She didn't want to come here. Insisted the nurse was exaggerating. Fortunately, I went to get her anyway—her pinky was twice its normal size, and I wouldn't take no for an answer."

I hung on her every word, hot and cold flashes washing over me. *Get to the point! Where is she?*

"You—" Brandy pursed her lips, her hand cramping into a fist where it rested in her lap. "She has marks... all over her arm. That's why she didn't want to come here. She knew she'd have to take off her sweater."

I squeezed my eyes shut. "Marks? What do you mean, marks?"

She let out a bitter laugh. "It's my fault, I guess. There's been nothing but drama since you showed up. I should have known it was a bad idea to let you back in their lives."

An alarm went off inside me. "What are you talking about? I haven't done anything. I would never—"

"Not you, Ms. Wolff," the doctor said. "Grace appears to have been engaging in self-harm behaviors. It's an expression of—"

"She knows what it is," Brandy spit out. "Grace was fine. And now look where we are."

There was a knock on the door, and a nurse opened it to let Grace in. Her hand was in a splint, and she kept it clutched to her chest with the other arm.

She saw me and flinched. "What are you doing here?"

"If you'll excuse me," the doctor said. "I'll give you a minute to talk."

I waited for him to leave the room then faced my daughter. "Grace," I said on an exhalation. "Why didn't you say something?"

"I was at school."

"Not about that. You've been hurting yourself?"

Her eyes widened, and her gaze flicked briefly to her arm. Most of it was bandaged, but the gesture said enough.

"You told her?" Grace scowled at Brandy. "I asked you not to."

"Grace, I'm your mom." I stood, trying desperately to get her attention. "I would have understood." All this time when I thought she was better, there must have been signs. *How did I miss them?*

She took a step back, shaking her head. "I don't want to talk about it. It's none of your business."

"But you need help," Brandy said behind me. "You're cutting yourself. That's not... *normal*."

My nails dug into my palms. She was making things worse. "Grace."

"No! Stop ganging up on me." She glared at me. "It's no big deal. It's not as if I'm gay or something like Connor. Should we tell him he's not normal too?"

"Grace!" She must have seen my alarm, for her mouth immediately clamped shut, and her face grew pale.

Behind me, I heard Brandy gasp and her chair scrape. "Connor's what?"

"Nothing," I said over my shoulder, but there was no retracting it.

"Connor thinks he's *gay*?" Her voice dripped with distaste.

Grace looked miserable. I wanted to wrap her in my arms, tell her all was fine, and whisk her away. But first, I had to deal with the dragon in the room.

"No." Brandy huffed. "There's no way. Joel would not have stood for that."

I spun around. "Joel would have loved him either way. As do I."

She stepped closer to me. "You knew?" Then, in a tight voice, she said, "Grace, could you give us a minute, please. The grown-ups need a word."

I tried to communicate silently with my daughter to let her know I wasn't mad at her, but Brandy shut the door so fast, I wasn't sure Grace saw me.

"I should have known," Brandy said, her composure melting. "You come back here, insert yourself into our lives again, and bring all your turbulence along. I should have heeded the red flags and turned you away, but Shane reminded me that is not the Lord's way. And this is the reward?" She jabbed a rigid finger inches from my chest. When she spoke again, her voice was low and trembling. "You are foul. My brother died because of *you*. You broke his heart. You condemned two innocent lives by leaving them motherless to fend for themselves. And when we'd finally built them up again and helped them reclaim some of their lost innocence, you strip it all away."

My tongue felt swollen in my mouth, my eyes dry and cold. Was this what she'd thought of me from the moment I came back? Did others agree? "I don't think..." I started, searching for the right words. "I didn't know about Grace. And she was far from fine when I got here." It was a poor defense, but it was all I could say. *She didn't start self-harming because of me, did she?*

Brandy blinked slowly as if to steady herself. "Connor, confused and corrupted, Grace hurting herself." She'd retracted her finger, but her words were like poison arrows aimed directly at me. "I am telling you right now, these kids need protection and morals, and clearly, that is not your forte. I am leaving here today, and I'm filing that motion to adopt. You will get these children back over my dead body."

Then she muttered as an afterthought, "It won't take much. You're unstable and dating a drug dealer. No court will let you anywhere near them when I'm done."

She looked at me as if expecting a rebuttal, but I no longer knew how to form words. Somewhere in the depths of my brain, a war was being fought, a need to counter her arguments and defend myself on one side, the fear of her being right on the other. They were in a deadlock, frying all synapses.

When I didn't say anything, she huffed, grabbed her purse, then stormed outside. I heard her call for Grace to follow before the door slammed shut.

I lifted my hands halfway to my face but found them shaking too hard, so I let them drop again. My breathing was shallow and insufficient, black dots dancing in front of me. Unable to do anything else, I sank into the nearest chair. Brandy's words sounded on repeat in my head like an echo chamber in a fun house. Mocking. Taunting.

Grace was like me. Cursed. I hadn't been able to protect her from it. And as soon as Brandy got hold of Connor, he would have even more reason to hate me. It didn't matter that Grace had been the one to say the words. The bridge was burning.

CHAPTER 36

I didn't remember getting in my car, but suddenly, I was on Avenue D driving north past fast-food joints and grocery stores, my knuckles white from gripping the steering wheel. My whole body vibrated from the strain of keeping at bay the thoughts that wanted to take over. They tapped like a hammer at the base of my skull, a persistent echo that wanted in.

Foul.

You're foul, Annie.

"I'm not." I pressed my head against the headrest. "I'm trying."

My eyes stung as I turned right at one intersection, left, then right again, not thinking about where to, only about forward motion. I circled the same few blocks several times before I had the presence of mind to choose a different route, a new street I didn't recognize. The houses and backyards were quiet that time of day, still lifes blurring in my peripheral, much like my insides that had turned to an unidentifiable mush. Another two left turns, another right. The streets started to look familiar, the park, the house with the glassed-in porch. Suddenly, I knew where my subconscious was taking me, and I didn't object. I let it happen.

I hit the brakes much too fast, jerking to a stop at the curb across from my kids' old elementary school. The scene of the original crime.

A sob traveled through me, too overpowering to fight. The sun sparkled in the windows of the building, glinting through my tear-stained vision like the memory of that terrible day. I hadn't been there since then, but it hadn't changed.

I dove into the memory, inhaled it, and relished the deep stabs within. A righteous pain to linger in.

I'd watched my kids line up outside the school doors with their friends, Grace trudging toward the kindergarten door, one blond ponytail among many others, while Connor ran up to body check his best friend Dean. I heard Dean exclaim something and Connor laugh.

I knew I would never hear him laugh again, and it ruined me.

The bell rang. The teachers put on their business faces, and the cacophony of voices quieted down. Grace turned slightly and waved, a half smile on her face. I waved back, every ounce of self-restraint focused on not running to her, scooping her up, pressing her to me, and never letting go. Then she turned back to face Ms. Halloran and started walking. I covered my mouth to hide the scream that wanted to break loose from my chest.

Next, the second-graders jostled into something at least resembling a line and started moving. I willed Connor to turn around for one last glimpse of his always-animated face, but he was explaining something to Dean and probably didn't even notice they were moving.

One by one, the school building swallowed them up, and I couldn't move. I looked from window to window, my eyes seeking frantically, but only the reflection of a light-blue April sky met my desperate gaze. Fluffy white clouds. Rustling green leaves. Such mockery.

The other parents left. I held my breath and started backing away across the blacktop. One foot behind the other, my head spinning from the lack of oxygen and the paralyzing sense of loss. Connor and Grace had become the very air that I breathed, and now that I was no longer to be their mom, there was also nothing to fill my lungs.

I reached the fence that marked the end of the school grounds and stopped, my left foot hovering off the pavement for just a moment. Then I walked away. For them. Fittingly, it had felt like saying goodbye to life itself.

A KNOCK ON THE GLASS next to me yanked me from the blurry vision buried deep within. I wiped my cheeks and lowered the pane.

"How you doin', miss?" The school's octogenarian safety patrol officer, Mr. Peters, peered down at me with the same light-blue eyes I remembered from being a student there myself. His hair was whiter now. "There's no parking here. Gonna have to ask you to move along."

He didn't recognize me. Small blessings. "Of course. I'm sorry. Just, um, getting my bearings."

"Need directions or anything?"

I didn't even know where I was heading next. I just knew I needed some time to sort out the tangled mess of thoughts in my head. "No, no. I'm okay." I flashed him a paltry smile.

"All righty, then. You have a nice day now." He took a step back but kept watching me until I pulled away from the curb.

How did it come to this? Another failure, another disappointment. I was on the road again, aimless. The demons in my head wanted to run. *Everyone would be better off*, they said. *Coming back was vain. Even being here, you weren't able to protect your children.*

The voices weren't wrong. It was just that I had promised. Unlike eight years ago, I couldn't leave—*wouldn't*—but I also couldn't face any of them. Everything had gotten so much harder than even I'd expected it to. Maybe Kara was right, and that was just the nature of parenthood. Or perhaps there was something innately wrong with *me*. Maybe I wasn't cut out for navigating the intricate emotional rollercoaster of a family where multiple wills, personalities, strengths, and weaknesses had to coexist. Maybe I really was ill-equipped for putting myself last in the way being a parent required. I'd been gone eight years. That was a long time to go without obligations to anyone but myself.

On the other hand, I had made progress with Grace and Connor. I'd messed up, too, but I knew I hadn't imagined our connection. When I was with them, I felt it in my bones—I was their mother. I just didn't know how to translate that knowledge into practice. Because somehow, every other choice I made backfired.

For the first time in years, I missed my own mom. She smiled at me before my mind's eye and put a plate of food down in front of me.

I gasped as the pain of loss swept through me. It pierced through my fog and offered a moment of clarity.

That was where I needed to go.

I pressed down harder on the gas pedal and sped onto the northeast-bound road toward the cemetery in Everett where my mom was buried. The sun was low. Somehow the afternoon had disappeared, but I had nowhere I needed to be. I should have returned to Mina earlier, but it was late enough that the urgency had passed. Wic would be home soon, anyway, and I was in no state of mind for more confrontation. *I could text her,* I thought, reaching over to the passenger seat for my purse to get my phone. The seat was empty.

"What the...?" *Did I leave it at home? At the doctor's office?* I glanced at the floor, but there was nothing. "Damn it."

Too late now. The cemetery gates were up ahead, and I wasn't turning around.

My mom's headstone was a humble ground plate carrying only her name and the dates of her interrupted life. With the sun gone, the temperature crept toward freezing. I wrapped my coat tighter around me and sank onto the damp grass. It pricked through my jeans, but I ignored the chill, sitting back on my calves. She was number sixty in the row—I'd counted before, and it still held up. A full clockface's worth of lived lives. Three twenties. An orderly comfort.

Streetlights lit up the paths and grounds around me, and plenty of other graves in the huge cemetery had candles and lanterns burning, so there was no real dark to be scared of. The ghosts haunting me were already in my head anyway. A few more would make no difference.

"Hi, Mom," I said, my voice oddly loud in the quiet evening. "Sorry, it's been a while." I swallowed hard. Closing my eyes, I could see the three of us—my parents and me—in glimmers of my childhood playing like a reel before me. Good and bad.

"How is Dad?"

My question was met by nothing but stony silence. Of course.

My father's wish had been to be interred in his family grave where he grew up in Pennsylvania. I knew it didn't make sense, but that made him feel further out of reach.

Fifteen minutes passed, fifteen more. My legs fell asleep.

Eventually, I let out a deep sigh, my breath billowing like a cloud of smoke. I shifted closer to the stone, planting my gloved hands on it. "You're still gone," I mumbled, shaking my head. "I needed you, and you left me."

Motherless.

Wasn't that what Brandy had called my kids too? Connor had thought I was dead, so to them, my actions were really no better than my own mother's. After Mom died, I'd blamed myself for a while—for not looking after her well enough, for not being enough of a reason for her to stay. I wondered if Connor had done the same.

"I messed up, Mom. And I almost fixed it, but now, I need someone to tell me what to do."

A magpie in the tree above me let out a sharp "caw." I looked up just as the first snowflake drifted slowly down to settle on my nose. I caught another few in my palm. Perfectly whole and each perfectly unique. Not an answer to my plea but a small distraction. Ten of them in my hand then twenty. Thirty.

I used to build snowmen with my kids when they were little. One year, we made a whole family with scarves, carrot noses, and everything. They lasted several weeks in an unusual cold spell. Just like my mom, I had not been an altogether bad parent. For a long time, it had just been easier to focus on the failures because they'd justified what I'd done. My running away.

"Is that what you did?" I asked my mom's silent memorial. "You forgot about the crafts and rolling meatballs and bedtime stories? Forgot about love?"

The snow came down faster, big flakes lighting up like fireflies in the gleam of the lamp posts, softly coating the dark. I watched in wonder as they tumbled toward the ground in a jumble that matched my thoughts.

I had tried to forget the love part, but it had proved impossible. I'd loved my kids even before they were born, and I knew I'd had moments when I'd been the mother they deserved. I wanted to believe I could still be that person. I wanted to bake cookies with Grace, watch Connor on stage, do movie night on the couch together. I knew the mom in me was still there.

That was the difference between my mother and me, I supposed. She *wasn't* there—would never be. And maybe that was worth more than any similarities between us.

I brushed a fresh layer of icy flakes off my mom's headstone. "You robbed yourself of a second chance. I didn't."

I was still far from perfect, and I was bound to trip and fall a million times over yet. But I could also decide to shake it off and try again. Sometimes, I might even get things right. Yes, I'd failed to prevent Grace's self-harm, but I'd known something was off before anyone else. My gut told me she needed me to be there for her. And Connor—as upset as he might be with me today, I knew in my heart he would be in a safer space with me than under Brandy's roof. I'd made my kids come around once. No matter how out of step we were at that very moment, the only thing that would make it final was me treating it like it was.

And I wouldn't.

I would work for them, fight for them, and show them that my love for them was real. And then, at the end of my long life, that was what would matter most. That was what would count. Not my mistakes, no matter how grievous.

A warm tear trickled down my frozen cheek, fell to the ground, then disappeared in the snow. I wiped my face with the back of my glove and pushed myself up off the grass.

"Thanks, Mom," I whispered.

I was ready to go home.

CHAPTER 37

It was a little after half past eight when I pulled into Wic's drive-way. Kara's car was parked askew near the walkway to the house, which made little sense, since we hadn't agreed to meet up. The snow wasn't sticking, and one of her front tires had made a muddy dent at the edge of the lawn.

Chilled to the bone after all those hours at the cemetery, I couldn't wait to get inside and into dry clothes, but I still went through the front door instead of my own entrance to see what was going on. As soon as I stepped into the kitchen, three pale faces turned my way.

There was a split-second pause, then Kara flew into my arms. "Oh my God, Annie!"

"What?" I looked from her to Wic, whose features were set in stone. "What's wrong?"

"What do you mean, what's wrong?" Kara let go of me and stepped back. "We've been worried sick. You've been gone for almost nine hours, and no one could reach you. Where were you?"

Mina regarded me with poorly concealed wariness. I'd done it again. Another misstep.

"I had to clear my head. There was some stuff. Earlier, I mean."

"You could have called. We thought..." Wic ran a hand over his hair.

"I would have, but I forgot my purse at urgent care." A shiver coursed through me, and I pulled at my damp jeans to get them off my skin. "I'm so sorry. I didn't mean to—" I was going to say, "scare anyone," but I realized then that I should have known better. With my history, of course they would be alarmed at my absence. "I'll explain, okay? But would it be all right if I changed first? I'm freezing."

"You'd better," Mina said from her chair. "Wouldn't want you *catching your death.*"

"Mom!" Wic glared at her.

"I'll be right back."

I hurried up the stairs, and it wasn't lost on me that as soon as I was out of view, the three of them resumed a hushed conversation that I could only assume was about me. It was all fine. I could deal with it. One step at a time. The new me was determined to recover from mistakes.

When I returned to the kitchen, Wic, Mina, and Kara were all seated around the table. A mug of steaming tea waited for me. I pulled the sleeves of Wic's oversized sweatshirt over my hands and sat down.

"I'm sorry," I said again. "I promise, I didn't run away."

"And what about the, uh, other stuff?" Wic's expression was still on guard, but his gaze had softened.

"Were you going to hurt yourself?" Mina asked, to the point as always.

"No." I locked eyes with Wic. "I really wasn't."

He let out a deep breath and rubbed a hand across his forehead. "You have to understand. Mom called me when a couple of hours had gone by, and you didn't come home. She called Brandy and Kara. We didn't know what to think."

"I'm so sorry." I reached for his hand and squeezed it.

He gripped mine in both of his. "You can't do stuff like that."

"I know."

"So, what happened?" Kara asked. "According to Brandy, you seemed fine at the clinic. Worried about Grace, but that's all."

I let out a sad laugh and shook my head. "She *would* tell you that." I gripped my mug and brought the hot beverage to my lips. It warmed its way deep into the icy pit of my stomach. "Not quite what went down."

I explained about Grace's injured finger and that Brandy had found out some other things were going on with her and Connor, not mentioning either the cutting or Miles. I told them about Brandy's rant, her adoption threat, and the panic I'd felt. "But again, I promise I wasn't leaving. I went to Mom's grave, lost track of time. That's all."

Kara put her arm around my shoulders. "I believe you. And I'm sorry you had such a rough day. I'm just glad you're okay."

I leaned my head against hers. "Thank you. Where's Logan, by the way?"

"No worries. He's with his dad." She sat back, yawning. "But I should probably head back. It's getting late, and I have to be at work early."

"I'll walk you out."

When I returned, Mina also announced it was time to tuck in. "Glad to have you back," she said to me. "And next time, keep your phone with you."

"I will. I really am so sorry."

"Good."

"I'll give you a hand, Mom," Wic said. He turned to me. "Don't go anywhere. I'll be right back."

I finished my tea while I waited for Wic, my body feeling heavier by the minute. He returned wearing one of the soft T-shirts he usually slept in and carrying a pillow. When I raised an eyebrow in question, he put it down on the table then pulled me up by my hands and into his arms. We stood there in the kitchen for a long time, his strong arms around my shoulders, mine around his waist, just breathing, not moving. His heart beat steadily beneath my ear.

"You'll sleep upstairs tonight?" I asked.

"I'd like to but only if you want me there. I'd feel better having you close." He inhaled deeply. "Annie, I was so worried. I didn't know what to think. I—" His voice caught, and when I looked up into his face, his eyes welled.

"No." My hand went to his cheek, wiping at the moisture spilling over. "No, I wouldn't. I'm okay. I promise." I got up on my toes and placed a chaste kiss on his lips.

He nodded.

"Come on. Let's go to bed. I think I could sleep until noon."

A small smile. "I should probably text Shane first. They're worried too."

"I doubt it. I have a feeling Brandy will be disappointed."

"She won't. I know you guys have your issues, but deep down, she cares about you."

"Very, very deep down." He was about to object again, so I backtracked. "Fine. I know we have to come to some sort of understanding. I'm not going to let her take the kids."

"We'll figure it out. Tomorrow."

I fell asleep with his arms wrapped tightly around me, endlessly grateful he'd said "we."

IT WAS STILL DARK IN the room when we both jolted awake to the incessant ringing of Wic's phone. Why he insisted on that old-school ringtone I had no idea.

"Who's calling?" I groaned, still half-asleep.

Wic jumped out of bed and grabbed his phone from the charger. "It's Brandy."

"Now?" I sat up, instantly more awake.

"Hello?" He'd picked up the call with his back to me, but not ten seconds in, he spun around, his expression one of alarm. "Are you sure?" he asked. "Yeah, they're not here."

"What's going on?" I whispered.

He covered the speaker. "Get dressed. I'll explain in a sec." Then to Brandy, he said, "We'll go drive around. Keep us posted." He hung up.

The set of his jaw intensified the feeling of dread growing in my stomach. "Is it the kids? Did something happen?"

"They were gone when she woke up. Note on the fridge. Apparently, they've gone after you, and they're not answering their phones."

My stomach dropped. "What do you mean? I'm here."

"But they don't know that."

My thoughts were like molasses, synapses firing in slow motion as I tried to figure out where they might have gone. I pictured Connor and Grace alone on the road somewhere, easy prey for all kinds of nefarious circumstances. Accidents could happen, and human trafficking was a thing. *What if they get separated?*

A sharp sob left me. *Oh my God. What have I done?* I had to set things right and bring the kids back safely. I wouldn't risk them for anything.

Wic was instantly there at my side. "Hey, we'll find them. What can I do?"

I straightened and shook my head to clear it. *Where do we start?* I looked around the room, willing some coherence into my brain. "We have to get my purse and phone. They might have messaged me. What time does urgent care open?"

"Probably not until eight."

"Shit." I gnawed at my lip, thinking. "I believe Kara knows one of the nurses. Maybe she can help."

"That's good." Wic was already dialing. While he spoke to Kara, I finished getting dressed. "She's calling her friend," he informed me as I was putting on my boots. "Let me grab a warmer sweater, and I'll be right there."

"No, you have to stay here. Your mom will wake up soon."

He stopped in his tracks, looking torn. "You're right. But the minute you know anything, you call me, okay?"

His phone beeped with a message. "Kara's friend will meet you at the clinic in twenty minutes."

"Okay." I opened the door, ready to head out.

"Annie, wait." Wic opened the fridge and handed me a banana and a bottle of water. "Good luck."

Lord knew I was going to need it.

CHAPTER 38

T hank goodness for the kindness of strangers. As soon as I had my phone in my hands again, I plugged it into the car and waited for it to come alive. Those five minutes felt more like hours. At the first beep, I clicked it open with shaking hands and was met with a stream of missed messages.

Wic's texts flickered across the screen. *Mom called. Where are you? Is Grace okay?*

Another read, *I'm worried about you. Don't do anything stupid.*

I paid them little mind, eager as I was to find any sign of life from my children. The ones from Connor made the pounding in my head worse. He'd texted last night, too, in three separate pleas.

7:05 p.m.: *I overheard B and S say you've left again. Is it true?*

9:10 p.m.: *Where are you? You can call me. Or Grace. She's here too.*

11:22 p.m.: *Hello? Did you go back to Albuquerque? Are you mad at us?*

The irony was that by the time Connor sent the last message, Wic had already let Shane know I was back. Clearly, that had not been communicated to the kids. And now, they were gone.

"And then what?" I asked out loud. "Where are you now?" I pulled up Connor's contact and dialed. According to Brandy, their phones were off, but I wasn't as sure. You could dismiss a call if you didn't want to answer. All I could hope was that my name lighting up his screen wouldn't provoke that same response.

One signal went through then a second. On the fourth, he picked up, and I let out the breath I'd been holding.

"Mom?"

"Connor! Thank God you're okay. Where are you?"

"It's her," I heard him say on the other end—I assumed to Grace.

"Is your sister with you?"

"She's here. Where are you?"

I laughed between the tears that had started up again. The relief at all my dark premonitions not coming true was overwhelming. "I'm home. I know you think I left, but I didn't. I promised, remember?"

After a long silence, he said, "But you were missing."

"Just driving around. I'm so sorry. Are you safe?"

"So you're not in Albuquerque?"

"What? No. I don't have my place there anymore."

"Oh."

"I told you," Grace said in the background.

"Connor, what did you do?" I asked.

"Promise you won't be mad? We got on a bus. We thought you'd left, and we... we didn't want that."

I let that sink in. As misguided as their actions were, they hadn't given up on me. I pulled out of the urgent care parking lot then sped off. "Okay, I'm coming to get you. Do you know where you are right now? Where's the next stop?"

"I'll ask." He came back a minute later. "We should be in Ellensburg in an hour."

"Okay, then you get off there. Find a cafe or something where you can wait, and I'll get there as soon as I can. And Grace..."

"What about her?" Connor asked.

A rustle sounded on the line, a sharp "Let me talk to her."

"Hold on," Connor said, handing me off.

"He doesn't know," Grace half whispered.

"Sweetie." Hearing her voice again made my heart swell. I should have been there for her, paid better attention. All those times when Connor came over, and she stayed away. If only I'd asked questions, tried harder.

"I'm sorry, Mom. I know you're mad at me, but I just wanted you back."

"I was never gone. And Grace, I'm not mad at you. I'm upset with *me*. I should have known better. I should have seen—"

"Just stop it, will you?" She raised her voice. "It's not you. I'd done it before you came back too. I don't know what it is. Sometimes, I just feel weird. All I know is, I don't want to live with Shane and Brandy anymore."

Connor came back on the line. "Yeah, me neither."

And there it was. They wanted me like I wanted them—admitting that to myself after all the turmoil was nowhere near as complicated as I would have thought. Instead, it seemed almost a given. We were family. Wrongs could be righted.

I was Atlas, shrugging off the weight of the world. I was a bubble of air rising to the ocean surface. I was alive.

"Mom?"

"I'm here. We'll figure it out as soon as we're together again. I'm on my way, okay."

"Just you? You won't call Shane?"

"I won't call Shane. I'll let Wic know I'm getting you just so they don't worry, but I'll come get you myself. Just be safe, okay? If anything happens to you—"

"We'll be fine. Don't worry."

Ha! Don't worry. Does he not know me at all? "I'm going to hang up now and focus on driving. Keep me posted, and I'll do the same."

"Will do."

"And Connor, I really am sorry—for everything." I clutched my phone tight to my cheek.

"That's all right, Mom," he mumbled. "Just get here."

Before I pulled onto the expressway, I texted Wic like I'd promised Connor. I kept it brief. *They're safe. On a bus a couple of hours away. Picking them up and coming home. More later.*

He did the same, responding with a thumbs-up. Then I turned the radio on and cruised.

CHAPTER 39

I reached Ellensburg around ten Friday morning. I'd had enough gas station coffee that my whole body felt like it was vibrating, but it had served its purpose, so I ignored the discomfort. With the help of my phone, I navigated off the I-90 toward the Greyhound station. Connor had texted that they were waiting at the brunch place next door.

My fingers strummed the steering wheel, still keeping the beat of the music I'd turned off. I wouldn't be able to relax until I saw them.

Finally, I pulled into a parking space near the door and practically ran inside. My legs felt like jelly, and I was surprised they carried me as well as they did.

"Table for one?" the host called.

I rushed past her to the booth by the windows, where Connor's red jacket stuck out.

"Mom!" Connor flew off the seat and into my arms.

Grace was slower to react. "That took a long time," she said with a yawn, joining our embrace.

"Thank God you're safe," I said, pulling her to me. "Don't you guys ever do something like this again." Brandy's call yesterday from the urgent care felt like a lifetime ago. I'd been on such a rollercoaster since then that the fact that I was now standing in a restaurant in Ellensburg, hugging my kids, seemed completely outlandish but also almost to be expected.

I didn't censor my tears. Until that moment, I'd never known true relief. I held them close, burying my face in their hair. Long gone was the baby smell I'd once inhaled through tears of a different kind, but their scent was still a balm to my soul.

"Can I get you some coffee?" A young waitress with heavy eyeliner and a retro-looking apron interrupted our reunion.

"Did you eat something?" I asked the kids.

"I had a pop," Grace said. "I could eat."

"Okay," I took a breath. "Let's sit for a bit. No coffee for me," I told the waitress. "But I'll take a menu, please."

"For sure." She smiled.

"What do we do now?" Connor asked after she'd disappeared.

I sniffled even as I smiled at his practical nature. "We get some breakfast, we talk, then we drive back home."

Between bites of chocolate chip pancakes, Connor and Grace filled me in on their version of yesterday's events. After school, Grace had locked herself in her room, not wanting a continuation of the urgent care drama, and she'd refused to come out for dinner. Later, when Connor had tiptoed through the kitchen to sneak her some food, he'd overheard a hushed argument between his aunt and uncle about me having fled once more. While Shane had left room for the possibility that I would show up again, Brandy had been adamant. I'd broken my vows once—I was bound to do it again.

"But you didn't," Connor said. "She was wrong."

"She was. I just really wish you'd double-checked before taking off." Sometimes, I forgot how young they still were. Still children. "Brandy loves you too. She means well, and Lord knows I've made plenty of mistakes in my life—mistakes I can't undo." I made sure to look both my kids in the eye. "But I'm not giving you up. I'm going to prove her wrong."

"Will you tell her we're going to live with you?" Grace asked.

Connor set his empty juice glass down. "She's not going to like it."

I pressed my lips together. "Yeah. I'll be honest, I don't know what she'll do. But I know what I want, so I'll just have to deal with it."

"We'll deal with it," Connor said, bumping his shoulder to mine.

We. Again, the word resounded like a soft chime in my head, a stark contrast to the clamorous opuses I'd hidden behind for so long. I held tight to that tune as we started our journey back. A new melody for a new future.

GOING ON A ROAD TRIP with the kids was vastly different from doing it alone. My car had never been so full of life. It was also a perfect opportunity to begin righting the miscommunications that had made things go awry, starting with my commitment to staying in Snohomish with them for good.

"If you have any questions at all," I said, opening up the floor, "about your dad, my depression, my life in Albuquerque, anything. I don't want you to worry anymore or to guess."

"I want to know what's going on with you and Wic," Connor said right away. "Do you love him?"

I glanced at him and caught him watching me intently.

"I think I could." It was the truth.

"I like Wic," Grace said from the backseat. "He's cool."

High praise indeed from a thirteen-year-old.

"Yeah, I like him too," Connor said. "But..."

"It's not between you and him." I reached for Connor's arm. "And believe me, if it was, I'd choose you. I didn't expect him to come into my life any more than I expected to be allowed back into yours, but here we are. He means a lot to me. But if me taking a step back from him for now is what you need, I will."

Connor considered this. "No, I don't want that."

Phew. "And I *know* I shouldn't have told him about you and Miles. That was out of line, and I'm very sorry."

"God, grown-ups are *so* clueless," Grace said. "I knew he was your boyfriend ages ago."

"You did?" Connor and I asked in chorus.

"Well, duh." She didn't elaborate further.

"Guess everyone knows now," Connor said.

"Not everyone. And you should take your time. Come out when it's right for you."

"Miles is going to tell his parents."

I nodded. "Is he nervous?"

"Yeah. But they're cool. I think it'll be okay."

"I'm sure it can be overwhelming—what you're going through. But you know if you ever need someone to talk to, I'm here for you."

He smiled. "I know."

"Mom," Grace said. "Who do you talk to when you're overwhelmed? Like when you drove around and didn't come home yesterday. Is it Wic?"

The car in front of me braked to exit the expressway, and I slowed with it. "I have a therapist in New Mexico. But I'm going to find someone local now, I think. You should go, too, Grace. But we can talk more about that later." I looked at her in the rearview. A professional pair of eyes and ears would be good. While I still felt bad I'd missed the depth of her distress, part of me knew it was because I'd been stretched thin, distracted by my own issues. And, I reminded myself again, I'd been right to stay in the first place. In that sense, I *had* come through for her. Like a mom.

She held my gaze for a moment then nodded. "Yeah, maybe."

It was late afternoon by the time we approached Seattle and hit the Friday commuter mayhem. Normally, it would have driven me nuts, but on this cloudy January day, I relished the added minutes. I wasn't quite ready for what lay ahead, not yet daring enough to walk into whatever awaited us at the end of this road without some trepidation. Connor had kept Brandy and Shane posted on our progress, as I was sure Wic had, but a mountain of bold words still towered between Brandy and me. My personal Mount Everest. I wasn't sure where we would go once we hit Snohomish town limits. I could drop the kids off at their house or claim them immediately, dive right into the fight. It wasn't an easy decision.

Ten miles per hour was a more conducive pace than sixty for such quandaries.

When we reached Woodinville, Connor pointed out I hadn't said a word since Issaquah forty minutes earlier.

"I'm thinking," I said.

"Don't brag."

It was such a Joel-like quip that a sharp cackle burst out of me. It startled Grace, who'd been listening to music in the back, making her stir with a dopey "Wha—?" that made us crack up even harder. The joke wasn't all that funny, but we needed a good laugh.

Her trance broken, Grace looked up and must have recognized where we were. "We're almost home already?"

"Ten more minutes." I tried to smile, but my cheeks wouldn't cooperate.

"Where are we going?" Grace asked, putting words to all the thoughts stewing inside me.

It occurred to me then that I didn't have to solve this all on my own. We could talk about it like a family.

"I'm not sure. Your things are at Brandy's. And your beds and everything. They probably expect me to take you there, but you know where I stand. After all this, it would feel better not to drop you off. Wic's couches are pretty comfortable too." I bit my cheek and looked to Connor. "Though you might not want to go there."

He gave me a half smile. "It's okay. Like you said, he is a good guy, so I'll try harder."

"Thank you. Really." I gave them some time to consider what I'd put in front of them, then I asked, "What do we think?" I tried to make my question light. I didn't want them to feel the burden.

"It would be weird if you just dropped us off." Grace's voice was tentative. "But I'm sure they've been worried too."

"I prefer the couch if I have a choice," Connor said.

I nodded. "Okay. I think I need to speak to Shane and Brandy, see where we stand."

"What about the guest room?" Grace asked. "Could you stay there? That way we'd still be together."

After what Brandy had said to me, I cringed at the thought of staying a moment longer than necessary under her roof. But then again, maybe it was necessary.

"I can ask. Would that work for you, Connor?"

He grumbled a bit but then agreed. Outside, the view changed as the trees along Route 9 gave way to the valley that announced we were home. My second return in four months. To an outsider, they might have appeared like echoes of each other, but I was not the same as before. My one objective now was to keep us together no matter what. With all I had to live for, I would put safeguards in place to keep me on the side of the living. The darkness of my family legacy would stop with me.

THE THREE OF US APPROACHED Shane and Brandy's door as a united front. It was a feeling I could get used to. As soon as we set foot on the front step, the door flew open.

"Oh, thank heavens!" Brandy's face was flushed. "Come here, you two." She pulled my kids into a quick embrace.

"Glad you're all right," Shane said, his features tenser than usual. "We'll talk about this later, but for right now, why don't you go up-stairs and wash up? Annie." He nodded to me.

My kids looked at me over their shoulders. I nudged them on, hoping my expression conveyed I had things under control.

"Thanks for getting them, I guess." Brandy said to me. She was rubbing her distended belly.

I took another step into the house. "Could we talk for a bit?"

"Can it wait?"

I forced myself to keep eye contact. "No."

"I'll go put on some coffee." Shane disappeared into the kitchen.

Brandy let out a sharp breath, her hand stopping its movement for a second. Something disconcerted flickered in her gaze.

"Are you okay?"

She raised her chin. "Fine. What did you want to talk about?"

No going back now. Suddenly, I wasn't sure what to do with my arms. "The things you said yesterday." I grabbed onto my purse strap. "You were really out of line."

She scoffed. "Is that so? The kids have never run away from home before. Are you telling me that had nothing to do with you?"

"No, of course not." I straightened. "But the reason they did was because they heard you say I'd left again—which I hadn't."

"Well, I didn't know that."

"No, you assumed. And I guess that's what I want you to stop doing. I feel like I've shown you time and time again that I'm serious about staying, about being a family again, but you're so stuck on the other stuff that you don't see it."

"So now it's about me?"

"Yes. You and me and Shane and Wic and Mina and everyone else in the kids' lives. We all want what's best for them, right? Sure, I do some things differently than you and Shane, and no, I'm not perfect. But I am their mom."

"You're making things so complicated for them."

"They disagree. They want to live with me." Ignoring her darkening features, I pressed on. "And I'm telling you, I will fight for them. With everything I have."

Her eyes narrowed. "If that's the case, then I will—" Her brow twitched, and her whole body went rigid. "No," she whispered, looking down toward her feet.

A wet stain was spreading on the thighs of her blue maternity jeggings.

She took a step toward me and reached for my arm, her face a mask of alarm.

Her water had broken, and she wasn't due for another six weeks.

CHAPTER 40

Mina was a godsend, peppering the kids for details of their adventures as soon as they entered the house. It was a good way to take their minds off the chaotic scene that had been Shane rushing Brandy to the hospital. He'd promised to let us know what was going on as soon as he knew.

Once the kids were settled on the couch in front of a movie, Wic and I snuck up to my room for some privacy. He pulled me close—so close my ribs hurt—and I, in turn, clung to him with equal relief.

"You did it," he said. "The kids are safe."

"I feel like I've aged five years since yesterday."

He chuckled, his breath warming my hair. "I bet."

I silenced him with a kiss that he deepened gradually, hands roaming up my back into my hair. If we could have stayed there, we would have. It took self-control of the grandest kind—the parent kind—not to linger. There would be time for us later.

"Do you mind if the kids stay on the couch tonight?" I asked. "I'd put them up here, but I think they'll be more comfortable in the living room."

"They wouldn't rather sleep in their own beds? I have a spare key."

"I think Connor does, too, but he said he didn't have it with him."

"You think he's making that up?"

I shrugged. "Besides, if I'm there with them, you'll be here all alone." I linked my fingers with his. "We can't have that."

He smiled. "Couch it is."

Reluctantly, I stepped away from him, though I kept his hand in mine. "We should go back downstairs, or they'll assume things."

"I suppose." He pouted. "I'm going to try Shane, too, and see if they have an update."

"They'd better have good news." My heart ached thinking of Brandy possibly losing another baby. I couldn't imagine.

Wic watched me without speaking for a bit. "You know it says a lot about a person that they can feel compassion for someone they're at odds with. After the cruel things she said to you—"

I shook my head. "Feels like another lifetime. And just because she said hurtful things doesn't mean I want to see her suffer. If anything, I want her to have some joy in her life. Maybe then she won't be so quick to judge. That said, if she wants my kids, I'll see her in court."

He squeezed my hand as we descended the stairs. "You're amazing, you know that?"

Little fireworks went off inside me. I couldn't remember the last time someone had called me that. Maybe no one ever had. "You're not so bad yourself."

SHANE DID HAVE GOOD news, and a week later, Wic and I stepped out of the elevator up from the hospital parking garage, the smell of disinfectant stinging our nostrils. I had a small stuffed elephant in my hand, and Wic carried a bouquet of multicolored tulips. Grace and Connor had stayed behind with Mina. Even though Brandy and her new baby daughter had only had to stay in the NICU for a couple of days after she was induced, the Special Care Nursery they were in now also discouraged families from bringing children to visit.

"You're sure it was the second floor?" I straightened my jacket.

"That's what Shane said. Stop fidgeting. You're fine."

"I don't know why I'm so nervous." I did know. It would be the first time I saw Brandy since that row in her foyer when her water had broken. Shane said they would welcome a visit to break up the day, but I wasn't convinced she felt the same.

We checked in at the nurses' station, where one of them gave us the room number and offered a vase for the flowers. He also asked us to wash our hands before going any farther down the bustling hallway.

"It's so noisy," I said as we made our way to the room. "I pictured lullabies and hushed voices, not all this beeping."

Wic squeezed my hand. "It's a hospital."

We knocked on number eleven and entered at a faint "Come in."

Shane met us at the door while Brandy lingered behind him on a sleeper sofa. Her hand rested on a large plastic cube at her side.

"These are for, um, you guys, I guess." Wic handed Shane the flowers with an awkward smile. "Congratulations, man."

Shane grinned as he accepted the gift. "Thanks. Glad you could make it. Come on. Let me introduce you to our perfect little God-sent miracle." He gestured toward the cube.

It was an isolette—a small bed enclosed by clear plastic to keep the little one in a controlled environment. I trailed behind the men, my feet leaden as I closed in on my sister-in-law. She finally looked away from the cot when I was only a step away.

"Annie," she said, her gaze meeting mine.

"Hi." I fidgeted with the stuffed toy I was holding until I realized what I was doing and held it out for her. "Oh, this is for you. Um, for your daughter."

Her inscrutable expression quivered as if something had moved beneath its surface, and before I could prepare myself, she smiled. "It's adorable," she said in a soft voice. "It'll be perfect for the nursery once we go home. Look, Shane. Isn't it cute?" She held out the plush elephant for him to see. When he turned, I got the first clear view into the covered bed where a tiny doll-like creature slept, her fists balled tightly to the chin as if she were preparing for a boxing match.

Brandy saw me staring and stood. "This is Camryn." Her voice carried the name like one would a delicate gift. "Camryn Hope Joelle Hemingway."

My throat constricted. "Bee, she's beautiful."

She grinned. "I know."

"Honey, do you mind?" Shane held up two cigars. "We'll just step out for a few minutes."

"Go ahead. But only a puff or two. You can't come back in here stinking."

"Cross my heart." Shane and Wic disappeared out the door with a gleeful shuffle.

"Men." Brandy clicked her tongue, but a glint in her eye suggested she quite liked hers, cigar or not. "Where were we?"

I returned my focus to my niece. "We had established Camryn is beautiful, I believe. How is she doing healthwise?"

Brandy caressed the top of the plastic cover and leaned closer to it. "She's great. She was a bit jaundiced, but that seems to have cleared up. We're still working on latching, and she'll have the oxygen monitor a while longer, but then, God willing, we get to come home." She sounded surprised as if that was a foreign concept to her. It might well be considering how long they'd tried for a baby.

"I remember bringing Connor home like it was yesterday." I conjured the film reel inside my head. "I couldn't believe they were actually going to let us walk out of the hospital with him. We had no idea what we were doing—we were still little more than kids! But there we were, strapping the car seat in, pulling out into traffic. I kept expecting someone to come after us and say it was a mistake."

She nodded. "When did it sink in that it was real?"

I chuckled at the memory. "That first night, we didn't sleep at all. He was colicky and wouldn't stop crying no matter what we tried. Finally, Joel turned on some music—I think it was Bon Jovi or some other light rock like that—and he bounced with Connor in his arms in time with the music. Full-on squats. The crying stopped instantly. That's when we got it. No one was going to hold our hand through this new phase in our lives. We had to figure it out. That's about as real as it gets."

Brandy didn't respond at first. She gazed at her daughter, who now looked to be dreaming. Camryn's leg twitched, then her little face scrunched up as if she was about to cry before she settled again. It boggled my mind what she could possibly have to dream about after only three days on this earth. Maybe the birth trauma or cold air and the novelty of human touch. Or maybe it was something grander and more profound like memories of a different existence still lingering within.

"I was thinking," Brandy said, interrupting my train of thought. She was still intent on Camryn. "I'm going to be here with her for another week or so. And Shane comes in after work every day." She paused, sucking in her lips. "Maybe the kids could stay with you a bit longer? If Wic and Mina don't mind, of course. He has a key to the house, so if they need anything, you can stop by at any time. I was just thinking they might be better off with adults around. Safer, you know." She glanced at me. "The rest we can talk about later."

The rest. "Bee, I…"

"I mean it." She gave me a sad smile and shook her head. "I don't want to bring that up now. Not here. This is Camryn's room. But I'm thankful you brought them back. You should know that."

The air in my lungs grew heavy. Her reluctance to resolve things now could mean she still wanted to take Grace and Connor away from me. I wanted to believe she was past thinking me unfit, but I wouldn't be certain until she said the words. She *had* suggested the kids stay with Wic and me a while longer, though. *Surely that's a good sign.* Even if Shane was busy during the day, he was home at night, and it wasn't like the kids couldn't mind themselves for a few hours after school. I burned to lay it all on the table, state my case, and be done with it.

"She's waking up." Brandy stuck her hand through a hole in the side of the cot. "Hi, baby girl," she cooed. "Did you have a nice sleep? Mommy is right here."

She continued to whisper sweet nothings to her child, leaving me in limbo about what would happen to mine. With her attention diverted, my opportunity was gone. Shane and Wic returned a short while later, and after that, there was nothing left but to take our leave.

"Keep us posted," I said before we headed out, the unspoken words still nagging at me. "And congratulations again. To the both of you."

They waved—a brief absentminded gesture—but had already turned back to their daughter before the door closed behind us.

"I NEED TO MAKE SOME preparations," I told Wic a few days later while watching him sand a board to a silken finish. We were in the garage, warm air blowing at us from a space heater but just barely keeping the chill off our backs. Not knowing what would happen when Brandy and Shane once more settled into their regular routine at home was eating at me. I wasn't sure how to ready my mind for a possible conflict—especially considering what they'd just gone through. It was hard to be angry with someone who'd just given birth to a preemie after multiple miscarriages while caring for her dead brother's teenagers. Somehow, I felt like I owed Brandy deference despite the harsh words she'd had for me. I was also done waiting for the ax to fall.

"I know what I want—a home, soccer games, violin recitals, plays, homework, college applications, curfews, holidays, road trips, meals not eaten alone, companionship, a future... And I feel like I'm this close." I held up my fingers to demonstrate.

Wic put the sandpaper down and came around to where I was sitting. "What can I do to help?"

I rubbed the back of my hand with the other. "If she tries to take the kids—"

"For what it's worth, I don't think she will."

"She threatened to use your past against me."

A look of alarm came over him. "What? Why didn't you tell me?"

"I was afraid you'd remove yourself from the equation. I wasn't ready for that."

"But if me being out of the picture would help you get the kids—"

I raised my chin. "I already have the kids. They want to be with me. And your past is your past. I've decided a judge would see that too."

He nodded slowly.

"I do need a lawyer, though. Just in case. Kara gave me a number. If I have to go see him, will you come with me?"

He crouched in front of me. "Of course."

"And I need to be able to show I have room for the kids. Income, housing—that type of stuff. They can't keep sleeping on the couch." That, I had yet to figure out. I could try to find a teaching job locally in addition to my online courses, but nothing was guaranteed. My CV was less than impressive, and without a bigger income, there was no way I'd be able to afford a place for the three of us. I'd stayed up late the past few nights, crunching numbers, but no amount of arithmetic acrobatics made any difference.

"Actually..." Wic returned to his board, placing his hands on it. "I've done some thinking in that direction."

"Really?"

"But I don't know how you'd feel about it." He reached for an envelope with finer grit paper, pulled out a sheet, then put it down as if not sure he wanted to use it. The fan in the heater hummed like a deranged bumblebee off to the side. "It's just a suggestion, but it could be a temporary solution at least. It was actually something Mom said that gave me the idea."

"And do you maybe feel like sharing this idea sometime today?" I smiled. Wic wasn't often reticent with his words.

He let out a low snicker and smoothed invisible strands of his tied-back hair off his forehead. "What if I cleared out the office and my room for the kids. There's plenty of space in here for storage." He gestured to a corner that held nothing but a few paint cans and a tarp. "The rooms are smaller than what they're used to, but they'd at least have a door to close for privacy, a bed, desk, bookcase, closet." He shrugged.

I was speechless. If anything, I'd expected him to suggest places where I might apply for work, not offer his house up. "But what about you? You can't sleep on the couch. That's ridiculous."

"Well, Mom's original idea was to offer you the office and have the kids share the space above the garage. Clearly, she's forgotten what teenagers are like."

I laughed. I could just imagine Grace and Connor being forced to share a room. There would be mutiny within ten minutes.

"But then I thought," he continued, shuffling and reshuffling the sandpaper envelopes, "between the four of us, there are actually two who, potentially, maybe, could share a room." He glanced sideways at me and waited.

Oh.

"I know it's soon and everything, but I'm already sleeping up there most nights. We'd just need a bigger bed. And maybe a better desk if I'm going to use it as my office too. Of course, you'd have to talk to Connor and Grace about it."

He kept talking while, in my head, the missing pieces of the puzzle fell in place. *Can it really be that simple?*

"Annie? Say something."

I stopped trying to shoot holes in his idea and snapped to it. "You're asking to move in with me?" I got up. Walked toward him.

"Well, I'm..." His forehead wrinkled. "Yeah, I suppose I am."

"Into my room above the garage?" I reached him and put my hands on his chest. "You know, the landlord is pretty strict. I don't know that I'm allowed to make that call."

He wrapped his arms around my shoulders, eyes glinting. "Is that a yes?"

I reached up and kissed him. "We'll have to check with the landlord."

His soft laugh mingled with mine. "Already did. He says yes."

"Are you sure? It's a big change."

"I'm sure. And it would help, right?"

"So much." I leaned into his embrace. "But if we do this, promise you'll tell me if it gets to be too much. Mina too."

"She loves them."

"I know."

For a while, we didn't speak. He held me and I him, the image of the possibility growing brighter and more colorful each time I conjured it. We could live here, the kids and I. Together. Wic and I would be official, and Mina would have more company. I could look for a job locally, but if I didn't find one for a while, we would still be fine if we pooled our incomes. The image showed a whole life. We would be a family.

The only remaining cloud in our sky was Brandy and the battle still to be fought.

CHAPTER 41

Grace insisted on five purple balloons and five yellow.

"But it's a girl," Connor said. "We should do pink."

"Do you see me wear pink ever?" Grace crossed her arms. "Not all girls like pink. Purple is close enough, and the nursery is yellow. Trust me."

There was no point arguing. I didn't have a strong opinion either way. It was the day Brandy and Shane would get to bring home Camryn, and I was certain they would have more important things on their minds than the color of balloons adorning their doorstep.

We left the party outlet with a bag full of streamers and signs, heading next to the grocery store for the cake. Wic and Mina were meeting us at the house to help set everything up. They were bringing lasagna. If we'd had more time, we could have prepared a fancier welcome-home dinner, but as it was, Shane had texted Wic last night with the news we'd all been waiting for. That meant a quickly improvised celebration or nothing at all.

"Do you think they'll let me babysit when she's older?" Grace asked when we made our way down the aisle to the bakery counter.

"I'm sure they will. You'll be the best big cousin any little girl could ever ask for."

Grace rewarded me with a small smile. She wore her hair down for once, a blue hairband keeping it behind her ears. Her skin was smooth like velvet even beneath the harsh fluorescent lights. Since we'd been back, her mood had seemed more even-keeled, and she'd already had one meeting with a new therapist. She still didn't want to talk to me about her self-harming other than to assure me it had only happened "a couple of times," but that was fine with me for the moment. I wasn't overly keen on sharing my personal experiences with that, and I suspected once she opened up, I would have to do the same. It had messed with my head to realize I was like my mother—I could only hope that I would be able to cushion the blow for Grace when that day came. I would spend a lifetime assuring her she wasn't already doomed if that was what it took. I would never stop.

Connor had slowed his pace and fallen behind. I pretended to browse a nearby shelf to let him catch up. He hadn't said anything, but I knew he had mixed feelings about seeing Brandy again. It was in how his eyes turned down when we talked about them and in his lack of interest in the baby. With each day bringing us closer to the imminent reunion, he'd withdrawn further into himself. It didn't take a mind reader to guess he was anticipating judgment, dreading it, but I had hoped he would be able to shake it off. He and Miles were good, and Miles's parents had not been the least bit surprised at their son's coming out. I certainly had no issue with his sexual orientation, and neither did Grace, Wic, or Mina. But he'd known Shane and Brandy all his life—I could understand why he wanted their acceptance too. It was time for me to step in as reinforcement to get him ready to face them.

"Should we get cupcakes, too, or just the cake?" I asked him when he reached me. Grace had run ahead to browse the sheet cakes. "Or cookies, maybe? Chocolate chip is always a hit."

He grabbed the handle of the cart. "Whatever is fine."

"What?" I made a dramatic move to check his temperature. "Are you feeling all right today? Not interested in cookies? Something must be seriously wrong."

Despite himself, a smile tugged at the corner of his mouth. "Ha ha."

I put my arm around him as we started walking. "What bothers you the most? What are you worried about?"

He halted as his head jerked in my direction. "How did you know?"

"I can tell. I'm your mom."

His jaw tensed. "I'm not looking forward to this. That's all." He paused for a beat. "She was so mad when I got home from school that day. I mean, I know she was upset about Grace, too, but... She'd gone through my room." His face flushed. "I had this one picture on my computer. It wasn't bad, I promise—just a screenshot from a fundraising firemen calendar that Miles had emailed me because he thought I looked like one of them. It was stupid, and I'd forgotten I had it, but she went completely unhinged. I left when she started with the whole sin sermon. Spare me, you know?" He scoffed.

"Oh, bud. I'm so sorry."

"I know."

"But I'll be there today. And I will never let her talk to you that way again. I promise."

He shrugged. "It's not like I really care."

"But it still hurts."

He nodded. "I guess."

I wanted to tell him about the plans Wic and I were making right then. We'd kept our thoughts to ourselves, not knowing how the next few days and weeks would play out. But while we hadn't wanted to get their hopes up, we weren't talking about them moving back to their aunt and uncle's either. Fortunately, the kids grumbled surprisingly little about still having to sleep on the couches. Somehow, the oddness of the situation had settled into a new normal.

"Is there anything I can do to make you more comfortable?" I rubbed his shoulder as we caught up to Grace.

"Nah." He attempted half a smile. He acted so much like Joel when he was stressed but didn't want to show it. "Like you said, you'll be there, and I'm sure they have other things on their minds right now."

"What are you guys talking about?" Grace asked. "Brandy bashing on gays?"

"Excuse me?"

She ignored me. "I'll be there, too, and Wic and Mina. And I don't think Uncle Shane really cares. He's more of a Jesus-loves-all Christian."

My heart melted, but Connor squirmed where he stood, clearly not entirely comfortable with being the focus of his sister's protective side.

"Okay, can we just pick out a cake already?" Connor said. "At this rate, we'll still be here tomorrow."

"This one," Grace announced. It was double chocolate with the word Congratulations written in white frosting on top. Multicolored sprinkles surrounded three beautiful flowers made out of purple, yellow, and white frosting. "It'll match the balloons we bought."

It was perfect. I was sure not even Brandy would be able to stay mad when faced with such sweetness.

WHEN BRANDY AND SHANE arrived home, Camryn was asleep. After muted welcomes, the new parents disappeared upstairs to the nursery to see if she would take to the crib. Shane reemerged a short while later, beaming but with dark circles under his eyes. He'd been working for the past week and spending time at the hospital every minute he was free, and it had taken its toll.

"You guys, you shouldn't have." He tapped one of the bouncy balloons lightly. "That's so nice."

"I picked them out." Grace looked pleased with herself.

He ruffled her hair. "Good taste, kiddo."

Wic offered Shane a beer, which he took with a satisfied hum. Together, they walked over to the couch and settled in.

"What about the cake?" Grace whispered to me.

"We'll wait for Brandy."

"Aw, can I at least have a cookie?" Connor asked.

"Sure. And one for me." Stress eating seemed to run in the family.

It was another thirty minutes before Brandy joined us, Camryn in her arms. She held the little one tucked close, one shoulder higher than the other. I knew from experience that would hurt in the long run, but today was not the day to warn her of the dangers of nonergonomic baby carrying. With any luck, we would have time for that later. If she was willing to listen.

"Yay, cake!" Grace flew up from her seat and disappeared into the kitchen. "Con, come and get the plates."

They returned moments later with their loot and had to clear their throats several times before they had everyone's attention. Brandy only had eyes for her daughter.

"Mom," Grace whispered, indicating I should say something.

"Oh." I straightened. "Right. Um, this is to wish you welcome home—the three of you. We're so happy to have Camryn in our lives and wish you all the best." I raised my pop can. "To family."

Wic's gaze met mine, and he gave me a reassuring smile. "To family."

Camryn whined in Brandy's arms in seeming agreement that made everyone laugh.

"If it's all the same to you, I'll be considering myself this one's grandmama," Mina said. She was seated closest to Brandy, almost as mesmerized by the new life as its mother. "And I will spoil her rotten." There were no grandparents left on either Shane's or Brandy's side, and Mina knew that.

Brandy looked up. "We'd be honored." Then she cooed to Camryn, "Won't we, sweetie?" She took Mina's hand and squeezed it. "Truly honored."

"Well, since we're bestowing gifts..." Wic pushed off the couch and pulled a large wrapped package out from behind it. "Made you something." He gestured for Shane to open it then came over to stand by me.

Shane tore the paper off to reveal a beautifully handcrafted cradle. I'd seen it in the garage, of course, but that was when it had been unfinished. Now it gleamed a dark-walnut color that went perfectly with the furniture in the room.

"I thought you could maybe keep it down here for nap time. Not that you have to use it," he hurried to add. "It can be a decoration too."

While he was talking, Brandy joined her husband in admiring the handiwork. "It's perfect. I can't believe you made that." She walked over to Wic and kissed his cheek. I didn't know who was most surprised—Wic or me.

"Yeah, thanks, man." Shane caressed the smooth side panels. "Remind me again, why aren't you doing stuff like this for a living?"

Wic and I exchanged a knowing smile. That was the goal. Construction was a paycheck, but he was an artist at heart, and I would help him get there no matter how long it took. It was the least I could do.

Wic brought Mina home when the afternoon dwindled. The kids disappeared upstairs, and Shane ran out to the grocery store for smaller diapers. I'd just finished putting our plates in the dishwasher and wrapping up the leftover cake when Brandy joined me. My pulse quickened as soon as she sat down at the counter. She yawned and reached for one of Camryn's socks that I'd found on the floor and picked up.

"She's still too small for the newborn stuff," she said with a little laugh. "I have all these cute outfits, and she can't wear them."

"Yet. She'll grow into them soon." I filled up a glass of water and had a sip. Then I took a deep breath. "We should probably talk."

Brandy looked at me for a beat then nodded.

I dove right in. "I know you're angry with me, and you think I've somehow damaged my kids by coming back. And yes, I have flaws, and I've made some bad decisions. Several," I added. "But I'm not giving them up. I may not be a perfect mother, but I am theirs, and for some miraculous reason, they want me here. Grace is already seeing a counselor, and Connor—there's nothing wrong with him. He's gay. Big deal. This is the twenty-first century. What he needs is acceptance and support, and he'll be just fine. I can give him that."

Surprisingly, Brandy remained silent. I took a breath and continued. "I want the kids to move in with Wic and me—permanently. He and Mina are on board. We'll rearrange the rooms. We've got it all figured out. And by the way, that whole thing about Wic—that was a low blow. You know him. You know he's not some kind of degenerate."

She had the decency to look a bit bashful at that, but I pushed on. "You do what you have to do. Try to adopt them, spread rumors about Wic and me—I'm not backing down on this. I'll get a lawyer, too, if I have to."

"No." She was about to say something else when Camryn let out a surprisingly sound cry on the baby monitor for someone so little. "Oh, hold on a second."

A million and one thoughts stirred in my head before she returned. *No, what? No, you can't have the kids, or no, don't get a lawyer?*

With a practiced hand, Brandy undid her top and put Camryn to her breast. She was a natural, I realized. I would have never thought.

"There." She let out a long breath and looked at me in earnest. "About the kids. I'm not going to lie, I still have some concerns, but I was wrong to blame you for everything. I was scared. It was too much at once, and I overreacted. So no lawyers."

For the first time in weeks, the icy knot I'd carried around in my belly started to thaw. "You mean it?"

"I do. If anyone tried to take her—" She paused to gaze down at Camryn. "I'd lose it. I'm really sorry, Annie. If the kids want to live with you, I won't stop them. But they'll always have a place here, and I plan on telling them as much." She switched Camryn from one breast to the other. I remembered a lot of fumbling at that stage of motherhood, a lot of trial and error. Not so for her. "For the record, they actually seem... pretty happy." Her eyebrows shot up as if, for the first time, she'd realized that was true. "But, while I promise to extend some benefit of the doubt here, you should know I've been angry with you for years. That's not possible to erase overnight. When you left—I thought we were friends. Or friendly at least. And I know Joel loved you." She fell silent for a moment. "I'll never understand it. Especially now." She nodded toward Camryn. "But maybe I don't have to. Maybe forgiveness is the key. And I can work on that."

I didn't know what to say at first. I'd never actually considered how my leaving might have impacted those not in my immediate family. Back then, in my mind, I'd been the appendix of my world—a dormant threat that no one would miss. Remove me, and life would go on much the same. I'd been wrong. I'd left a permanent scar.

"It really does seem like a lifetime ago."

Her mouth pulled sideways. After a long pause, she asked, "Are you really different now? That day you disappeared—"

"I didn't leave, Bee. I was fifteen minutes away the whole day. Should I have found a way to communicate that? Yes. But I didn't leave."

She nodded. "So what's changed?"

"Everything." An airy lightness inflated my chest. "I'm not hiding anymore. Grace and Connor see right through me, and I let them. I'm honest about who I am. That's the difference. When everyone around you sees you for who you are, they also hold you to being your best self. We're making an action plan for the possibility of my depression spiraling again. And it might—I'm not pretending otherwise."

Camryn was done eating, and Brandy lifted her to her shoulder and patted her bottom gently. "What can I do?"

I blinked at her. "Do?"

"If you spiral."

"Oh." My cheeks heated. "That's... wow."

"I don't mean to make you uncomfortable. I just want to know. So I can help."

"I didn't expect the question is all. I guess remind me. Of this. This conversation, what I have, who I am now."

Camryn let out an impossibly loud burp for her size, and we both smiled. "And who is that?" Brandy asked, settling the little one again.

The answer came to me without a struggle. "Grace and Connor's mom, Wic's girlfriend, Camryn's aunt, your sister-in-law, a teacher, a friend. Someone who loves the little things. Loves... living." The truth of it filled me up. *I love living. Who would have thought?*

"You're crying."

I touched my fingers to my cheek. "I am?"

Brandy got up. "I think you'll be fine, Annie." She nodded in the direction of the family room. "I'm going to try to put her down, okay? How about you and me start over?"

I wiped my eyes with my sleeve and smiled. "Sounds good to me."

She nodded once then disappeared into the other room, where Wic's cradle was waiting.

Yes, I would be fine. I had no idea what life would throw my way, but I did know I was ready for it. Excited for it. And I would not go down without a fight.

EPILOGUE

One Year Later

Rain pelted the windshield as I pulled into the high school drop-off lane and waited for the minivan in front of me to let out its passengers. Another Tuesday morning goodbye, but it was vastly different from the one long ago that had caused my deepest torment.

"Do you have your lunches?" I asked as Grace and Connor pulled on their backpacks. "I put them on the counter this morning."

They grumbled sleepy affirmatives.

"Good luck with the science test, Grace. Don't forget, Selena's mom is picking you up after practice today. Remind her to drop you at Shane and Brandy's."

"Like I could forget. You've been living and breathing this party for the past two weeks." She leaned forward from the back seat and kissed me on the cheek.

"It's not every day your niece turns one." Finally, it was my turn, and I pulled up and put the car in park. "Connor, you'll be there too? No later than five."

"I'll be there."

They pushed open the doors, letting the damp chill into the cabin. I shivered in my yoga wear under Wic's thick parka. Kara and I had taken up the meditative exercise a few months back when a new place opened down the block from her.

"Have a great day!" I hollered as they hurried through the downpour into the school building. Mina thought I spoiled them by driving them every day, and maybe I was, but it was mostly for me. Those extra fifteen minutes in the car with them before the day commenced could not be traded for anything—not when I'd wasted so many years away. Now each morning, I was raring to go.

I returned home and scurried up the walkway through the front door. "Brrr. We might get snow if it continues like this!" I called to Mina, who was at her usual spot by the kitchen table.

"That would be nice. Don't get me wrong, I don't much mind the rain, but the gray gets to me. I need light."

Heavy footfalls coming down the stairs made us both turn. "Morning." Wic hurried into the kitchen, kissed me on the lips, and grabbed a piece of bread for the toaster in one quick motion.

"And to you."

"There's a certain pep in your step today, son." Mina raised one eyebrow. "Should I give Annie credit, or are you in a good mood in general?"

"Mom!" The verbal slap on the wrist came with a chuckle. Wic bumped me with his shoulder as he put his toast on a plate then gave me a playful wink. "Well, normally, it's Annie. But today is my second meeting with Evergreen Interiors."

"Ah, the barn doors."

"That's the one."

A few months back, we'd attended one of the big farm shows in the area. Wic had had a booth where he'd displayed his signs, flower crates, and other smaller crafts, but he'd also brought two handmade barn doors to use as a backdrop, and they had drawn the attention of a local interior decorating firm that wanted to know if he would be willing to do commissioned work for them. He was still with the general contractor and liking it fine, but the new opportunity could be the opening he needed to get his name out there. The first step to creating his own business.

"Are you nervous?" I asked.

"Not really. We've practically shaken on it already. Today is more about details—time frames, scope, that kind of thing. Sealing the deal."

"And then you'll start building?"

He grinned. "Fingers crossed. I should be back by four." I opened my mouth to speak, but he beat me to it. "I know, I know. Party, five o'clock."

"You've still got the presents in your trunk?"

"Aye, aye." He kissed me again then hurried into the foyer and pulled on his jacket. "Need anything else?"

I followed him to the front door then reached up to smooth back a strand of inky hair that had gotten caught on his collar. "Nope. I'm good."

He stilled beneath my fingers as if I'd reminded him to breathe and leaned his forehead to mine. "Are you sure we can't tell everyone tonight?" he whispered.

My hands found his. "It wouldn't be right. It's Camryn's day. Besides, we don't even have a ring yet."

"Hmm." He nuzzled the tip of his nose to mine. "Sorry, I couldn't wait."

A low laugh percolated in my chest, but I managed to stifle it before it came out. As open as Mina was about Wic's and my relationship, she didn't need to hear all our sweet nothings. "You're so not sorry."

He brought my left hand to his lips and kissed the finger that would not stay empty for long, if my memory of last night served me right. I'd said yes.

"Got me there. But maybe I should have waited and made a grand gesture. Flowers, dinner, a romantic walk along the river—"

"Ugh."

"Yeah? You actually preferred me asking when you were half-asleep?"

Our embrace had turned into a swaying dance in front of the door, arms around each other's shoulders, faces close. Our own little cocoon. "Spooning has never been more romantic."

"But we're not telling anyone today?"

I shook my head. "Soon. Kids first."

"Think they'll approve?"

"You know they will."

I meant it. Once Brandy and I settled most of our differences and Wic and I officially asked the kids to move in, we had never looked back. Sure, there'd been times in the year since—especially before we got the room situation in order—when everyday life had been less than smooth sailing, but we got through them, and now it almost felt like we'd never been apart.

Almost.

I still discovered things about my kids that any other parent would have known. I'd found Grace's first communion dress in a box, and one day, Connor had shown me a scar where he'd had stitches after a close encounter with a bike rack at age nine. There were things I'd missed that I would never get back, but the many chances to make new memories helped me not to dwell on what was lost. I lived for them, loved them—vocally and ferociously—and I was not so obtuse that I couldn't see they thrived on it.

Wic had stepped back initially to let everyone get acclimated, but soon, his true nature had reemerged, and he fit right in. I'd been anxious about how Connor would react to the news about living with him, but I need not have worried. Wic was very clear about not wanting to take Joel's place and aware enough to allow me space to be "Mom." The kids respected him, and in some ways, I dared to think he had become a sort of father figure for them regardless of his intentions. Our home was three generations of multiple bloodlines, but we were family, and that was what mattered most.

"You should get going," I told Wic. "Knock 'em dead. I'll see you tonight."

"THERE'S THE BIRTHDAY girl." I dropped to the floor and scooped Camryn into my arms.

Her face lit up as she wrapped her arms around my neck. "Nannie." Chubby fingers dug into my hair, and she bounced up and down in my lap.

"Someone's excited. I hope you had a good nap today, baby girl, because we're taking over the house."

"It wasn't the worst nap." Brandy rubbed her face at the kitchen table. She had a pile of crackers in front of her that she nibbled on without pause. Her voice went up in pitch as she said, "But Mommy sure could have used another few hours of rest, sweetie pie. Yes, she could."

"How are you feeling? Still nauseous?"

"It's terrible. Did Shane tell you? The only thing I can eat are boiled potatoes with lemon. That's it. And crackers. I think I'm driving him a bit up the wall. You should have Wic take him out for a guys' night. He needs it."

"Maybe it's another girl. You were pretty sick with Camryn too."

"Anything is possible. But it's a blessing either way, and I'm not complaining."

I gave her a sympathetic pout. "So..." I turned Camryn in my lap so she was facing her mom. "What can I start getting ready?"

She broke another cracker in half and considered it carefully before bringing it to her lips. A faint quiver of disgust traveled across her face. She put it down again. "I think I need a minute," she said, getting up. "Ask Shane. He's ordering the pizzas."

After she left, I pulled a soft, squishy book from Camryn's bin of toys nearby and opened it in front of her. "I guess we have some time. How about your favorite aunt reads you your favorite book?" I kissed the top of her downy head. "Would that be good?"

She banged a fist against the fabric pages in approval.

"I'll take that as a yes."

It was closer to six when we all assembled at the dinner table. Shane said grace, but Wic and I held hands underneath the table instead of folding them in prayer. He'd only just arrived, and I had yet to ask him more than a cursory question about his day. His smile assured me the conversation could wait.

The girl of the hour wiggled and squirmed in her high chair to the point where I was afraid she'd topple it. Before we could load our plates with pizza, Shane scrunched up his face and sighed. "You know what, guys? I think today is a day for dessert first. Connor, will you get the small one and put one candle in it?"

Without question, Connor disappeared into the kitchen, reemerging a minute later with a small white frosted cake that he placed in front of Camryn. She stilled, instantly mesmerized by the flickering flame of the single candle.

"Oh, look. She's not sure what to do," Grace said. To everyone's surprise, she had joined the cheerleading squad at the high school in the fall and was fresh off practice in her gear. "Blow, like this." She leaned forward, pretending a sharp exhalation.

Birthdays... Not long ago, mine had seemed so threatening. Such a sinister countdown. But I'd be thirty-eight this year then thirty-nine, forty. I didn't even doubt it anymore. Not a day went by that I didn't consider that change a small miracle.

"You'll have to help her," Shane said to Grace, bringing me back to the present.

After that was said and done, the extinguished candle was removed, then Grace pointed at the cake. "Dip your finger in it," she said to Camryn. "Like this." She mimed doing so then licked her digit with great flourish.

Camryn's eyes widened, and she giggled. She stared at the cake then back at Grace. "Huvh," she said, pointing at the pastry.

"No, for you." Grace pushed it closer to Camryn. "You eat it."

"This will not end well," Mina said merrily to my left. "Not for the rug anyway."

As if on cue, Camryn lifted both hands over her head only to bring them down on top of the cake with enough force that frosting flew all the way to Connor's seat at the other end of the table. There was a moment of stunned silence before the room burst into laughter.

Spurred on by the apparent approval, Camryn repeated her feat over and over until not much more than crumbs remained. She may have gotten some of it in her mouth, but mostly, the dessert was stuck to her hair, her bib, her face, the table, and her parents, who sat closest. No sooner did she run out of cake than she yawned and rubbed a grubby fist across her face.

"Well, that's it, folks," Shane said. "If you'll excuse me, the little princess needs her beauty rest."

"Can the rest of us start eating?" Connor asked.

Camryn wailed as Shane tried to clean up the worst of the mess.

"She says yes, you'd better, or the pizza will get cold."

Grace reached for the box but stopped. "Wait. We didn't sing to her."

Brandy waved. "Oh, that's okay—"

"No. We *have* to sing. It's her first birthday." She looked to Shane, who had started bouncing Camryn to settle her down.

"Sure," he said. "Of course. Let's do it."

Grace took up the tune, and the rest of us followed. Camryn quieted and watched us all intently—from Grace to Connor and Wic then to me, Mina, and her mother. When we were done, a blissful smile crept upon her lips.

"'Ray," Camryn said, echoing our hoorays at the end. She repeated it several times as Shane brought her upstairs.

Brandy yawned.

"Do you want to join them?" I asked. "It's okay if you do. I know how that feels."

Her pale face lit up. No doubt the vision of her soft pillow seemed little more than a mirage these days. "Are you sure? She usually sleeps best in the beginning of the night, so if I go up now, I'll get several hours." Her voice caught on the last word.

I smiled. "You go. Only family here. No one will mind."

"But the clean-up."

"I'll take care of it. Don't worry. I've got this."

She paused. "You really do, don't you?" She looked first at me then at each of the people around the table, who were now busy stuffing themselves with food.

She patted my arm before she walked away. I turned back to the table, where Connor had just thrown a napkin at Grace, which she threatened to reciprocate with a piece of pepperoni.

"Grace," I said, using my newly acquired mom voice modeled after Kara's.

The bickering instantly died down, and the pleasant hum of conversation started up again.

Yes, I've got this, I thought.

I'd found my second chance, and it was as good as they came. Never again would I forget that each new day marked a *first* in the journey of the rest of my life.

ACKNOWLEDGEMENTS

How lucky am I that I get to follow my authorly whims and write books in more than one genre? As this, my first women's fiction title, is made a Real Thing in the World, I want to thank those who made that possible.

First, I am deeply grateful to my tireless agent, Kimberley Cameron, for not giving up on this story and always believing it would find a readership. I so appreciate your persistence! Thank you also to the whole team at Red Adept Publishing—especially to Lynn, Erica, Sara, Marirose, and Virge—for finally bringing this story to readers in the best possible shape it could be.

I wrote this book back in 2018 on the heels of taking part in Pitch Wars, and there were many people in my class who supported the effort from the beginning. Whether you read an early version, answered questions to help deepen the story, or simply encouraged me, I am so grateful. Specifically, I want to mention Carrie Pulkinen, Em Shotwell, Jessica Holt, Kristy Gillespie, Megan McGee, Piper Grayson, Robin Lemke, and Tobi Iott. Your contributions were instrumental to Annie's story getting to this point!

This book took its good old time finding a home, and as any writer will know, it is crucial to develop a thick skin, perseverance, and patience along the journey. Doing so is much, *much* easier with like-minded people walking next to you. So, Rompire, while the writing of this book predates your invaluable friendship, you were still there for the weary (yet exhilarating) final miles of the race. Amy, Em, Julia, Lana, Lexie, Lisa, and Megan (who *was* there!)—you all are the bee's knees! I am so fortunate to have you in my life to cheer me on and to offer support, advice, and genuine care every single day. Love and hugs to you all!

To my family, who puts up with me holing up in the office for long stretches of time only to emerge bleary-eyed and light averse, mumbling about plot holes every so often—you are my everything. When you cheer for me, I remember to cheer too. Brian, thank you for always being up for brainstorming sessions (even though I'm not invited to yours...) and for being my partner in all the things life throws at us. I love you always. To Noah and Sophia, who just happen to be the same age as Annie's kids in this book as it's being published—know that this is a mere fluke. Any similarity is purely coincidental, except the portrayal of a mother's love for her children as an all-encompassing force. You've got me there, each of you holding half my heart forever.

I also want to give a shout-out to anyone who has shared news of this book on social media, posted reviews, and generally spread the word. You are awesome! And to you, dear reader, holding this book—without you, I'd be writing into a void. Thank you!

Finally, I want to recognize everyone whose life is touched in some way by depression, and there are a lot of us. I see you, and I've been you. Please know that you are strong even when you feel weak, you matter even when you feel insignificant, and you are needed even when you feel like a burden. Ask for help. Never give up. It will get better.

24/7 National Suicide Prevention Hotline: 800-273-8255

About the Author

Anna E. Collins was born and raised in Sweden, where she spent her early years hounding the local librarians for new reads. One American husband, two children, and two international moves later, she realized she had her own stories to tell, and once that proverbial lid was opened, there was no closing it again. She put her master's degree in educational psychology on the shelf and picked up the pen.

Anna currently resides in the Seattle area, where she writes about the lives and inner workings of women—their hopes, dreams, journeys, and relationships. Her goal is to make readers both laugh and cry. In 2019, she was a Golden Heart finalist.

When not writing, reading, or raising humans, she can be found exploring other creative pursuits like painting, woodworking, and baking as well as endlessly brushing her mini goldendoodle, Archie, who is a Very Good Boy.

Read more at www.aecollinsbooks.com.

About the Publisher

Dear Reader,

We hope you enjoyed this book. Please consider leaving a review on your favorite book site.

Visit https://RedAdeptPublishing.com to see our entire catalogue.

Don't forget to subscribe to our monthly newsletter to be notified of future releases and special sales.

Made in United States
North Haven, CT
19 May 2022

19358722R00193